A LONG TIME DEAD

Recent Titles by Sally Spencer from Severn House

THE BUTCHER BEYOND

THE DARK LADY

DEAD ON CUE

DEATH OF A CAVE DWELLER

DEATH OF AN INNOCENT

A DEATH LEFT HANGING

DYING IN THE DARK

THE ENEMY WITHIN

GOLDEN MILE TO MURDER

MURDER AT SWANN'S LAKE

THE PARADISE JOB

THE RED HERRING

THE SALTON KILLINGS

STONE KILLER

THE WITCH MAKER

A LONG TIME DEAD

Sally Spencer

severn
House

This first world edition published in Great Britain 2006 by
SEVERN HOUSE PUBLISHERS LTD of
9–15 High Street, Sutton, Surrey SM1 1DF.
This first world edition published in the USA 2006 by
SEVERN HOUSE PUBLISHERS INC of
595 Madison Avenue, New York, N.Y. 10022.

British Library Cataloguing in Publication Data

Spencer, Sally
    A long time dead
    1.   Woodend, Charlie (Fictitious character) - Fiction
    2.   Police - England - Fiction
    3.   Detective and mystery stories
    I.   Title
    8213.9'14 [F]

    ISBN-13:   9780-7278-6363-8 (cased)
    ISBN-10:   0-7278-6363-0 (cased)
    ISBN-10:   0-7278-9168-5 (trade paper)

Typeset by Palimpsest Book Production Ltd.,
Polmont, Stirlingshire, Scotland.
Printed and bound in Great Britain by
MPG Books Ltd., Bodmin, Cornwall.

For Dave Garnett

Prologue

The American sitting in the back of the Buick was wearing a pinstriped suit of the style much favoured by bankers and stockbrokers in the City of London, but even an untrained observer would never have taken him for a civilian.

It was not so much his haircut which revealed him as a military man – though, in the age of liberation which had been ushered in by the Beatles, his hair was very short even for a man of conservative tastes. Instead, it was his posture which gave him away. For whereas a lesser man might have taken the opportunity to luxuriate in the customized soft leather which had added so much to the purchase price of the vehicle, he sat ramrod stiff, his arms by his sides, his head held in place by an invisible high collar.

'We're very nearly there now, Major,' the chauffeur said cheerfully, over his shoulder.

'Good,' his passenger replied, without, it seemed to the driver, a great deal of enthusiasm.

The Major let his thoughts drift back to the day he was told he'd been appointed to the post of Military Attaché at the US Embassy in London. He'd considered himself lucky to be given such a plum job, and that feeling had remained – pretty much intact – until he'd received the phone call from Washington DC, a few hours earlier.

He didn't feel so lucky now.

Now, he wished he'd been posted to some obscure little South American country that no one in the Administration back home would have had very much interest in.

For some minutes, the Buick had been driving along a narrow country lane which ran parallel to an ancient chain-link fence. Now, it had almost reached a pair of large, open gates, manned by a couple of British bobbies wearing those

1

pointy hats which the Major had always considered faintly ridiculous.

'Haverton Camp, sir,' the driver said, flicking his indicator on, and turning the wheel.

One of the policemen, a kid who hardly looked old enough to shave, stepped into the roadway and held out his hand for the Buick to stop. The Major wound down his window, and held out his identification for the constable to see.

'Major Garrett?' the policeman asked, looking him in the eye and completely ignoring the document.

'No, son, I'm Betty Grable,' the Major replied.

The constable looked perplexed. 'Sorry, sir?'

'I'm Betty Grable,' the Major repeated. 'If you don't believe me, just check my ID.'

The constable did as he'd been instructed. 'You *are* Major Garrett,' he announced. A grin spread across his face. 'Was all that by way of teaching me a lesson, sir?'

Garrett nodded. 'Always put your faith in documentation over people, son. A document has no reason to lie.'

'I'll remember that, sir,' the constable promised. 'Shall I tell you where you can find the guv'nor?'

'That would be helpful.'

'Drive straight through the main camp until you reach an open space that used to be the parade ground. He's at the far end of it, studying the crime scene.'

'Appreciate it,' Garrett said.

The constable hesitated for a moment, then said, 'Do you mind if I ask you a question?'

'Not at all. What is it?'

'Who's Betty Grable?'

'You really don't know?' Garrett asked, amazed.

'No, sir.'

'She was an actress. A big, big, movie star.'

'Is that right?' the constable asked, plainly none the wiser.

'You must have heard of her! She starred in the movie *A Yank in the RAF*! With Tyrone Power!'

'And when would that have been, sir?' the constable asked, obviously still unenlightened.

'I don't know for sure. 1941? 1942? It was some time during the War, anyway.'

2

The constable looked somewhat dubious. 'Seems an awful long time ago, sir.'

Yes, Garrett agreed silently, it probably did, to a boy like him. From the constable's perspective, the Second World War must be almost ancient history. And that made the murder – which he had come all this way to see with his own eyes – ancient history too.

The Major suddenly felt very old.

The driver edged the car through the gates, and on to a concrete road which was rutted and cracked after nearly a quarter of a century of total neglect. The road was flanked by a series of long wooden huts, so rickety that it seemed that a single jab of a finger would bring them crashing down like a row of dominoes.

'Hard to believe that this is one of the places they launched the Invasion of Normandy from, isn't it, sir?' the driver asked over his shoulder.

'Yeah,' Garrett agreed.

The huts petered out, and ahead of the car lay a large concrete rectangle, dappled with patches of green where the grass and weeds had forced their way through. Beyond the parade ground was another chain-link fence, and standing close to it were a small group of men.

'Stop here,' Garrett ordered. 'I'll walk the rest of the way.'

'Are you sure about that, sir?' the driver asked. 'There's no need to worry about damaging the car, you know. The suspension will take it, as long as I drive slowly.'

'I'm *not* worried about the car,' Garrett told him. 'I need a little time to think.'

As he marched briskly across the ruined parade ground, Garrett looked neither to the left nor to the right. Instead, he appeared to be keeping his eyes focussed on the men standing around a slight depression in the ground. But even that was not strictly accurate. He was not so much looking *at* them as looking *through* them – gazing towards a possible future he would prefer to avoid, but suspected was unstoppable.

He came to a final halt at the very edge of the shallow hole, and gazed down into it. The human skull which lay there seemed – despite its lack of eyes – to be looking up at him, and, even without teeth, appeared to be greeting him with a macabre grin.

Nor was the skull occupying the hole alone. There were other bones in evidence, too – ribs, femurs, fingers.

The men who had partly disinterred this body had had no expectation of making such a dramatic discovery, Garrett thought.

And why should they have had?

They were not archaeologists, but builders. Their intent was not to uncover the past, but to construct the future. Yet it had fallen to them to finally reveal – by total accident – the corpse of a man whom the most powerful military machine in the world had failed to find, even when the trail was fresh.

'I'm Inspector Clarence Dudley of the Devonshire Constabulary,' said a voice.

Garrett looked up. The speaker was a man in his mid-forties. He was wearing a long white Macintosh, and the kind of bowler hat much favoured by actors playing British policemen in cheaply-made B pictures.

'Well, there's the corpse,' Dudley said, with a banality perfectly in tune with his B picture appearance.

Garrett looked down into the hole again. 'Are you sure this guy really *is* Robert Kineally?' he asked, his tone half-suggesting that he was hoping for a reply in the negative.

Dudley shrugged. 'That's what it says on his identification tags,' he answered.

Major Garrett knelt down, and examined the dog tags for himself. One of them, he noted, was partly obscured by a dark brown blob, which was made up of swirling lines.

'It's a bloody fingerprint,' Dudley said helpfully.

'Yeah, I'd just about figured that out for myself,' Garrett replied, over his shoulder.

The second set of tags, which had no evidence of blood-stains on them, had once belonged to a Robert T. Kineally, who had been immunized against tetanus, hailed from Connecticut and had listed Martha Kineally as his next of kin.

Perhaps it wasn't him, Garrett told himself.

These were undoubtedly Kineally's *tags*, but perhaps the body was somebody else's.

Yeah, right! he thought, with self-disgust.

In his time, he'd known soldiers who would sell army

4

equipment – and even their own weapons – if they thought that they could get away with it. But a man's dog tags were something else. They didn't *belong* to him, they were *part* of him – sometimes, when the battle was finally over, the *only* part of him which was still recognizable.

So whether Garrett liked it or not – and he most definitely didn't – he was forced to accept that he was now staring down at the last mortal remains of Robert Kineally. Which the State and Defence Departments were just gonna love, because what they *really* needed at that particular, delicate moment was flack from Senator *Eugene* Kineally.

The high-level meeting had started out amicably enough, but it was now in its third hour, and tempers were becoming heated.

'For Christ's sake, what's the problem here?' the four-star American General was demanding. 'First we fight a bloody war for you, then we step in to protect you from the goddam Ruskies. And what do we want in return? All we're asking for is a tiny piece of land, which, even in a rinky-dink country like this one, you'd never even miss.'

The civil servants flanking the Right Honourable Douglas Coutes, Minister of Defence, stiffened. The minister himself bit back the first words which had come to his mind, and forced a reasonable expression to invade his face.

'No one here disputes that you need land to site your military bases on, Jack,' he said smoothly. 'It's merely a question of which particular pieces of land we give you.'

'From the point of view of defending this country – *your* country – the choice of a location is obvious,' the General countered.

Coutes pressed the fingertips of both hands together, in what was a gesture of either contemplation or prayer. 'You're looking at the matter from a purely military perspective, Jack,' he said.

'Damn right, I'm—'

'Which is perfectly understandable, given your particular brief. But we, the government, have to consider the *political* fall-out of any decisions that we make, too. And not only would the site you propose despoil a great deal of open countryside – which would undoubtedly enrage both the nature freaks and any number of other bunches of crazies – but it

5

would also, and much more significantly, mean the compulsory purchase of property belonging to some of our most important and influential families.'

'Important families? Dukes and earls? Those kinda guys?' the General asked, aggressively.

'Those kinda guys,' Coutes agreed dryly.

'Are you trying to tell me that, even today, they're still calling some of the shots?'

'More than you could ever imagine,' Coutes said. 'Our last prime minister was, I scarcely need remind you, an earl. And even out of power, the aristocracy is a force to be reckoned with.'

'Jesus!' the General snorted in disgust.

'No country – not even your own great republic – is immune from such influences,' Coutes said. 'Your home-grown "movers and shakers" may not have titles, but their *modus operandi* is probably very similar to those of the lords you seem to despise.'

'Latin, already,' the General said, his disgust deepening.

There was a discreet knock on the door, and Coutes's Principal Private Secretary slipped into the room. 'There's a phone call for you, Minister,' he said. 'It's Mr Braithwaite.'

'Tell him I'm in a meeting,' Coutes snapped.

'I will, if you insist, but I rather think you *should* take this call,' the PPS said emphatically.

The minister sighed heavily. 'All right. Have the call transferred through to here.'

The PPS raised a warning eyebrow. 'Perhaps it might be wiser to have your conversation with Mr Braithwaite in private,' he suggested.

Back in his own office, Coutes wrenched the phone from its cradle, and jammed it against his ear.

'What's this all about, Braithwaite?' he demanded.

'We've been getting some disturbing signals from our intelligence sources in Washington DC,' the caller said.

'About the military base?'

'How did you know that?' Braithwaite asked, astonished.

'How did I know? How did I bloody-well know? I know, you bumbling idiot, because this Calderdale Camp issue has been dominating my life for the last two months.'

6

There was an awkward – almost embarrassed – pause at the other end of the line.

'Actually, it's not Calderdale I'm talking about, Minister,' Braithwaite said, almost apologetically. 'I was referring to Haverton Camp.'

'But that's been closed for years!' Coutes exploded.

'I realize that, but . . .'

'They shut it down soon after the Invasion of Normandy. The Ministry might still own the land, but that's just a legal technicality.' Coutes paused. 'Come to think of it, didn't the Chancellor get me to agree to selling it to some development company with plans to turn it into a garden city?'

'That's quite correct, Minister, but—'

'So why bother me with it now? Are you under the impression that because I served there briefly myself, I've developed some sort of sentimental attachment to the bloody place?'

'No, I . . . Minister, the signals from Washington concern a Captain Robert Kineally. Does that name mean anything to you?'

'Not a great deal, no,' Coutes said.

'You don't remember him?'

'Of course I *remember* him, but then I *remember* what I had for breakfast, and that doesn't mean a great deal to me, either.'

'It's . . . er . . . being said that you didn't get on with him very well,' Braithwaite said uncomfortably. 'In fact, it's being suggested that a high level of animosity existed between the two of you.'

'I couldn't stand the sanctimonious little prig. So what? There were a number of people I didn't get on with back then. Anyway, as far as I recall, the bastard disappeared just before the invasion of Europe.'

'So he did, Minister. But not, it would seem, of his own free will. And now that he's turned up again—'

'What!'

'—now that he's turned up again, there are people in Washington who rather feel that you have some explaining to do.'

7

One

When the phone on his desk rang, that damp early spring morning in 1965, Detective Chief Inspector Charlie Woodend was not thinking about the War.

But he easily could have been.

He often did.

'It never even enters my head any more, Charlie,' one or another of his old comrades would tell him at their reunions, after a few pints had been sunk. 'As far as I'm concerned, it's all over and done with. I can honestly say I've put it completely behind me.'

'Is that right?' Woodend would ask.

'It is, Charlie. It most definitely is.'

He didn't believe it. As far as he was concerned, the War wasn't something you forgot – it was merely something you tried not to dwell on too much.

Because when you'd sweated half your body weight away in North Africa, when you'd almost drowned during the landing on the beaches of Normandy and nearly frozen to death in the Battle of the Bulge, when you'd seen for yourself the horrors of the Nazi death camps – and *he* had done all those things – you couldn't entirely vanquish the memories, however much you might wish to.

Still, on that particular morning – as he sat twisting the paperclips on his desk into an intricate pattern and waiting for the arrival of a major case which might serve to distract him, at least temporarily – his thoughts were dwelling on matters much closer to home.

He was worried about his wife, Joan, and the heart condition which had first manifested itself on their holiday in Spain. He was fretting over the mental health of Inspector Bob Rutter, who'd had a nervous breakdown shortly after his own wife, Maria, had been murdered. And he was very concerned about the emotional balance of Detective Sergeant Monika Paniatowski, who was not only his bagman and confidante, but also Rutter's ex-lover. So, all in all, it was hardly surprising that it came as something of a relief when the phone *did* ring.

'Charlie? Charlie Woodend? Is that you?' asked the caller.

He did not quite recognize the voice at first, though the shiver which ran down his back told him that when he did put a name to it, he wasn't going to like the result.

'It's me!' the caller said. 'Douglas Coutes! You surely remember me, don't you?'

Oh yes, a voice in Woodend's head said ominously, I remember you, all right. You bastard!

'What can I do for you, Captain Coutes?' he asked.

'No need to call me that now, Charlie,' the other man replied. 'The war's been over a long time, you know.'

He laughed, but Woodend could detect no humour in it – no sense of good-hearted joshing. Rather there was an edge to the laugh – a nervousness which almost bordered on hysteria.

'This isn't a social call, is it?' the Chief Inspector guessed.

'Not entirely, no,' Douglas Coutes agreed. 'Though, I must admit, I have been feeling guilty about not having got in touch with an old comrade like you long ago.'

You never felt guilty about anything in your whole life, Woodend thought – which is probably why you're a government minister now.

But aloud, he said, 'What do you want, Mr Coutes?'

'Douglas, Charlie!' Coutes said reprovingly. 'After all we went through together, I think you can call me Douglas.'

'Is it somethin' *official* you wanted to talk about, Mr Coutes?' Woodend asked, flatly.

'Semi-official,' Coutes told him, ignoring the deliberate slight. 'Do you remember an American called Robert Kineally?'

Of course I remember him, Woodend thought. He was a rare bird indeed – one of those few officers it was a pleasure to work with.

'What about him?' he asked.

'You remember that he completely disappeared, just before the Invasion of Normandy?'

'I was told *later* that he'd disappeared,' Woodend said,

choosing his words carefully. 'If you recall, I'd already been posted on by then.'

'Of course you had,' Coutes agreed. 'You missed all the fuss – the American military policemen turning over the camp, the helicopters they brought in specially so they could search the whole area from the air—'

'Like you said, I missed all that,' Woodend interrupted.

'There were those who thought he'd fallen into the sea, and those who said he'd deserted.'

And what did *I* think? Woodend wondered. To tell the truth, I was already on the battlefront when I finally heard the news – an' with everythin' that was goin' on around me, I hardly thought about it *at all*.

'There were even those who thought he was a Nazi spy, and had fled before his cover was blown,' Coutes continued.

Woodend sighed. 'There's always folk who'd rather think the worst of other people, but anybody who really knew Robert Kineally would never have believed he was a Nazi,' he said.

'Well, exactly,' Douglas Coutes agreed. 'He and I may have had our differences, but—'

'Could you get to the point, please, sir?' Woodend interrupted.

'It turns out none of those things had happened. It turns out he was *murdered*.'

'So?' Woodend asked, though he was finding it hard to disguise the quickening of interest in his voice.

'Don't you want to know *how* I know he was murdered, Charlie?' Coutes asked.

'It was all a long time ago, and I'm not sure I—'

'I know he was murdered because I've just been informed that they've found his body!'

'Where?' Woodend asked, resignedly giving in to his ever-increasing curiosity.

'I don't know exactly. They haven't released all the details yet. But I believe it's somewhere near Haverton Camp.'

'After such a long time, how can they be so sure it's him?' Woodend wondered. Then the answer came to him. 'Of course, he'll have had his dog tags on him, won't he?'

'Yes, he had his dog tags,' Coutes agreed. 'And the American authorities have also checked his dental records, and come up

10

with a perfect match. So I'm afraid there's absolutely no doubt about it. It really is him.'

Woodend reached for a cigarette, and lit it from the large box of kitchen matches which he always kept on his desk.

'So Robert Kineally was murdered,' he said. 'How?'

'Stabbed, apparently.'

'Well, he's been a long time dead, so there's not much chance of them solvin' the crime after all this time,' Woodend said. 'I doubt they'll even try.'

'I've . . . I've been told there *is* going to be an investigation,' Coutes said. He paused and took a deep breath – as if he'd been putting off what he had to say next for as long as possible, but now recognized that the moment had finally come. 'And apparently, the Americans consider me one of the main suspects,' he finished in a rush.

'Why would they do that?' Woodend wondered.

'They've . . . they've apparently found one of my fingerprints on Kineally's dog tags.'

'After all this time? I'm no expert on fingerprints, but I'm surprised they could still lift it.'

'It . . . it was a bloodstained fingerprint.'

'Bloodstained? In that case, you might as well confess straight away, don't you think?'

'But I didn't *do* it!'

'Then how do you explain the fingerprint?'

'Isn't it obvious? Whoever killed Robert Kineally must have decided to frame me!'

'How?'

'I don't know, for God's sake! You can't expect *me* to think like a murderer. But there must be hundreds of ways.'

'Name one.'

'Maybe I touched the dog tags while Kineally was still alive. Maybe the killer made a wax impression of my fingerprint, and somehow transferred it to the dog tag. I'm no expert in these matters. That's why I'm calling you.'

Woodend stubbed out his cigarette. 'If you're tellin' me all this because you think I might have some influence with the people they put in charge of the case, then you're just wastin' your breath,' he said.

'You! Have influence!' Coutes scoffed. 'I'm the one with

11

influence. I'm a *government minister*, in case you've forgotten.'

That's better, Woodend thought. That sounds more like the Douglas Coutes I came to know and heartily dislike – the Douglas Coutes who was arrogant to the point of megalomania.

'So why *are* you ringin' me?' he asked.

'Because you're a detective.'

He's flipped, Woodend told himself. The man's gone completely off his rocker.

'You want *me* to investigate the case?' he asked.

'Obviously!'

'I can't.'

'Can't?'

'That's what I said. I don't care how much influence you've got, it won't be enough to get me assigned to the investigation. The local police would never stand for it. An' even if they were made to buckle under pressure, the press would make a field day out of it. Besides, if I'm to have any involvement at all, it will be as a witness – because I was there just before it all happened.'

'It's because you were there – because you know what it was like – that I want you on the case,' Coutes said doggedly.

'In what capacity?'

'I'm not sure. I haven't really had time to work out all the details yet,' Coutes said impatiently. 'We'll come up with something. Perhaps we'll call you a "ministerial advisor".'

'But what I'd really be is some kind of private eye!' Woodend said incredulously. 'A gumshoe!'

'It doesn't matter what your exact status is,' Coutes said. 'All that really matters—'

'I won't do it,' Woodend said firmly.

'Why not?'

'Because I don't think it *can* be done, Mr Coutes. It's amazin' that after all this time they've been able to produce evidence against you – but it'd take a real bloody miracle to uncover any more evidence that could possibly be used in your defence. Besides . . .'

'Besides what?'

'Given the fact that they've lifted your bloody fingerprint from his dog tag, I'm a long way from bein' convinced you *didn't* do it.'

'How dare you!'

'I'm just lookin' at the facts. You were a real nasty piece of work back then, and you an' Kineally certainly had enough reason to hate one another, didn't you, Mr Coutes?'

'I don't know what you're talking about.'

'You surely haven't forgotten Mary Parkinson, have you?'

'Who?'

'Mary Parkinson. Farmer's daughter. Sweet little thing. You met her in the Dun Cow.'

'Oh, her,' Coutes said dismissively.

'Her,' Woodend agreed.

'You surely don't think I'd have murdered Kineally over a piece of skirt, do you?'

No, given what little value he placed on women in general, he probably wouldn't have, Woodend thought.

'Still, on the face of it, things are certainly lookin' bad for you, aren't they?' he asked.

'I've already given you my word that I didn't kill him,' Coutes said, somewhat impatiently.

'The word of an officer an' a gentleman?' Woodend asked. 'Well, you never were much of an officer—'

'Now just listen here—'

'—an' you were nothin' at all of a gentleman.'

'I may be in trouble at the moment,' Coutes said, with a new, threatening tone seeping into his voice, 'but even weakened, I still have sufficient power to either make, or break, someone like you.'

'Maybe you're right,' Woodend agreed. 'Maybe you can – an' maybe you will. But whatever happens, I'll do nothin' to help you.'

'Listen, Charlie, I seem to have got a bit carried away,' Coutes said, wheedling now. 'If you'll just reconsider—'

'Not a chance,' Woodend interrupted. 'I'm goin' to hang up the phone now, Minister.'

'You can't just—'

'I'd wish you good luck – but we'd both know I didn't mean it.'

Two

Chief Constable Henry Marlowe looked up at the big man who was standing in front of his desk. He had not liked Charlie Woodend from the moment they had met, and the longer they knew each other, the deeper that dislike had grown.

Woodend, it seemed to Marlowe, paid scant regard to anything that really mattered. His lack of concern *began* with the way he dressed – hairy sports jackets instead of the smart lounge suits favoured by other senior officers – but went on to include so many other things.

When Woodend bothered to show any deference at all, it was *mock*-deference. At best!

In addition, he had a habit of ignoring standard procedures (as clearly laid down by his betters) and instead chose to blunder around any case he was assigned to like a rampant dinosaur.

But perhaps the worst thing about 'Cloggin'-it Charlie', the Chief Constable was forced to admit, was that – despite the appalling way he carried out his duties – he usually got results. No doubt that was more due to luck than judgement – and no doubt his luck would one day run out – but until then, his very presence on the Force was a source of continual irritation to the forward-looking senior policeman who had to deal with him.

All of which helped explain why the arrival of the visitor from the capital – the man now sitting behind the desk next to the Chief Constable – had been so welcome. Because when he went away again, he wouldn't be going alone. And the thought of being without Woodend – even if it was only for a week or so – was more than enough to instantly give Marlowe a rosier view of life.

'This is Mr Forsyth,' the Chief Constable told his Chief

Inspector. 'He's come up from London, specifically to see you.'

'I *am* honoured,' Woodend said.

There was nothing wrong with words the Chief Inspector had used, Marlowe told himself. It was the *way* Woodend had used them. The bastard simply refused to be impressed by anything.

The Chief Constable rose to his feet. 'Since the matter that Mr Forsyth wishes to discuss with you is outside the ambit of my operational control, I have decided to absent myself from this meeting,' he said, moving towards the door.

Forsyth waited until Marlowe had left the room and closed the door behind him, then stood up and said, 'Well, this is all very formal, isn't it?'

'Mr Marlowe likes formality,' Woodend said. 'Thrives on it, as a matter of fact.'

'Yes, that's certainly the impression I gained myself,' Forsyth said thoughtfully. 'But without wishing to interfere with Mr Marlowe's usual arrangements and procedures in any way, I'm sure we'll both be much more comfortable sitting over there.'

He was indicating a pair of easy chairs, placed on opposite sides of a large coffee table.

This 'relaxing area' was a relatively new feature of the Chief Constable's office, and had been added when Marlowe had read about it in one of the management magazines he so enjoyed perusing in the time he should have been devoting to police work.

Woodend lowered his heavy frame into one of the chairs, and made a rapid assessment of the other man. Forsyth was in his fifties, he guessed. He was wearing an expensive herringbone suit, and heavy glasses which – perhaps by accident, but more likely by design – matched the cloth perfectly. His short grey hair was neatly trimmed, his hands looked as if they had been recently manicured.

A civil servant, Woodend thought.

But not one of those who helps the unemployed to fill out forms in the dole office, and then goes home and worries about his mortgage. No, this man would have a large mahogany desk somewhere in Whitehall, and, at the weekends, would escape to his country residence for a spot of hunting and fishing.

'Do you have any idea why I'm here?' Forsyth asked, as if he were genuinely curious to hear the answer.

'I can only imagine that it's somethin' to do with Douglas Coutes,' Woodend replied.

Forsyth laughed. 'Right on the button,' he said. 'Our Minister's in a bit of a bind.'

'So I believe,' Woodend said, noncommittally.

'A bind that you, apparently, expressed absolutely no interest in helping him to get out of.'

'That's correct.'

'May I ask why?'

Woodend sighed. 'It's a long story.'

A very long story. A story that started – in a sense – before he ever even met Coutes.

Everybody, and that included the Germans on the other side of the Channel, knew the invasion of France was coming – but very few people knew exactly when or where it would actually happen. For the vast army, gathered on, or near, the south coast of England, it was therefore merely a matter of training as hard as it could and then waiting to be told on which battlefield it would quite possibly lay down its collective life.

Charlie Woodend, newly promoted to sergeant, was at home in Whitebridge when the order came through that he was to be a part of that invading army. It was the first leave he had had for four years, and though he knew his home town like the back of his hand, he still found it hard, after being in the desert for so long, to come to terms with the absence of sand.

There were other things he found difficult to accept, too.

His parents' terraced house, which had seemed huge to him as a child, now felt dwarf-sized.

The parochial feel of a place which had been weaving cotton for a hundred years – and blandly assumed it would continue to do so for another thousand.

Yet the difficulty was not with the house or the place, he recognized. They were as they had always been. He was the one who was no longer the same.

It had been with much trepidation that he had gone to see Joan. He'd been carrying her image around his head all the time he had been away. But what if – in the process – his mind had modified that image of her? What if – like the town – she now seemed an almost alien creature to him?

Their first meeting had done little to calm his fears. Physically, she had changed a little over the years, for though she was still a slim young thing, it was now possible to detect the beginnings of the thickness which would set in as she approached middle age. That didn't really bother him. But what if she had started to develop a thickness of the soul? Or if such a thickness had always been there, but he'd never noticed it before?

'What would you like to do?' he asked flatly, almost as if he were talking to a virtual stranger.

'We could go the pictures if you like,' Joan suggested. 'They're showin' Casablanca, with Humphrey Bogart and Ingrid Bergman, an' I missed it the first time round.'

'All right, let's do that,' he agreed lethargically.

He had expected no more from the picture than a temporary respite from his confused feelings for Joan. Yet he soon found himself captivated by the plot, and when Rick – who had constantly claimed throughout the picture that he stuck out his neck for nobody – decided to make the noble self-sacrifice, Woodend felt an uncharacteristic tear trickling down his cheek.

'You could have knocked me over with a feather when Rick didn't get on that plane with Ilsa,' Woodend said, as he and Joan were leaving the cinema.

'Could I?' Joan asked.

'Didn't it come as a surprise to you, an' all?'

'Not really.'

'So what was it that you saw, an' I missed?'

'That you an' Rick are a lot alike.'

'Come off it, lass!' Woodend said, suddenly starting to feel a little hot around the collar. 'Rick's a Hollywood hero, an' I'm just an ordinary workin' class feller.'

'But when push comes to shove, you'll both do what's right, however much it might cost you,' Joan said firmly.

Woodend shook his head. 'I'm not as big a man as you're givin' me credit for,' he said.

'Maybe you're not,' Joan agreed. 'But you will be – given time.'

Woodend felt all his fears – all his misgivings – melt away, and before he knew quite what he was doing, he had flung his arms around Joan and was hugging her to him.

'Steady on, Charlie Woodend! You're almost crushin' me to death,' Joan gasped.

He relaxed his grip a little. 'If I manage to get through this war in one piece, I want to marry you,' he told her.

'You'll get through,' she assured him, and the way she said it made him believe that he really would.

'You haven't said if you want marry me or not,' he said, almost fearful of her response.

Joan smiled. 'There didn't seem to be much point in statin' the obvious, Charlie.'

But what if things hadn't happened like that? Woodend asked himself, as he viewed his past from the easy chair in Marlowe's office.

What if he hadn't been granted leave, and so never had the opportunity to go back to Whitebridge?

What if he *had* gone back home, but he and Joan had decided to spend the evening in the pub, instead of the cinema?

Or they'd gone to the cinema, but watched some other film, rather than *Casablanca*?

Would he, then, have been the man he was that first time he met Mary Parkinson – or would he have been a different man, who would have reacted to her quite differently?

And if he *had* reacted differently, would Robert Kineally have spent the last twenty-one years lying undiscovered in a shallow grave?

'I seem to have lost you, Chief Inspector,' said a smooth, carefully-modulated voice.

Woodend snapped himself back into the present.

'Sorry, sir, you're quite right, I was miles away,' he told Forsyth. 'What was it you were sayin'?'

'I was asking you if I've got all my facts right. As I understand it, you first met the Minister in the early spring of 1944. Is that correct?'

'Yes, it is.'

'And it turned out to be a very short-term posting, didn't it? You actually served under him for just two months?'

'Aye,' Woodend agreed. 'It doesn't seem long, does it, when you put it in those terms?'

'What terms would *you* put it in?'

'Coutes was hard work,' Woodend said. '*Bloody* hard work. An' even after only a couple of months with him, I came away feelin' as if I'd earned a long-service medal.'

Three

'*You're to be assigned to work with Captain Coutes,' the quartermaster told Woodend, when he arrived at the camp. 'He left instructions that he wanted to see you as soon as you got here.'*

Woodend looked down at his heavy military kitbag. 'I'll just dump this in my billet, sir, and then I'll—'

The quartermaster laughed. 'You don't know our Captain Coutes, do you, Sergeant?'

'No, I—'

'When he said as soon as you got here, that's what he meant. He's in the officers' mess.'

'Still an' all, it won't take me more than two shakes of lamb's tail to go to my billet an—'

'He'll check up later, you know. He'll want to know, to the second, when you arrived. And if there are even a couple of minutes left unaccounted for, he'll have your guts for garters. So if I was in your shoes, Sergeant – and I wouldn't be, not for a king's ransom – I'd get over to that mess sharpish.'

The officers' mess was only distinguishable from the other wooden huts which surrounded it by a large notice nailed to the wall, and by a corporal posted on guard beside it. The notice said that 'other' ranks were prohibited from entering, unless with the explicit permission of an officer, and the corporal had clearly been charged with seeing that the edict was obeyed.

The corporal gave Woodend's pay-book a cursory glance, then said, 'He's at the bar. Says you're to report to him there.'

Inside, the mess was as unimpressive as its exterior had suggested it would be. There was a bar, and a few tables and chairs, but all in all, it was far less inviting than the average pub.

20

Ah, but anybody *could go into a pub,* Woodend *reminded himself, whereas officers' messes were exclusive – and exclusivity mattered to some people.*

Apart from the steward, the only man in the entire place was a captain who was sitting at the bar, sipping a pink gin and reading a newspaper. Woodend marched smartly over to him, deposited his kitbag on the floor, and came to attention.

'Sergeant Woodend, reporting for duty, sir!' he said.

The officer looked up, nodded vaguely, then turned his attention back to his newspaper.

Coutes kept him standing there for a full five minutes before folding his paper and giving him the briefest of inspections.

'So you're my new dogsbody, are you?' the Captain asked.

'Yes, sir.'

Coutes took a thoughtful drag on his cigarette. 'Surprised you didn't try to get out of this show altogether.'

'I beg your pardon, sir.'

'Served in North Africa, didn't you?'

'Yes, sir.'

'I heard it was rough.'

'It could be. On occasions.'

'So I'd have thought you'd have had a pretty good case for claiming battle fatigue, and putting in for some kind of clerical post.'

'It was suggested that I might.'

'Then why didn't you?'

Woodend shrugged. 'I've never been very keen on sittin' behind a desk. Besides, the job's not finished yet.'

'What job?'

'Defeatin' Hitler.'

Coutes snorted, then signalled to the steward that he wanted another drink. And though he would have been quite within his rights to order a drink for his new sergeant, too, he showed no signs of doing so.

Captain Coutes was slightly younger than he was himself, the sergeant decided. The Captain had a thin, pointed face and sharp little eyes. It wouldn't have been accurate to call him ugly – Woodend could think of any number of girls who might find him quite handsome – but there was definitely something untrustworthy and devious about him.

'So you think that it's your job to fight Hitler, do you, Sergeant?' Coutes asked.

'I think it's all our jobs, sir,' Woodend replied.

Coutes nodded. 'I suspected you were probably a death-or-glory boy the moment I saw you, and you've not disappointed me.' He lit a fresh cigarette from the butt of his old one, but did not offer the packet to Woodend, nor suggest that the sergeant stood at ease. 'Do you know what our job really is, Sergeant – I mean mine and yours?'

'We're to be a liaison with the American Army, based in Camp Haverton, aren't we, sir?'

'That's the fancy way of putting it. What it boils down to is keeping an eye on them until the time comes for us to ship them across the Channel to be used as cannon fodder. And I'm not just talking about the white farm boys here. We also – God help us – have to nursemaid the niggers.'

'The situation that we find ourselves in is particularly delicate because it involves not one, but *two,* important people,' Mr Forsyth explained to Woodend. 'The first is my minister, the Right Honourable Douglas Coutes. He's important not so much because he *is* a minister as because he's a *bloody good* minister in a *bloody difficult* ministry. The Yanks like him, the Russians respect him. And getting them both on your side, to a certain extent at least, is no mean feat.'

'So you're sayin' he's indispensable?'

Forsyth shook his head. 'Of course not. Nobody ever is. But we'd be pushed to find a replacement half as good as him.'

'If he goes down for murder, you won't have much choice,' Woodend pointed out.

'Exactly,' Forsyth agreed.

'Who's the other important person?' Woodend asked.

'Senator Eugene Kineally, Robert Kineally's older brother. He's braying loudly for Douglas Coutes's head on a platter, and he has such a powerful voice in the US Senate that the American government is – extremely reluctantly – joining in on the chorus.'

'What would have happened if Robert Kineally hadn't had such an important brother?' Woodend wondered.

'The case would have gone away,' Forsyth said flatly.

'I beg your pardon?'

'Douglas Coutes is involved in matters which will affect the fate of millions of people. The Americans, as I've already said, have the greatest possible confidence in him. Thus, if they could have looked the other way, they almost certainly would have done.'

'Even though Coutes killed one of their citizens?'

'Now, now, Chief Inspector,' Forsyth said, wagging his finger, almost playfully. 'All we know for a fact is that there is *some* evidence which might *tend* to implicate the Minister in the killing.'

'Are you talkin' about the bloody fingerprint?'

'Yes. Certainly that. But there's also a knife which appears, on the face of it, to have been the . . . er . . . murder weapon.'

'So they've found that, have they?'

'Yes, indeed. As a matter of fact, it was there in the grave – right next to the body.'

'That's convenient,' Woodend said. 'What kind of knife is it?'

Forsyth looked sheepish. 'A Prussian Army knife, of the kind the German Infantry used in the First World War.'

'One of them with a channel in the blade which allows the victim's blood to drain from the wound?'

'Exactly.'

'Coutes had a knife like that.'

'I know. To be frank with you, it's almost certain that the murder weapon did actually *belong* to the Minister.'

'So there's his prints on Kineally's dog tags, an' his knife was used to do the killin'?'

'As I said, some of the evidence does tend to implicate the Minister. But that's a long way, as I'm sure you'll agree, from concluding that the Minister wilfully and deliberately murdered Robert Kineally.' Forsyth paused. 'Any questions so far, Chief Inspector?'

'Yes,' Woodend said. 'Why are you tellin' *me* all this?'

'Because our working assumption is that the minister did *not* kill Kineally – and we want you to prove it.'

'Charlie Woodend, PI,' the Chief Inspector said.

Forsyth laughed politely. 'Not exactly. You will be granted some kind of semi-official status, because the Americans can quite see the need for us to have a presence in the investigation.'

'A presence?' Woodend repeated. 'We should have more than a bloody presence in the investigation! This was a murder committed in *England*.'

'Actually, it wasn't,' Forsyth corrected him. 'The body was discovered within the boundaries of Haverton Camp, which, at the time, was considered to be American soil.' He paused. 'Are you familiar with the Visiting Forces Act of 1942, Chief Inspector?'

'I can't say I am,' Woodend admitted.

'It was an act of parliament which authorized the Americans – acting through their own court martial system – to impose the death penalty, even within the confines of the United Kingdom. Of course, actual executions, when they were carried out, were left in the hands of an *English* hangman, but nevertheless, the general principle was established that it was the Americans who had the right to—'

'Hang on a minute,' Woodend interrupted. 'Douglas Coutes is a British citizen.'

'But he was on secondment to the American Army at the time the murder took place. They argue – and they seem to have very strong legal grounds for doing so – that that places him under their jurisdiction.'

'So if he's brought to trial, it'll be an American court martial that he appears before?'

'That seems to be the current thinking.'

'An' if he's found guilty, he'll be executed?'

'That eventuality seems highly unlikely, however much the senator pressurizes his government. But I think we're getting ahead of ourselves here. We don't want the minister to be even brought to trial. And that, of course, is where you come in.'

'Even if he's never tried, won't just the fact that he's been implicated in the investigation destroy his credibility?' Woodend wondered.

Forsyth chuckled. 'Of course not. This whole matter is being kept completely confidential. The official version of events is that the minister is still involved in intense negotiations with the American military.'

'An' what happens when the press get hold of the story?'

'They won't. And even if they did happen to, we'd slap D Notices on them, and they wouldn't be able to print a thing.

So you see, Chief Inspector, if there is no trial, it will be – to all intents and purposes – as if there had been no investigation, either.'

'I can't become personally involved in the investigation,' Woodend said. 'I was a witness.'

'You raised that objection with the Minister, too,' Forsyth said mildly. 'But it's not actually true, is it? At the time of the murder, you'd already been posted to the Isle of Wight. And what the Minister told *you* is perfectly correct. It's *because* you were there then that we want you there now. It's hard enough investigating a twenty-one year old murder, without having to try and imagine the atmosphere and circumstances in which it took place. But you don't have to imagine it, do you, Chief Inspector? Because you lived it!'

'I won't do it,' Woodend said flatly.

'I'm rather afraid that you will, you know,' Forsyth contradicted him. 'I am acting on the orders of the highest authorities, and you simply have no choice in the matter.'

The man from the Ministry reached down for an attaché case which was positioned – suspiciously conveniently – by the side of his chair. He opened it on his lap, took out a single sheet of paper, and laid it on the coffee table.

'Sign this,' he said.

'What is it?' Woodend asked.

'It's a copy of the Official Secrets Act. It commits you not to reveal anything you may discover during the course of your investigation, on penalty of imprisonment. Sign it.'

'Don't you think that it might be wise of me to read it through first?' Woodend said.

Forsyth shrugged. 'You can if you wish. But it doesn't make any difference. You may not like what it says – very few people who read it actually do – but you'll have to sign it anyway.'

Woodend took out his pen and scrawled his signature at the bottom of the document. 'Happy now?'

'I won't be happy until this rather unpleasant business is completely resolved,' Forsyth said. 'And perhaps not even then.' He picked up the document and returned it to his attaché case. 'There is one more thing I should inform you of, Chief Inspector.'

'An' what might that be?'

'You won't be conducting the investigation alone.'

'Are you sayin' that even though it's not a Central Lancs case, I can still take my sergeant with me, instead of just relyin' on local help?'

'No, I'm not saying that,' Forsyth replied. 'Although, if you do wish to take your own sergeant with you, I can certainly see no harm in it.'

'Ah, then we're back to this vague word "presences" that you were bandyin' around earlier,' Woodend said.

'Yes, we are,' Forsyth admitted. 'I'm truly sorry to have to tell you this, Chief Inspector Woodend, but Senator Kineally doesn't really trust the British police force—'

'Don't tell me that – it'll only make me cry,' Woodend said sarcastically.

'—but you shouldn't be too offended, because he doesn't trust the American military police, either.'

'Well, that's all right then. So who *does* he trust?'

'He trusts the Federal Bureau of Investigation. That's why you'll be working in tandem with one of their special agents. Don't worry, he's a good man – I've seen his service file.'

'Was he there, in Haverton Camp, at the time Robert Kineally disappeared?' Woodend asked. 'Is *that* why the Yanks have chosen him?'

'No, he wasn't there,' Forsyth said. 'As a matter of fact, he didn't even serve in the War.'

'Why not?

'He was far too young at the time.'

'Too young!'

'But he did attend Harvard University. And he has an excellent post-graduate degree in law.'

Woodend groaned. 'At least Bob Rutter only went to grammar school,' he said, almost to himself.

'What was that?' Forsyth asked.

'Education's a wonderful thing, but you can sometimes have too much of it – especially in my line of work.'

'I'm sure that's not true,' Forsyth said.

'That's easy enough to say when you've never actually been involved in a murder investigation yourself,' Woodend countered.

'I am to take it, then, that you have an objection to working with the special agent?'

'Now why ever would you think that?' Woodend asked. 'Let's look at the facts for a minute, shall we?'

'All right.'

'First of all, I'll be investigating a twenty-year-old case,' Woodend said, beginning to count off the points on his fingers. 'Secondly, at least half the witnesses will probably be dead by now – and the rest will have as vague a memory of the whole affair as I have myself. An' thirdly, I'll be under pressure to come up with one answer by the British government, an' another quite different one by this Senator Eugene Kineally. Have you got all that?'

'Yes, I think so.'

'Now, as you would imagine, given those circumstances, I'll be absolutely delighted to be workin' with some feller from the FBI – a man who wasn't long out of nappies when the murder happened, an' probably has no idea what it was like to live through those times. In fact, "delight" isn't a strong enough word for it. Workin' with this feller will be like the icin' on the bloody cake for me.'

'I'm pleased to note that you're adopting such a positive attitude,' Forsyth said, with a face so straight Woodend was sure that only a civil servant could have managed it.

Four

R unning a petrol station on the A49, just south of Ludlow, could scarcely have been called the world's most challenging or stimulating work. But as Wilfred Tattersall, the owner of that particular station, liked to tell his cronies in the local pub, any job was no more and no less than what you made of it.

'I don't just fill their tanks and check their oil, you know,' he'd say, when he'd had a few drinks.

'No, of course you don't, Wilf – sometimes you clean their windshields and put air in their tyres, as well,' one of his drinking companions would invariably counter.

'I use my time at the station to improve my knowledge of human nature,' Tattersall would continue, ignoring the interruption.

'You use your time to be a nosy parker, more like.'

'And what's *wrong* with being a nosy parker?' Tattersall would reply with dignity. 'Albert Einstein was a nosy parker. So were Sir Isaac Newton and Charles Darwin.'

'And which petrol company did *they* work for?' his so-called friends would ask, smirking into their pints.

But their scepticism did not bother Wilfred Tattersall – at least, not a great deal, and not all the time – and he continued in his quest of observing people and trying to work out just exactly what it was that made them tick.

The couple he served that Wednesday mid-morning – travelling in a Wolseley which had seen better days – provided him with ample material for speculation, since, unlike the commercial travellers and lorry drivers who made up much of his business, they were not easily classifiable.

For a start, he thought – as he gazed in at them through the windscreen that he was lethargically washing – they were showing no inclination at all to talk to each other. Yet there appeared to be none of the frostiness between them which suggested they'd had a row – a luxury that men and women often found themselves indulging in when they were forced to spend a long time in each others' company.

Nor did the two of them emanate any of the easy intimacy some married couples displayed – nor yet show the mutual contempt which other couples often opted for.

Even so, there was definitely something going on between them – the woman studied the man, as if attempting to anticipate his needs; the man was conscious of this scrutiny, and seemed to take it as his due.

'You'll be wearin' that windscreen away if you rub at it much longer,' the man said.

'Just finishing up now,' Tattersall replied, realizing that, in his fascination with this pair, he did seem to have been cleaning at the same spot for at least a couple of minutes.

Stepping away from the front of the Wolseley, Tattersall made a decision to mentally separate the subjects of his study – to confine each to a different chamber of his curious mind – in the hope that if he could understand each individually, he would be able to make more sense of them when he joined them together again.

The man – a big middle-aged bugger, whose head scraped against the car roof – was wearing an old sports jacket and cavalry twill trousers, which blended in well with the essential shabbiness of his vehicle. His lined face suggested he had seen much during his life – and would have preferred to have forgotten most of it – yet there was no sense of world-weariness about him. Rather, the philosopher of the petrol pumps decided, he was a man who had accepted that while there was a great deal about the earth which was rotten, it was still in the hands of every individual to do a little to improve things.

The woman was younger – not above thirty. She was dressed well – not expensively, but with style. She had blonde hair, and though her nose was perhaps a little large, she had a pretty face and a stunning body. There were no visible signs of despair on her face, and yet, for reasons he could not quite put his finger on, the attendant saw her as essentially a tragic figure.

The man got out of the car and stretched his legs. 'Do you sell newspapers?' he asked.

'I do,' Tattersall replied, excited by the thought of gleaning new information from his subject's choice of reading matter. 'Which one would you like? The *Daily Mail*? Or are you more of a *Telegraph* man?'

'I'll take a copy of every paper you've got.'

'Including the *Daily Worker*?'

'*Especially* the *Daily Worker*.'

'It's the official newspaper of the Communist Party, you know,' Tattersall said, almost as a warning.

'So I've heard,' his customer told him.

When Tattersall returned with the armful of newspapers, he saw that the woman had now slid across into the driver's seat.

'I'd never have put the big bugger down as a man who'd allow a woman to drive his car,' the garage owner told himself. 'But then again, I'd never have thought he'd buy the *Daily Worker*, either.'

The man paid for the petrol and the papers, then climbed into the passenger seat. The woman slipped the car into gear and pulled away at what was almost a racing start.

As the Wolseley disappeared down the road, Tattersall took off his cap and scratched his bald head. The pair of them were a team of some kind, he decided – and they were facing a problem which neither of them was quite sure how to handle.

As they drove further south, the stack of newspapers on Woodend's lap gradually diminished in size. But it was not until they were approaching a roadside sign which welcomed them to glorious Devon that the Chief Inspector finally threw the last of the papers over his shoulder, to join the pile which had already accumulated on the back seat.

'Well?' Monika Paniatowski asked.

'I didn't believe that feller Forsyth, when he told me him and his people could keep a tight lid on the whole affair,' Woodend told her. 'But, bugger me, if he hasn't gone and done just that!'

'So there's no mention of Haverton Camp in the papers?'

'Oh, there's a mention – it would have rung alarm bells in some quarters if there hadn't been – but it's the right *kind* of mention.'

'The right kind of mention?'

'Take the *Daily Express*, for example. There's a couple of paragraphs, buried deep inside it – right next to an advert for laxatives, as a matter of fact – which report that a body's been discovered at the camp. But there isn't even a hint that the Right Honourable Douglas Coutes might be involved. An' the *Daily Worker*, which would dearly love to do anythin' that might embarrass the government, hasn't given it any column space at all. Too busy expoundin' the principles of Marxist-Leninism, I expect.'

'None of which makes our job any easier, does it?' Monika Paniatowski asked. 'I mean to say, how are we expected to question the witnesses about Coutes, without them figuring out that he's the prime suspect?'

'It'll require footwork that'd leave Fred Astaire himself in awe of us,' Woodend said. 'But since we've both signed the Official Secrets Act, we have to find *some* way to make it work.'

'And what if, despite all the obstacles, we *do* prove that Coutes was, in fact, the murderer?'

'Ah, then it's what the Americans would call "a whole new ball game",' Woodend explained. 'If Coutes is guilty, all bets are off. The D Notices are withdrawn, the papers can print what they like, and the government will just have to come to terms with the harsh reality that one of its most senior members is a killer. Which, accordin' to our friend Mr Forsyth, will create an international crisis, the depth of which nobody can yet even begin to gauge.'

'So it would be best, all round, if Douglas Coutes turned out to be completely innocent?'

'Undoubtedly.'

'And do you think that he is?'

'That's not what the evidence uncovered so far would seem to suggest,' Woodend said cautiously.

'But what's your gut instinct, sir?'

'I don't know if I have one,' Woodend admitted. 'Douglas Coutes was a real nasty piece of work when I knew him – but the world is full of nasty pieces of work, an' not all of them turn into killers.'

'So it's possible he *was* framed, as he claims?'

'Yes.'

'But unlikely?'

'The only thing that Coutes has got goin' for him is that he's not a *stupid* man by any means,' Woodend mused. 'An'

31

if he *is* guilty, he made not one, but two, incredibly stupid mistakes – the first at the time of the murder, an' the second much later.'

'The one at the time would have been using his own knife to kill the American?' Paniatowski suggested.

'Yes, that's right,' Woodend agreed. 'I saw him with that knife myself, an' there must have been dozens of other people in Haverton Camp who'd done the same. So why not use some other weapon instead? Why not a bayonet, for example? That would have done the job – an' he could certainly have got his hands on one, easily enough.'

'Yes, I imagine he could,' Paniatowski said.

'An' even if he *did* use his own knife,' Woodend continued, 'whatever would have possessed him to leave it in the grave with his victim?'

'He could have panicked,' Paniatowski suggested. 'Killers do make incredible mistakes when they lose their nerve.'

'True enough,' Woodend agreed. 'But Coutes never struck me as the panicking sort.'

'What about the second mistake he might have made?' Monika Paniatowski asked.

'That was very recent. In his position as Minister of Defence, he must have been consulted on the matter of selling Haverton Camp to a firm of property developers.'

'And if he'd known that Kineally's body was buried there, he'd have done all he could to block the sale?'

'Exactly. But accordin' to what Forsyth's told me, Coutes showed very little interest in the sale at all. So either he *is* innocent or he's *so* arrogant that he thought that even if the body was discovered, he'd get away with it.'

'Which is highly unlikely, because of the knife,' Monika Paniatowski pointed out.

'Which is highly unlikely because of the knife,' Woodend agreed. 'So what we're left with, Sergeant, is a situation which doesn't add up *however* you rearrange the clues.'

'You mentioned a girl,' Paniatowski said.

'Did I?' Woodend asked, sounding suddenly troubled.

'I think you said that her name was Mary Parkinson.'

'I should never have brought that name up.'

'Why?'

'Because I'd like you to keep an open mind about this case,

32

Monika, an' if I start tellin' you all about Mary Parkinson, it'll slam at least a couple of your mental doors tight shut.'

'What does that mean, exactly?' Paniatowski wondered.

'That once you've told me all about her – and how she fits into this case – I'll feel inclined to think that Coutes is guilty?'

'More or less.'

'I still think I should know.'

'An' I don't,' Woodend said firmly. 'It's bad enough that I should be prejudiced against the bastard right from the start, without you gettin' in on the act as well.'

'But if I don't have the full picture—'

'Talk about somethin' else,' Woodend said, in a tone which was not quite an order – but came perilously close to it.

'They want me to back off!' Senator Eugene Kineally told his Chief of Staff, that crisp Washington DC morning which was to see the first of the cherry blossom come into bloom. 'Those sons-of-bitches at the other end of Pennsylvania Avenue are pressuring me to back off!'

It was undoubtedly true that they were, the Chief of Staff thought. And, in some ways – given the international situation – he could quite sympathize with the White House's position. But if this Administration – or indeed *any* administration – really believed that it could bully Eugene Kineally into submission, then it didn't know him at all.

Kineally had been so badly wounded at the Battle of Guadalcanal, in February 1942, that his doctors told him he would never walk again. They had further hinted that his best course of action would be to grab his disability pension with both hands, and settle down to a life as a chronic invalid. Kineally had treated that advice with the contempt he felt it deserved. In November 1944, leaning heavily on a walking stick, he had been elected junior senator for Connecticut by a margin which left his opponent reeling with shock. Now, twenty-one years later, he was the senior senator for his state, the chairman of one of the most powerful committees in the Senate, and though he still walked with a slight limp, his leg only really troubled him when he was either very tired or very angry.

This was not a man, then, the Chief of Staff thought, who was going to be pushed around by anybody lower down the scale than the Lord God Almighty – and even against God, he might resist a *little*.

'I want justice for my kid brother,' the Senator said, 'and if I don't get it, I'll block every piece of legislation this penny-ante Administration tries to force through the Senate.'

'They are doing what you wanted them to,' the Chief of Staff reminded him. 'They may not like it – they'd probably reverse it if they possibly could – but they are *doing* it.'

The Senator grimaced, as a shooting pain passed through his leg. 'The FBI's already on the case, is it?' he asked.

'Mr Hoover's told us that he's already sent one of his best teams over to England.'

'And how are the Brits taking it?'

'Very well – under the circumstances. They've assigned one of their own investigators to the case.' The Chief of Staff consulted his notes. 'A Chief Inspector Charles Woodend. It seems he knew your brother.'

'Chuck Woodend!' the Senator exclaimed. 'Sergeant Chuck Woodend!'

'You've heard of him?' the Chief of Staff asked, amazed.

'Damned right, I've heard of him,' the Senator replied.

Five

The first official acknowledgement that Haverton Camp actually existed did not appear until the Wolseley and its occupants were only a few miles from the place itself. And when it did come, it was in the form of an old and battered signpost which – as if to make up for the previous lack of information – indicated the camp both to the north and the south.

'That's because it's on a loop,' Woodend explained. 'You can't approach the camp directly, you see. You have to go through either Haverton Village or Coxton first.'

'Which is quicker?' Paniatowski asked.

'Through Haverton Village,' Woodend said.

'Then should I—'

'But I think we'll go via Coxton.'

'Any particular reason for us going the long way round?' wondered the sergeant, who had been behind the wheel for over three hours and was about ready for a break.

'Aye, there is,' Woodend told her. 'It'll give you the opportunity to see for yourself what we now know to be the Trail of the Red Herring.'

Coxton was a pretty village which since the arrival of the railway, some time in the nineteenth century, had been doing its very best to pretend it was actually a small town. The station which was the basis for such pretensions was located at Coxton's southern end, and looking at the station now – with its Victorian cast-iron work and wooden crenellations – Woodend found himself swept up in a sudden and unexpected wave of nostalgia.

'Coxton Halt was the last place in this area I ever set foot in,' he told Paniatowski. 'I boarded a train there, one dark night in May 1944, an' I've never been back here since.'

'How did you feel about it at the time?' asked Monika Paniatowski, who, during her own wartime ordeal, had left more places behind her than her boss had had hot dinners.

'I suppose I left with mixed feelings,' Woodend confessed. 'Part of me was glad to be movin' on, because I knew the *reason* I was bein' transferred was that the invasion must be gettin' very close.'

'And like the gung-ho young man you probably were back then, you just couldn't wait to cross the Channel and into the thick of the fighting,' Paniatowski said, a little mischievously.

'Nearly right,' Woodend said. 'It's true enough that I did want the fightin' to start. But that was only so we could get it all over an' done with – only so I could get back to my real life.'

'What about the other part of you?' Paniatowski asked.

'What?'

'Since you say you had mixed feelings about it, I take it there was a part *didn't* want to go.'

'True enough, there was,' Woodend agreed. 'I hadn't been in Haverton Camp for long, but it had been long enough for me to meet some very nice people – an' in wartime, meetin' nice people is one of the few things that seem to make life worth livin'.'

Mary Parkinson had been a nice person, he thought.

He recalled seeing her, still standing on the platform, as the train had pulled out – a small and delicate creature made even smaller and more delicate by her obvious misery.

He wondered whether he'd made the right decision in choosing not to brief Monika on Mary – and thought that he probably had.

Coxton Woods lay about half a mile beyond the railway station, and the road cut right through the middle of them.

Woodend had not remembered them as being so extensive. But then, he supposed, a lot could change in twenty-one years. Some things had got older, some things had died, and some things – like the woods and Douglas Coutes's power – had gone from strength to strength.

'So here we are on the Trail of the Red Herring,' he told Monika Paniatowski.

'Meaning what, exactly?' Paniatowski asked.

36

'Meaning that when Robert Kineally went missing, his jeep went missing as well. An' this wood is where they found it.'

'Where *who* found it? The American military police?'

'Not them, no. Although, accordin' to what both Forsyth and Coutes told me, they'd certainly been lookin' for it hard enough.'

'Because they thought that if they found the jeep, they'd find Robert Kineally as well?'

'Exactly. But, as things turned out, it was actually discovered – purely by chance – by a local lad, some ten days after the search began.'

'You say it was abandoned in the woods?' Monika Paniatowski said, thoughtfully.

'That's right.'

'How *deep* into the woods?'

'Not very deep at all, as a matter of fact. No more than a short stroll from the station.'

'Then why . . .?'

'Wasn't it found earlier?'

'Yes.'

'It was covered with American Army-issue camouflage – which they managed to trace back to Haverton Camp. So what conclusion do you think the MPs came to?'

'That Robert Kineally had camouflaged it himself. Because the longer it took his pursuers to find the jeep, the longer it would take them to realize that he'd caught a train.'

'Just so. An' for anybody who didn't know he was already dead and buried, it'd be a perfectly logical conclusion to reach. Anyway, as far as the American MPs were concerned, that pretty much ended their part of the investigation into his disappearance. Wherever he'd gone after he boarded the train, he was now somebody else's problem.'

'Which is, of course, just what the killer must have wanted them to think,' Paniatowski stated.

'Too right. And the ruse worked for *twenty-one* years! But not any more. *Now*, the FBI will claim it was Coutes who drove the jeep, in an effort to cover his own tracks.'

'Though *whoever* killed Kineally would probably have done the same thing,' Paniatowski pointed out.

'True,' Woodend agreed.

But I'd so like it to be Douglas Coutes, he thought to himself. I really *want it* to be Douglas Coutes.

'What was your impression of Robert Kineally as a person?' Paniatowski asked.

A smile – half-warm, half-regretful – found its way to the Chief Inspector's lips.

'I liked the feller,' Woodend said. 'I liked him a lot.'

Captain Robert Kineally was tall, and had the kind of even white teeth that British dentists would dream about but never expect to see. His face was pleasing, rather than handsome, but – above all – it was earnest.

'I guess I'm what you might call a relationships kinda guy,' he explained to Woodend and Coutes over pints of warm beer at the Dun Cow, which was the nearest pub to Haverton Camp.

'A relationships kinda guy,' Coutes repeated, with something bordering on contempt.

'Sure,' Kineally agreed, missing the tenor of Coutes's words completely. 'The way I look at the situation, we're all in this big battle against the Nazis together, and I kinda see it as my job to ensure that everybody becomes friends and stays friends.'

Coutes took a sip of his beer, grimaced, pushed it to one side, and ordered a pink gin.

'Very nice – but a million miles from the truth,' he said.

'Yeah?' Kineally asked.

'Yeah,' Coutes mimicked. 'What your job really boils down to, Captain Kineally, is passing on messages from your boss to us, so that we can pass them on to our bosses.'

Kineally looked troubled by the statement. 'Is that all *you see it as, Captain Coutes?' he asked.*

'No,' Coutes replied.

'I'm sure glad about that,' Kineally said, looking relieved.

'The other part is a little more complex,' Coutes continued. 'When your bosses screw up – and they will *screw up, trust me on that – then it's your job to convince us they haven't actually screwed up at all.'*

'And what's your job?' Kineally asked, looking troubled again.

'Our job is to pretend to believe whatever pathetic reason you come up with to excuse your boss's incompetence. Of course,

38

it works the other way round as well, and you'll have to prac-
tice pretending to believe the excuses that we come up with
to explain away our *boss's cock-ups.'*

'There's surely more to it than that?'

'Not at all. Neither of our countries wants to lose more
men than it has to in the fighting, and so we're splitting the
risk. Which means that, even if we come to hate each other,
we have to put on a united front. And that's what we're here
for – to paper over the cracks.'

Kineally's *frown deepened. 'See, I think there's a more posi-*
tive role that you and I could play,' he said.

'And that is . . . ?'

'I think we could work to make our armies understand each
other a little better.'

'They don't need *to understand each other,' Coutes said*
disgustedly. 'They're here to learn how to fight. And while
they're learning how to fight, they should also be learning
how to obey orders without question.'

'You make them sound like machines,' Kineally said,
sounding increasingly bewildered.

'I wish that's what they were,' Coutes told him. 'Machines
are much easier to handle. Big guns stay in position and fire
when they're told to. Squaddies, on the other hand, are born
with a tendency to cut and run.'

'Squaddies?' Kineally repeated.

'Ordinary soldiers,' Woodend supplied.

'Oh, grunts,' Kineally said. 'Yeah, it's the grunts I'm mostly
concerned about. I'm from Connecticut, which can be a pretty
sophisticated kinda place, and I've travelled to Europe before.
But most of the men who make up our army have never left
the States. Hell, most of them have never even left their own
state *– or their own* part *of their own state. And suddenly*
they're the other side of the pond, having to deal with a people
whose English they can hardly understand, and a way of life
which they've only ever seen in old movies.'

'So what?' Coutes wondered.

'I'd like them to get something out of the experience of
being over here,' Kineally said. 'When they go into battle, I'd
like it if they were fighting not only for their own country but
also for the ordinary decent folks they've met while they were
over here in Britain.'

39

'If you want to make that your hobby, then by all means go ahead,' Coutes said coldly. 'But don't ever confuse it with the job you're actually meant to do. And don't try to drag us into it.'

Kineally turned his attention to Woodend. 'What do you make of all this, Chuck?' he asked. He paused, and almost reddened. 'You don't mind if I call you Chuck, do you?'

'I don't mind at all,' Woodend said.

'So, do you think I'm right?'

A picture of Joan came uninvited into Woodend's mind, and he knew that however difficult things became in the future, that picture would somehow pull him through.

'I think you've got a very good point, sir,' he said. 'In my experience, men always fight better when they've got something to fight for.'

He should never have said that, he thought, noticing how Coutes was glaring at him.

But it was the simple truth as he saw it, and he could not bring himself to regret speaking the words.

Once they'd left Coxton Woods behind them, the roads got narrower, and soon they were travelling along a high-banked country lane which was bordered by spring primroses. It was a twisty-turny lane, one of those which dutifully respected the boundaries of fields which had existed long before there had been any metalled road there at all.

'Are you absolutely sure we're going the right way, sir?' Monika Paniatowski asked.

Woodend grinned, and though he already knew the answer to the question he was about to put, he said, 'Now why on earth would you ask that?'

'I suppose it's because I was probably expecting something altogether more . . . more . . .'

'Impressive?'

'Yes, that's probably what I mean,' Paniatowski agreed. She paused, as if searching for a tactful way to phrase what she wanted to say next. 'It was a *proper* camp that you were based at, wasn't it, sir?' she continued.

'Depends what you mean by "proper",' Woodend said. 'It had all the things that most camps had.'

'Including heavy vehicles?'

'Most certainly including heavy vehicles.'

'Tanks?'

'No, none of them, as it happens. They were either on Salisbury Plain or down on the coast. But we had most of the rest – jeeps, armoured cars, trucks. We even had a couple of bulldozers.'

'Why?'

'We needed them to clear away any obstacles we'd meet when we eventually landed in Normandy.'

'And all of that came down this lane?' Paniatowski asked. 'The trucks? The armoured cars? Even the bulldozers?'

'They had to. There *was* no other way.'

'So how the hell did they manage it?'

Woodend grinned again. 'Slowly – and with great difficulty,' he said. 'You have to understand, Monika, that though the Invasion of Normandy was probably the biggest amphibious landin' that the world has ever seen – an', with a bit of luck, is ever likely to see – a lot of the decisions about how it was to be run were made entirely on the hoof.'

'It all sounds very amateur.'

'I suppose it was, in a way. There was no laid-down procedure for an operation on that scale, you see, so the planners invented them as they went along. An' while it would have been better to have nice wide roads runnin' to all the camps, neither the time nor the resources were available, so the planners decided we could do without them.'

'Why is it the British always seem to make a virtue out of having to put up with botched-up jobs?' Paniatowski asked, the Polish side of her nature – for once – coming to the surface.

'It might have been botched-up, but you can't deny that it worked,' Woodend said, surprised to find himself suddenly so much on the defensive.

'True,' Paniatowski agreed. 'But given the way that things were run back then, it's hardly surprising that Robert Kineally's body could have lain undiscovered for over twenty years, now is it?'

41

Six

The last remaining soldiers had finally departed from Haverton Camp in 1946. They left behind them enamelled signs which proclaimed that what lay beyond the chain-link fence was Ministry of Defence property, and that trespass was strictly prohibited, but neither the army nor the ministry itself had given much thought to the place since then.

Had there been a church on the camp, thieves would no doubt have descended on it and stripped the lead from the roof. Had it been close to a large town, then it might well have been squatted in by those unwilling to continue paying high urban rents. But as it was stuck out in the middle of the countryside, with nothing in it worth stealing, it had pretty much been left alone – except by courting couples anxious for a little privacy, and bike-riding kids in search of an adventure.

With the boom in house building and the extension of private motor car ownership, all that had changed. Suddenly, the camp did not seem so far from civilization any more. Suddenly, it ceased to be a decaying relic of another time, and had become a prime development site.

And then the body had been discovered by the team making the developers' preliminary survey, and the camp had come alive again *as a camp,* Woodend thought as they approached the main gate. Now, for the first time in nearly twenty years, the Stars and Stripes fluttered from the flagpole, and the entrance was guarded by two stern-looking men in white helmets.

The Wolseley pulled up at the barrier, and Woodend wound down his window and produced his warrant card.

The military policeman examined it carefully, then stepped back to look at the car. 'You come far, sir?' he asked, conversationally.

'About two hundred and fifty miles,' Woodend said.

'In *this* thing?' the policeman asked, sketching out the body of the Wolseley with his hands, as if trying to establish whether what he was seeing was actually what was there.

'What's *wrong* with my car?' Woodend asked, stung.

'It's kinda small,' the military policeman said. 'Jeez, a vehicle like this would fit into the trunk of *my* automobile.' He paused, and coloured slightly. 'No offence meant, sir,' he continued.

'None taken,' Woodend assured him.

After all, it wasn't really his fault, the Chief Inspector thought.

The Yanks he himself had known during the war had been just like this one – surprised by the minuteness of everything they came across, from the size of the country they found themselves in (which their education officers had informed was slightly smaller than Oregon), to the size of the rations on which the British people were expected to subsist. They'd got used to it in time – so much so that they didn't even really see it as abnormal any more – but their initial shock had been almost comical to observe.

'When did you arrive in Britain, son?' he asked the military policeman. 'Yesterday? The day before?'

'Flew in yesterday, sir. How did you know that?'

Woodend grinned. 'I'm a detective. Says so on my warrant card.'

The MP returned his grin. 'Sure does,' he agreed.

'An' I imagine there was more than just the two of you on that plane who were heading for this camp,' Woodend hazarded.

'Hell, yes,' the MP agreed. 'I'd guess there must have been a hundred guys in all.'

A hundred guys, Woodend repeated to himself.

His own government had sent him and Monika – and Monika was only there because he'd asked for her. The American government, on the other hand, had sent *a hundred guys*.

He should have remembered, from his days at the *old* Haverton Camp, that the Yanks never did things by halves. And this time they weren't just demonstrating their natural inclination to be thorough – this time they had the additional incentive of being spurred on in their actions by a powerful politician who was *demanding* results.

*   *   *

43

It was like travelling back in time, Woodend thought as the Wolseley followed the MP's jeep through the old camp. No, he corrected himself, it wasn't *like* travelling back at all – it was the real thing.

Driving past the endless rows of barrack huts, he felt the young Charlie Woodend entering him; the Charlie who didn't have a wife with a heart condition and a daughter who was training to be a nurse; the Charlie still to discover that murder was rarely simple, and the motives behind it often amazingly complex; the Charlie who, despite three years of war, was yet to kill another living being face to face – was yet to look into the eyes of a man whose life he was just about to steal from him.

They had left the huts behind them, and were approaching the open space which had once been the parade ground.

But it wasn't an open space any more! A whole encampment of caravans now covered the area where formerly there had been only a sea of concrete.

'Christ!' Paniatowski gasped.

Woodend knew exactly how she felt. It wasn't just the *number* of caravans which had taken her breath away, it was their *magnitude*. These caravans were not the fragile tin boxes on wheels which normally held up traffic on the narrow Devon roads during the summer holiday months. Instead, they were monsters – as long as some houses.

'Where, in God's name, do you think they got those bloody big things from?' Monika asked.

'From the same place they got the MPs,' Woodend said. 'They've flown them in from the States.'

The jeep came to a halt in front of one of these juggernauts, and Paniatowski parked the Wolseley behind it.

The MP turned around. 'That trailer just in front of you is Mr Grant's, sir,' he said.

Then he put the jeep into gear, and pulled away.

'Who's Mr Grant?' Paniatowski asked.

'My guess is that he's our oppo from the Federal Bureau of Investigation,' Woodend replied.

Edward Grant was not quite the fresh-faced college boy Woodend had feared he might turn out to be from Forsyth's description, but there was no doubt that he was still approaching thirty with confidence, rather than walking away from it with a vague sense of foreboding.

Despite the fact that he had been totally alone in his caravan before they had arrived, Woodend noted, the Special Agent was still dressed formally, in a sober suit, white shirt and dark tie. The shine on his black shoes would have satisfied an inspection by the most critical of Regimental Sergeant Majors, and his even teeth gleamed like stars.

He gave Woodend a firm manly handshake, and Paniatowski a more restrained, genteel one.

'Would you like a soda in my trailer first, or should I take you to your own quarters right away?' he asked.

'Neither,' Woodend replied. 'Before we do anythin' else, we'd like to see where the body was found.'

Grant grinned, good-naturedly. 'Gosh, you guys really *are* a pair of eager beavers.'

'Mr Woodend always likes to clog-it around the scene of the crime before he even thinks about doing anything else,' Paniatowski explained. 'He's famous for it, back in Lancashire.'

'Oh, OK, that's fine with me,' Grant said, though it was plain he had no idea what on earth she was talking about. 'The quickest way to get to the grave is to cut through J. Edgar Hoover City.'

'Cut through *what*?'

'J. Edgar Hoover City,' Grant repeated. 'It's the name that the guys have given this little set-up of ours.'

'Cute,' Woodend said, unconvincingly.

The caravans – the *trailers* – had been set out in neat rows, and each one had its own generator.

'We've got men out laying power lines right now,' Grant said, shouting over the generators' hum, 'so, with luck, we should be able to get rid of stone age technology by tomorrow at the latest.'

'Most impressive,' Woodend said.

And it was! After years of having to almost beg to secure the resources which he needed to do his job properly, this was like landing in Santa's Grotto.

'The trailers at this end are mainly accommodation,' Grant explained. 'The good stuff's at the other end.'

'The good stuff?' Woodend repeated.

'The crime labs,' Grant said airily, adding, in case Woodend had missed the point, 'the forensic laboratories.'

'You're speakin' in the plural. How many of them are there?' Woodend asked.

'Three.'

'An' how many technicians?'

'Eight.'

Woodend whistled softly to himself. This was another way of looking at the world entirely, he thought – though, of course, as with every other aspect of this particular investigation, it probably helped that it had Senator Eugene Kineally's total support.

'Are these technicians of yours the same ones who did the examination of Robert Kineally's remains?' he asked.

Grant shook his head. 'No, these guys are all just as new to the case as we are ourselves.'

'So who *did* carry out the initial tests on Kineally? Were they done at Scotland Yard?'

'No, not there, either,' Special Agent Grant said.

'Why not?'

'I have the greatest possible admiration for the British police and their methods,' Grant said, obviously choosing his words with the greatest of care. 'We, in the FBI, have learned much from studying your methods in the past.'

'But . . . ?' Woodend asked.

'But we must all accept the fact any workman is only as good as his tools, and that even with the best will in world, you simply can't make a silk purse out of a sow's ear.'

'I don't suppose you can, though it's not somethin' I've ever tried to do myself,' Woodend said. 'But I still have no idea what you're talkin' about, Special Agent.'

'May I be frank?' Grant asked.

'You can be whoever you like, as long as you answer my question,' Woodend told him.

Grant smiled, as if accepting that Woodend had just said something funny but still not quite understanding what it had been.

'We are the most technologically advanced nation in the world,' he said. 'We have pledged to put a man on the moon by the end of the decade, and I have no doubts that we will fulfil that pledge, whereas—'

'Whereas *we* can't get the Number Seventeen bus between Whitebridge and Darwen to run on time,' Woodend said dryly.

'I beg your pardon?'

'I think what you're tryin' to say is that the reason you had the body shipped back to Washington is because the FBI has labs which make ours look like junior chemistry sets.'

'I wouldn't put it quite in those words,' Grant said, though it was plain that was exactly what he *had* meant. 'The body would have had to be flown back to States eventually, anyway, because once this investigation is over, it will be buried in Arlington Cemetery, with full military honours.'

'From what I remember of Robert Kineally, that's the least he deserves,' Woodend said.

Just beyond the end of the line of trailers, half a dozen workmen were busily engaged in constructing a pre-fabricated – but nonetheless substantial-looking – building.

'What's that?' Woodend asked.

'The courtroom,' Grant said.

'Is it, indeed?' Woodend asked thoughtfully. 'You think you'll need it, do you?'

'We did consider other options,' Special Agent Grant admitted. 'But it somehow didn't seem quite right to hold anything as important as a court martial in an ordinary trailer.'

'You're missin' my point, lad,' Woodend said.

'And what point might that be?'

'A court martial is a bit like a theatrical performance – you might have all the props ready an' waitin', but you can't stage the production at all without your star turn.'

'True, but—'

'Or have I missed somethin' here?' Woodend interrupted. 'Has Douglas Coutes been arrested an' charged in the time it took me to drive from Whitebridge to here?'

'No, he . . . uh . . . hasn't been either arrested *or* charged,' Grant said, looked slightly embarrassed. 'At the moment he's just doing what I believe you British bobbies like to call "helping us with our enquiries".'

'Then isn't all this a bit like knotting the noose before the sentence is passed?' Woodend wondered.

'Hell, if we don't charge him, we can always take the court-room down again,' Grant said, trying to sound casual.

But you don't think that's going to happen, do you?

47

Woodend thought. As far as you're concerned, the whole deal's already done and dusted.

They had left the parade ground behind them, and were almost at the perimeter fence. The ground was covered with rough grass, except for one small area which had been excavated.

Woodend looked down at what had been a shallow grave. 'Remind me how was this discovered?' he said.

'The way I heard it, the surveyors were taking some kind of soil sample when they started uncovering bits of the stiff,' Grant answered.

'Robert Kineally,' Woodend said harshly. 'He wasn't a stiff! He wasn't a cadaver! His name was Robert Kineally.'

Grant looked shocked by the other man's sudden, unexpected vehemence. 'They started uncovering bits of *Robert Kineally*,' he corrected himself. 'Once they'd realized what it was they'd found, they cleared a little more earth to make sure there really was a body in here, then they called the local cops.'

'So if they'd decided to take their soil sample from somewhere else – say, a couple of feet to the left or the right – they'd have missed the body completely,' Woodend said thoughtfully.

'Damn straight!' Grant agreed. 'And there's guys in *both* our governments who wish they'd done just that.'

Woodend looked around. The parade ground was behind him, the perimeter fence in front and to the left, and the barrack blocks to his right. But what had been on the spot where he was now standing back in 1944?

This was where most of the motor vehicles had been parked! he suddenly remembered. The jeeps and the trucks, the armoured cars and motor cycles.

He pictured the killer moving silently across the camp in the dead of night, a corpse slung over one shoulder and held in place by one of his arms, while in his free hand he carried a shovel.

There had been night-time patrols at the time, he recalled, but they'd been on the other side of the fence, because attention had naturally been focussed on stopping outsiders getting in – not on preventing those *already* on the inside from burying the bodies of their victims.

So, the murderer had reached this spot without being intercepted. Then what had he done?

Chances were that he had begun to dig the grave close to where one of the armoured cars was parked – because when it pulled off, the following morning, its treads would all but eradicate any evidence of the night's work.

Woodend lit up a cigarette, and examined the grave again. The killer would have known that the longer he was involved in his grisly task, the greater the chances he would be discovered. But he would also have been aware of the fact that if he made the grave *too* shallow, there was a strong possibility that the army vehicles – churning up the earth – would uncover it. So he had made a calculated decision, and this grave – not too deep and not too shallow – was the result.

The man who'd dug it must have had nerves of steel, Woodend thought. And Douglas Coutes – for all his other faults – had just such nerves. So how likely was it that, having kept his cool thus far, he would then make the stupid mistake of leaving the murder weapon beside the corpse?

Woodend turned to Special Agent Grant. 'Let me ask you the big question now,' he suggested.

'And what might that be?'

'How the hell are we even supposed to even *begin* conducting this investigation?'

The American shrugged. 'I'm not overly familiar with your current methodology, Chief Inspector, but I would imagine you'll begin it pretty much the same way you begin every other investigation.'

'With every other investigation, I like to start by talking to the potential witnesses,' Woodend said tartly.

'Sure!'

'But that's not possible here, is it?'

'Why ever not?'

'Because all the potential witnesses in this case are either dead, or dispersed over two – possibly even three – continents.'

Grant smiled. 'Even a top-notch organization like the FBI can't do anything about the dead ones,' he said. 'But we've tracked down the live ones, and they should be here real soon now.'

'All of them?' Woodend asked incredulously.

'I believe so,' Grant confirmed.

'And how the hell have you managed that?'

Grant shrugged again. 'We employed a number of the various means at our disposal.'

'For instance?'

'Some of the witnesses agreed to come because they saw it as their patriotic duty. Others did it because they're government employees, and it was what Uncle Sam wanted them to do. That accounts for most of them.'

'An' the rest?'

'In the case of the more problematic ones, we found that sweetening the pot soon overcame any objections they might have had.'

'Sweetening the pot?'

'For the time they're here in this country, they'll be drawing the pay of a full colonel – which, for some of them, is more money than they've seen in their entire lives.'

'You've spent so much on this case already that you really *have to* solve it in the end, don't you?' Woodend said.

Grant grinned again. 'We've already solved it,' he said. 'We *know* we have. And this whole dog and pony show is only being laid on so that eventually *you'll* believe it, too.'

'Well, that's certainly puttin' it plainly enough,' Woodend said. 'Absolutely no frills at all.' He turned to his sergeant. 'I've got somethin' that I need to do alone, Monika. Can you find a way to keep yourself occupied for half an hour or so?'

'I expect so,' Paniatowski replied. 'What is it you'll be doing?'

'I thought I might as well go an' pay a visit on the condemned man,' Woodend told her.

Seven

Special Agent Grant had insisted that Paniatowski return to his trailer with him, in order to sample a cup of what he called 'real American coffee', and it was while she was drinking the brew – which wasn't half bad – that the large military truck pulled outside.

Paniatowski looked out of the window. 'It's loaded with boxes,' she said. 'And I mean *loaded.*'

Grant drained the dregs of his coffee, and placed his cup carefully back on the counter. 'Excellent!' he said.

'And are you going to tell me what's in all those boxes?' Paniatowski wondered.

'Sure,' Grant agreed. 'It's evidence.'

'Evidence?'

'Service records, reports, statements made to the military police at the time of Robert Kineally's mysterious disappearance, newspaper clippings – and the results of all the forensic tests which were carried out back at our headquarters in Washington.'

'In other words, they contain everything but the kitchen sink,' Paniatowski said.

Grant looked at her curiously. 'Is there a kitchen sink involved in this investigation?' he asked, and then, without waiting for an answer, stood up and walked over to the door.

A large MP had climbed down from the truck, and looked at him expectantly. 'Where do you want all this junk, sir?' he asked.

'Junk!' Grant repeated, his sensibilities clearly offended. 'It's very far from junk, my friend. What you have on the truck is the possible solution to an unsolved major crime.'

'Whatever you say,' the MP replied, indifferently. 'Where do you want I should unload?'

'The trailer next to mine,' Grant told him.

'You got it, sir,' the MP said, and began lifting boxes off the back of the truck.

Grant watched the whole process with obvious pleasure. 'It's kinda like being given a map to a secret buried treasure, don't you think, Sergeant?' he asked Paniatowski.

'Kinda,' Paniatowski replied, with none of the enthusiasm which the Special Agent seemed to be expecting.

The problem was, this wasn't her sort of work at all, she thought. Following paper trails – making dry, dusty documents yield up their secrets – was something her ex-lover, DI Bob Rutter, had excelled in. She herself was much more like Charlie Woodend – clogging-it around, ferreting out hidden thoughts from hidden corners of other people's minds.

She wondered how Bob was dealing with life at that precise moment.

Not well, she suspected.

Though she couldn't really *know.*

When she'd first heard about Rutter's nervous breakdown, her impulse had been to rush to his side and offer to nurse him through it.

But she hadn't done that, had she? Instead, she'd held back, because she simply didn't want to intrude where she wasn't wanted.

If he needed her help, she had argued to herself at the time, he would ask for it. If there was to be contact – of *any* kind – between them in the future, then he should be the one to initiate it.

And she'd always thought he *would* – which showed just what a lousy judge of human nature she'd turned out to be!

She thought about her current lover, Detective Chief Inspector Baxter, a man closer to Woodend's age than to her own. She had no idea how long that particular relationship would last – was not even sure if she wanted it to last at all. She did not love him, as she had once loved Bob (and perhaps still *did* love Bob) but she enjoyed his company – both in and out of bed.

'Since we've got time to spare while they're unloading the evidence, maybe we should take the opportunity to get to know each other a little better,' Special Agent Grant suggested.

'I beg your pardon?' Monika said.

Grant laughed. 'Oh gee, given everything I've heard all

about how you Brits are famous for your reserve and stiff upper lips, I suppose I should have been expecting that response,' he said. 'Still and all, it seems to me that if we were to fill in a little of our own backgrounds, it might help each of us to understand where the other one is coming from.'

What a strange way this American had of putting things, Monika thought. But she suspected that she knew what he meant.

Probably!

'All right,' she agreed, pushing her reserve and stiff upper lip to one side for the moment. 'I'm Polish by origin—'

'Yeah, I didn't think Paniatowski was much of an English name,' Grant interrupted her.

'My father was in one of the Polish cavalry regiments when the Germans invaded our homeland in 1939,' Paniatowski continued. 'By all accounts, the regiments fought heroically, but even they must have known that horses were never going to be any match for tanks.'

'I suppose your father must have been killed in action,' Grant asked, sympathetically.

'Yes, he was killed,' Paniatowski agreed. 'So many brave men were killed in such a short time.' She shuddered. 'Anyway,' she pressed on, more matter-of-factly, 'my mother and I spent the next six years wandering around Central Europe as refugees.'

'That must have been tough.'

'Well, it certainly wasn't the kind of life that I'd recommend to anybody else. We fed ourselves on things that even the pigs would probably have turned down, and when there wasn't even that available, we almost starved to death. Eventually, at the end of the war, my mother met an English officer in occupied Berlin. He asked her to marry him, and when she agreed, he brought both of us to England.'

'It's almost like a fairytale ending,' Grant said.

'Yes it is,' Monika agreed.

If you're prepared to overlook the fact that he made my mother's life a misery and sexually abused me, she added silently.

'Gosh, after the amazing life you've already led, mine seems so dull that I hardly dare tell you about it,' Grant said. He took a deep breath. 'But here goes anyway. I was born on

53

a farm in Wisconsin, and that's where I lived until I went to college.'

'Harvard, wasn't it?' Paniatowski asked. 'Just about one of the most famous universities in America.'

'Yeah, I got lucky,' Grant said dismissively. 'Anyways, I graduated, got a postgraduate law degree, and looked around for something to do. I suppose I could have gotten a job on Wall Street, but what I was really searching for was a worthwhile purpose to dedicate the rest of my life to, and joining the FBI seemed to pretty much fill the ticket.'

'Are you married, Ed?' Paniatowski asked, before she could stop herself.

'No ma'am, I certainly am not. I'm not even involved with anyone. How about you?'

'I'm semi-involved,' Paniatowski said, wondering how Baxter would feel about that particular description of their affair.

'Guessed you might be,' Grant said. 'It'd be a miracle if a pretty girl like you wasn't.'

Paniatowski found herself caught up in mixed emotions. One the one hand, she felt an urge to preen at still being called a girl. On the other, she couldn't quite avoid the suspicion that Grant had only said what he had because he knew *exactly* what effect his words would have on her.

'What's it like working for the FBI?' she asked in an effort to change the subject. 'Did it live up to your expectations?'

'It most certainly did. In fact, it exceeded them.'

'And what about the famous J. Edgar Hoover?'

'Mr Hoover *is* the FBI,' Grant said, going almost gooey-eyed. 'He's an inspiration to everyone working for him. His spirit imbues the whole organization with purpose, and when my immediate boss talks to me, we both know he's only talking as a representative of Mr Hoover. What about your boss? He's called something like a Chief Policeman, isn't he?'

'Chief Constable,' Paniatowski corrected the Special Agent.

'Yeah, that's it.'

'And he isn't my boss – Charlie Woodend is.'

'Sure,' Grant agreed easily. 'But I'm sort of assuming that, like my own boss, he's only standing in for—'

'Charlie Woodend's my boss,' Paniatowski repeated, with

54

a ferocity which took her by surprise. 'I couldn't give a tuppenny damn about any of his so-called superiors.'

Grant laughed. 'Well, that's plain enough for anybody to understand. So what's Charlie Woodend like?'

'Honest,' Paniatowski said. 'Honest and dedicated. I'd trust him with my life.'

Grant was starting to look at her a little strangely. 'You sound almost as if you're half in love with the guy,' he said.

'I *what*?'

'When you were talking about him just now, you kinda looked as if there was something special—'

'Let me assure you, Special Agent Grant, that I'm not in love with Chief Inspector Woodend now, nor have I ever been, nor am I likely to be in the future!' Paniatowski said hotly.

Grant held out his hands in front of him, as though getting ready to ward off an attack. 'Hey, hold on there,' he said. 'I wasn't trying to insult you. I was just making an observation.'

Paniatowski took a deep breath. 'Of course you were,' she said, more calmly. 'But you're way off the mark.'

'I'll take your word for it,' Grant said. 'So tell me, Monika, how do you think I'll get on with this paragon of an English policeman?'

'That depends.'

'On what?'

'On how well he decides you're doing your job. If he thinks you're playing straight with him – and are as dedicated to finding out the truth as he is – then you'll have no problems with him at all.'

Grant thought about it for a moment, then said, 'I think your Mr Woodend and I are going to get along just fine.'

Eight

The two American military policemen were standing near the trailer which had been assigned to the Right Honourable Douglas Coutes for the duration of the investigation. They could not have been said to be actually *guarding* it, but they couldn't have been said to be *not* guarding it, either.

Which was rather a neat way of exemplifying Coutes's current predicament, Woodend thought. The Minister of Defence wasn't under arrest – but he certainly wasn't at liberty, either.

When Woodend knocked on the door of the trailer, a voice from inside called out that he should enter. The Chief Inspector opened the door and stepped into the trailer's living room.

Coutes was sitting at the table, ostensibly – and possibly ostentatiously – examining the contents of his Ministerial Red Box, which was probably still being delivered to him on a daily basis. He looked up briefly, registered the Chief Inspector's presence, and then returned his attention to his papers.

Woodend took the opportunity to get a proper look at the man he'd once both served under and heartily despised.

Coutes had not been entirely untouched by the passing of the years, he decided, but that touch had been light, and any impartial observer, looking at the two of them together, would probably have guessed that the policeman was a good ten years older than the politician.

Another minute passed before Coutes looked up again, and when he did, he said, 'Well, well, well, this is quite like old times, isn't it?'

Woodend thought back to their first meeting in the officers' mess, all those years earlier.

'Quite like old times?' he repeated. 'Insofar as you've kept me standin' here like a puddin', waitin' until you feel inclined to speak to me, then I suppose it is. But a lot's changed, as well.'

'Like what, Sergeant Woodend?'

'For a start, I'm a Chief Inspector now.'

'Of course you are,' Coutes agreed.

He sounded, Woodend thought, as if he believed that a man in his position had no need to apologize for any mistakes he might make over another man's rank – or over anything else, for that matter – and possibly that was just what he *did* believe.

'I didn't do it, you know,' the Minister continued.

'Didn't do what?'

'I did not kill that man,' Coutes said emphatically. 'I did not kill him, and I did not place his body in a shallow grave.'

And Woodend – who knew from experience that Coutes would lie without a second's thought when the situation demanded it – was surprised to discover that he didn't think the Minister was lying this time.

'How did your knife come to be in the grave with the corpse?' Woodend asked.

'I can only assume it was there because the real murderer *put* it there.'

'How would he get his hands on it in the first place? Did you lose it? Or did he steal it from you?'

'He stole it. I'd never have been careless enough to lose that knife. I was very fond of it.'

'So when exactly was it stolen?'

'I'd guess it was five or six weeks before the Invasion, which would make it a week or two before Robert Kineally disappeared.'

'Where was it stolen from?'

'From here, of course. From this delightful little camp we liked to call home.'

'I assume, in that case, that there'll be some written record of the theft.'

'Written record? What are you talking about? Why would there be any written record?'

'Because, if you'd reported it missin', I imagine some clerk or other would have made a note of it.'

'I *didn't* report it missing.'

'Why not?'

'It would have reflected badly on me.'

'It would?'

'Of course. An officer who is held in so little respect by his men that they think they can steal from him with impunity, will very soon become a figure of ridicule.'

'But whoever stole it wasn't one of *your* men. If it disappeared here, it must have been stolen by one of the Yanks.'

'We were all part of the same glorious army of liberation – or so you used to tell me with monotonous regularity. Besides, the American officers looked down their noses at us Brits often enough as it was. I certainly didn't want to give them a further excuse to feel superior.'

'Pity, though, isn't it?' Woodend mused. 'If you had reported the knife missing, you'd probably be in the clear now.'

'If I had reported it missing, the Americans would now be claiming I only *pretended* it was stolen,' Coutes countered. 'Whoever decided to frame me back then had thought the whole thing through fairly carefully.'

'So you still think that the murderer had some kind of personal grudge against you?'

'I don't think he would have lost any sleep over me taking the blame for his crime, but his main aim in pointing the finger at me was probably to take the pressure off himself. And if we're talking about grudges, then the person who he must have had the biggest grudge against was surely Robert Kineally.'

'You had a bit of a grudge against Kineally yourself, didn't you, Mr Coutes?' Woodend asked.

'I wouldn't put it quite like that,' Coutes said. 'We had our disagreements, as any officers faced with a difficult situation will, but I—'

'A grudge,' Woodend interrupted firmly. 'A bloody *big* grudge. Which brings us right back to Mary Parkinson.'

'As I think I told you over the phone, she meant nothing to me,' Coutes said wearily.

'Not as a person, she didn't,' Woodend agreed. 'You never did care much about people as people. But as a *challenge*, I think she was much more important than you're now willin' to admit.'

They had been in the Dun Cow public house when they first saw her. Woodend would not, by choice, have spent his free

58

time in Coutes's company. But in the army it was the officers who decreed when an NCO's time was free, and Captain Coutes had decided – by a very narrow margin – that he would rather drink with Woodend than drink alone.

There were a number of women in the saloon bar that night. Some of them were Land Girls, mostly big, beefy lasses, who had taken over the agricultural work of the men who had gone into the army, and daily gave the lie to the popular belief that men were always the stronger sex. There were some local girls, too, on the lookout for Yanks who would sweep them off their feet and take them back to their ranches in Texas once the war was over.

'Slags, the lot of them,' Coutes pronounced, after surveying all the available women. 'I couldn't poke one of them unless she had a paper bag over her head and I had a clothes peg on my nose.'

Woodend took a half-hearted sip of his pint – beer consumed in Captain Coutes's presence never did taste quite right – but said nothing.

'Have you got some tart of your own, back home, that you're slipping it to, Sergeant Woodend?' Coutes asked.

'I rather think that's my own business, sir,' Woodend replied, hating to sound so stiff and wooden, but knowing that wooden words were a wiser response than smashing Coutes in the face.

'Didn't they teach you, during your basic training, that you should always answer an officer's question – whatever that question might happen to be?' Coutes asked.

'An' didn't they teach you, durin' officer trainin', that if you goad a worm long enough, it will eventually turn – and that could be dangerous when the worm has access to a bayonet?' Woodend countered.

The way the conversation was going, things could have turned nasty – especially for Woodend – but at that moment the door of the bar opened, and Mary Parkinson walked in.

Mary was nineteen at the time, and the daughter of a local farmer. She had a classic English peaches-and-cream complexion, and her blonde hair cascaded on to her shoulders in ringlets. She was wearing a floral dress which hugged her dainty figure. She wasn't beautiful, she wasn't even very pretty, in the conventional sense. But she had an aura – a kind of inner glow – which made Woodend think she was one of the loveliest sights he'd ever seen.

'Now there's a piece of totty well worth getting your knob out for,' Coutes said.

Mary glanced around the bar, and – not seeing the person she was obviously expecting to find there – first looked disappointed, and then a little lost.

'I'm in luck,' Coutes said, rising from his seat.

He walked over to where Mary was standing.

'Can I help you?' he asked the girl.

'I . . . I was supposed to be meeting my cousin, but she isn't here,' Mary said. 'I don't know quite what to do now. To tell you the truth, I'm not really used to public houses.'

'Perhaps your cousin's been delayed. Why don't you come over to our table and wait for her?' Coutes suggested smoothly.

'I don't know if I should,' Mary said hesitantly.

'She'll be disappointed if she does arrive and finds that you're not here,' Coutes pointed out. 'And if she doesn't turn up, my sergeant over there will drive you home. Now what harm could there be in that?'

'None, I suppose,' Mary said, allowing Coutes to take her by the elbow and steer her across to the table.

'I'm Dougie,' Coutes said, when they'd sat down. 'And this is my sergeant, Charlie.'

'Pleased to meet you, Charlie,' Mary said coyly.

Coutes ordered the drinks – a pink gin for himself, a pint for Woodend, a port and lemon for Mary – and then duly set about trying to impress the girl.

Woodend, for his part, stared into the corner of the room, and wished he were somewhere else entirely. But all the time Coutes continued with his patter, Woodend could feel the girl's eyes on him.

Finally, when the captain took a pause for breath, Mary said, 'And what about you, Charlie? Have you got a girlfriend?'

It would have been easy to say 'no' to this girl who made his heart beat faster just by saying his name, Woodend thought. But he had already made his choice – made his commitment – and wandering off the path he had chosen was not something he could bring himself do.

'Yes, I have got a girlfriend,' he heard himself say. 'Her

name's Joan. We're hopin' to be married when the war's over.'

'Well, that is nice,' Mary said, though she sounded just a little disappointed. She stood up. 'Excuse me for a minute,' she continued, and headed for the women's toilets.

'So what do you think, Sergeant?' Coutes asked, in a tone of leering confidentiality.

'I think you're wastin' your time,' Woodend said frankly. 'If you want to get your end away so badly, why don't you cosy up to one of them girls at the other end of the bar. Buy them a few drinks, an' they'll probably let you do what you like with them.'

'You're forgetting what I said earlier about the paper bag and the clothes peg,' Coutes told him.

'Mary's not goin' to give in to you,' Woodend said.

'I know she isn't,' Coutes agreed.

'Well, then?'

'At least, she's not going to give in to me tonight. Maybe not even this week. But eventually – who knows?'

'Why not just leave her alone?' Woodend asked.

'Because, before the war, I used to ride to hounds, and I got rather a taste for the thrill of the chase,' Coutes said.

Woodend did not know what to do or say even at that moment, and as the weeks went by – as Coutes's plan seemed to be coming closer and closer to fruition – he began to feel even more helpless.

He supposed he could have told Mary just what kind of man Coutes really was, but after the snow job the captain had given her, he doubted she'd believe him. It was, he thought, like watching an impending train crash – knowing exactly what was going to happen, yet being powerless to prevent it.

What he did not know – what neither of them knew – was that an obstacle would suddenly appear on the track to derail Coutes's train just short of what seemed its inevitable destination.

And that that obstacle would come in the form of Captain Robert Kineally.

'If push comes to shove, you can always claim that you killed Robert Kineally in self-defence,' Woodend suggested. 'Yes, I think you could make out a reasonable case for that.'

'I didn't kill him at all,' Coutes said coldly.

'Maybe not,' Woodend agreed, 'but if I could see I was goin' to be convicted of killin' somebody, whatever happened, I think I'd rather plead to a lesser charge than a greater one.'

'You're enjoying all this, aren't you, you bloody bastard!' Douglas Coutes demanded.

'"Enjoyin' it" isn't exactly the right phrase,' Woodend replied. 'But I have to admit I'm gettin' some satisfaction out of seein' you suffer, after what you did to Mary Parkinson.'

'I didn't *do* anything to her at all,' Coutes said. 'At least, nothing *illegal*. If I had, don't you think Kineally would have seen to it that I was brought up on a charge? Nothing would have made him happier than to see me spend the next fifteen years in gaol. But he took no such action. And why? Because he knew he'd never make anything stick!'

'Even so, he might still have the last laugh on you,' Woodend pointed out. 'The dead hand of Robert Kineally could yet see you where he'd have liked you to be back in 1944.'

'I wish we were both still in the army,' Coutes said. 'If we were, I'd make you suffer for this insolence. By God, I would!'

'You don't have to tolerate my insolence if you don't want to,' Woodend reminded him. 'The only reason I'm involved in this investigation at all is because you wanted me to be involved. So you've only to drop a word in the right ear, an' I'll be out of here before you can say "court martial".'

'It's tempting,' Coutes admitted.

'Then follow your instincts,' Woodend urged him. 'Tell whoever it is who set the wheels in motion to bring me to Haverton Camp that you don't want me here any more.'

'No, I don't think I *will* do that,' Coutes said. 'You've had your satisfaction in seeing me suffer. Now I'd like to get my revenge by completely turning the tables on you.'

'I've absolutely no idea what you're talkin' about,' Woodend told the Minister.

'Then I'll explain in such a way that even a simpleton like you can understand. You didn't like me from the very moment we met, did you?'

'No, it was dislike at first sight.'

'But, as time passed, it went beyond dislike. You grew to truly despise me, didn't you?'

'Very true. But I can't take all the credit for that – you made it really easy for me.'

'So when you prove me innocent of this murder – and you *will* prove it – it will be like thrusting a dagger in your own gut. And when you see me walk away – more powerful than I've ever been – it will be twisting that dagger round in the wound. And I'll enjoy watching that, *Sergeant* Woodend. Believe me, I'll *really* enjoy it.'

'You seem to be a lot more confident about the outcome than you were,' Woodend said.

'What's that supposed to mean?'

'That when you rang me up in Whitebridge, you were pretty near to shittin' yourself with worry. Now, you're takin' everythin' very calmly – almost *unnaturally* calmly.'

'I did go into something of a panic when I heard about all the evidence which seemed to implicate me in the murder,' Coutes admitted. 'But when I'd had time to think about it, I began to take a much more sanguine view of the whole affair. You see, since I'm innocent, I really have no need to worry.'

'The evidence hasn't gone away,' Woodend reminded him. 'It's still as strong as it ever was – an' it's still pointin' the finger at you.'

'But not for much longer. You'll soon find a way to discredit it,' Coutes said confidently.

The bastard was still so arrogant, Woodend thought. Still so bloody, *bloody* arrogant!

'I've been followin' your career through the reports in the newspapers for years,' he said to Coutes.

'I'm flattered at your interest,' the Minister replied.

'No, you're not,' Woodend corrected him. 'And you shouldn't be. As far as I'm concerned, you're nothin' but a carbuncle on the arse of humanity. I'd have wiped you from my memory years ago, if it hadn't been for the fact that there's one question about you that I've always wanted to find an answer to.'

'And have you finally found the answer you were seeking?'

'No, I haven't. To tell you the truth, I think I'm about as far away from finding it now as I've ever been.'

'Then why not ask me your question?' Coutes suggest. 'Why not see if you can get your answer straight from the horse's mouth?'

'All right, I will,' Woodend agreed. 'The old Douglas Coutes

– the one I knew – was not particularly principled, not particularly likeable, an' not particularly talented.'

'That's a rather harsh judgement to make, don't you think?' Douglas Coutes asked, and it was plain from the expression on his face that he was starting to enjoy himself.

'Harsh?' Woodend repeated. 'No, I don't think so. If anythin', I'm givin' you the benefit of the doubt. Anyway, that's not the point.'

'Then what is?'

'I've been in this room with you for less than ten minutes – an' already I can tell that you haven't changed at all.'

Coutes smiled. 'Then at least you have to give me full marks for consistency,' he said.

'So my question is this,' Woodend continued, ignoring the interruption. 'What's the secret of your success? How is it that you've managed to climb so far up the political ladder that some people are startin' to talk about you as a potential prime minister?'

'Perhaps you're wrong about me,' Coutes said, with the amused smile still in place. 'Perhaps I *have* changed over the years. Age may have mellowed me, and experience could well have taught me valuable lessons. Isn't it just possible that, in spite of what you seem to think of me, I have become a much better man than the one you knew all those years ago?'

'Aye, an' it's also possible that pigs might fly, an' the leopard might trade in its spots for stripes,' Woodend said. 'Come on, Mr Coutes, you know you're not goin' to fool me whatever you say, so why not break the habit of a lifetime, an' be honest for once?'

'Do you really want to know how I succeeded?' Coutes asked, growing more serious.

'I really want to know,' Woodend confirmed.

'I think I'm going to tell you,' Coutes said reflectively. 'But I won't do it to satisfy your childish curiosity – I'll do it because I know you won't like the answer, and that my answer will make it even harder for you, when you have to do the right thing and prove my innocence.'

'Even for a politician, you're takin' one hell of a time to say what you've got to say,' Woodend told him. 'So why don't you just forget all the neat phraseology an' cut straight to the chase.'

'Very well, I will,' Douglas Coutes agreed. 'Some people advance by playing to their own strengths. Most of my esteemed cabinet colleagues owe their current positions to doing just that. I, on the other hand, put much greater store in playing to *other people's* weaknesses.' He paused for a moment. 'I told you that you wouldn't like the answer.'

'Get on with it for God's sake,' Woodend told him.

'Everyone makes mistakes,' Coutes continued. 'Some people manage to get away with them, and others have their mistakes exposed to the full glare of public scrutiny. Now I've never exposed anybody else's failings in my entire life. But I haven't forgotten them, either – not a single one of them.'

'I'll bet you haven't,' Woodend said dourly.

'So now you have your answer.'

'Do I?'

'Of course. People help me to climb the ladder because they know that if they don't, I could damage them. In other words,' Coutes's smile returned, even more broadly now he was about to deliver his punch-line, 'in other words – and only *figuratively* speaking – I know where all the bodies are buried.'

Nine

'Welcome to the operational command module!' Special Agent Grant said cheerily, as Woodend opened the door of the trailer into which all the cardboard boxes had been unloaded.

Operational Command Module! Woodend thought. Sweet Jesus!

Grant might be nearly thirty years younger than Henry Marlowe – and come from the other side of the Atlantic as well – but he was fluent enough in gobbledegook to make even the Chief Constable jealous.

'So what do you think?' Grant asked eagerly.

'I like it,' Woodend said, 'but then I always have been partial to big caravans with a lot of table space.'

'Say what?' Grant asked.

'It's grand, lad,' Woodend replied, feeling slightly ashamed of himself for attempting to prick the bubble of Grant's enthusiasm. 'It's just what we need to get the job done.'

And he didn't need to be a detective to see that the job was obviously already underway. The table was covered with documents, most of them turned yellow with age, and Paniatowski and Grant, positioned at opposite ends of it, had begun the tedious process of sifting through the stacks.

'Well, Douglas Coutes was certainly here at Haverton Camp on the day that Kineally vanished,' Paniatowski said, looking up at her boss.

'In all fairness to the man, he's never actually denied that,' Woodend pointed out.

'And according to the documents I've examined so far, the last time Kineally was seen alive was on the seventh of May, 1944.'

'Which was just a couple of days after I'd left,' Woodend said, almost to himself.

A couple of days after I met Mary Parkinson – in tears – on that railway station, he added mentally.

'Well, if you weren't here at the time, sir – and you can *prove* you weren't – then I suppose that pretty much lets you off the hook as a possible suspect,' Paniatowski said.

Grant looked up from the table. 'I didn't realize Mr Woodend *ever* was a suspect,' he said.

So earnest, Woodend thought. So literal, and so bloody earnest.

'It was a joke,' Paniatowski explained.

Grant absorbed this new information carefully, and then laughed.

'Oh, sure, I knew that all along,' he said, unconvincingly. He reached for a pile of shiny photographs, which were balanced precariously on the edge of the table, and handed them to Woodend. 'Got some pictures here that just might be of interest to you.'

Woodend took the photographs from him, and found himself staring at the image of a knife which he had last seen, twenty-one years earlier, in the hands of Douglas Coutes.

The incident with the knife occurred on what might have been called Coutes's and Mary's third 'date' in the Dun Cow.

The two of them were sitting at a table. Woodend – who Coutes had banished from their company in order that he might pursue his relentless campaign of seduction – had fallen into conversation with a young man in civvies.

'I get heartily sick of almost everybody I meet asking me why I'm not in uniform,' the young man complained. 'Even when I tell them I'm a merchant seaman, it makes no difference, because then they ask me if I wouldn't be of more use in the "real" navy.'

'They just don't understand, do they?' Woodend asked, sympathetically.

'Too right, they don't! This country couldn't survive without the goods we bring over from America. And sailing in a convoy is no bloody cakewalk, even with naval protection. Do you know how many times ships I've been serving on have gone down?'

'Twice?' Woodend guessed.

'Three times!' the seaman told him. 'Because however many

battleships and cruisers you've got around you, it only takes one U-Boat to get through, and you're finished.'

'It must have been rough,' Woodend said.

'It bloody was! The first time, I was lucky enough to get into a lifeboat. But the second and third times, I was bobbing up and down in the water like a cork when I was rescued.'

'An' I imagine the North Atlantic can be quite cold in the middle of winter,' Woodend said.

The seaman grinned. 'It is a bit nippy,' he agreed. 'Still, I shouldn't complain. At least I was rescued eventually. Some of my shipmates were never found.'

'You all deserve medals,' Woodend said, with feeling. 'But since I'm in no position to award you one, how about a pint instead?'

'That's very kind of you,' the seaman said. 'And better than a medal, any day of the week.'

Up until that moment, Coutes's back had been blocking any view of Mary, but now, as he stood up and headed towards the toilets, she became clearly visible from the bar.

The seaman noticed her immediately. 'That girl looks familiar,' he said. 'You don't happen to know her name, do you?'

'Mary Parkinson,' Woodend said.

'That's right! Mary Parkinson! We were at school together, but I haven't seen her for years. She's certainly grown up a lot since we were both in Miss Eccles's class.'

'I imagine she has,' Woodend said. 'I imagine you have, an' all.'

The sailor grinned again. 'You're probably right about that,' he agreed. 'Look, if you'll guard my pint for me, I think I'll just go over there and have a quick word with her.'

There was too much general noise in the public bar of the Dun Cow for Woodend to hear what the seaman said to Mary, or Mary said to the seaman in return, but then he didn't really need to catch the actual words to be able to work out what was probably being said.

It was typical of most encounters between two people who hadn't seen each other for years – and had very little in common any more – he thought, as he watched them. They smiled, they each asked how the other was getting on, and then they covered the common ground of shared memories and old friends.

By the time five minutes had ticked away, they were running dry of conversation, and the sailor was glancing over his shoulder at the pint waiting invitingly for him on the bar. If they'd have been given another minute, they'd have found a graceful way to separate, and their unexpected meeting would have been over.

But, as chance would have it, they were not given that minute! Coutes re-entered the room, saw the sailor leaning over Mary's table, and immediately went black with rage.

The Captain tapped the sailor on the shoulder and said a few words to him, then the two men walked towards the door. Mary – innocent, young Mary – was left there alone, looking completely mystified.

Woodend still sat at the bar, wondering what to do next. On the one hand, he liked the sailor, and he did not like Coutes. On the other, Coutes was his boss and had the means at his disposal to make his life uncomfortable, whereas the sailor had no power over him at all. It was probably best, he decided, to keep well out of the whole business.

Yet even as this thought settled in his mind, he was following the other two men out into the yard.

Once outside, Woodend paused for a moment to allow his eyes to adjust to the darkness.

The government imposition of the Blackout in 1939 had created a very different night-time England to the one in which he had grown up, he thought. For the last five long years, there had been no street lamps, no car headlights, no dazzlingly illuminated advertisements, and though lights might burn inside the houses and pubs, the heavy blinds on the windows prevented that same light from spilling out onto the streets. Even so, the country had not lived in complete darkness. For a time at least, the fires started by Herr Hitler's bombing raids had lit up some areas as bright as day. And the moon and stars – unbowed by bureaucratic regulation, continued to illuminate the sky as they had always done.

There was a half-moon that night, and as Woodend's eyes grew accustomed to the gloom, he was able to see the drama unfolding by the skittle alley wall.

The sailor was pressed up against the wall, and Coutes was standing so close to him that their faces were almost touching.

'Stay away from Mary Parkinson,' the Captain said, in a voice which was almost like the growl of a wild animal.

'What are you getting so upset about?' the sailor asked, perplexed. 'I was only talking to her as an old friend.'

'I don't care if you were talking to her as her maiden aunt,' Coutes told him. 'Stay away from her!'

If the situation had only been handled a little differently, there would have been no trouble at all, Woodend thought.

If Coutes had simply told the other man that Mary was his girlfriend, the sailor would, in all probability, have immediately apologized for the intrusion. But no man who had been torpedoed three times in the middle of the Atlantic winter was going to stand for being pushed around by a soldier who had yet to see any action himself.

'I'm not in the army, you know,' the sailor said. 'You can't tell me what to do.'

Coutes laughed unpleasantly, and stepped back.

'Maybe I can't,' he agreed, reaching into his tunic, and pulling something out. 'But this can.'

He had produced a knife – a bloody big one, with a wicked-looking blade which glinted in the moonlight.

'Put that away!' the sailor said, with an edge of panic entering his voice. 'You could hurt somebody with that.'

'I could hurt you with it,' Coutes said. 'I could do worse than just hurt you. If I slice up your stomach in just the right way, it could take you several agonizing hours to die.'

'You wouldn't dare!' the sailor said, though he was sounding more and more as if he believed that Coutes might well carry out his threat.

'I'm an officer and gentleman, and you're nothing but scum,' Coutes said. 'If I claimed you attacked me, and I was only defending myself, who do you think the authorities would believe?'

'Please put the knife away,' the sailor said.

'No, I don't think I will,' Coutes said calmly. 'But I'm not going to kill you, after all. It's not necessary. All I have to do is put you in hospital for a few weeks. That should be more than enough to deter any other lout round here from thinking that he might try sniffing around in places he has no business to.'

'That's enough, sir,' Woodend said.

'*Mind your own bloody business, Sergeant!*' *Coutes shouted over his shoulder.*

'*I said, that's enough,*' *Woodend repeated. 'If you really fancy havin' a go at somebody, then let this feller leave, an' have a go at me.*'

Coutes hesitated for a second, then said to the sailor, 'Get out of here, you piece of shit!'

The sailor slid clear of the wall, but instead of making a run for it while he had the chance, he looked to Woodend for further instructions.

'*You go,*' *Woodend said. 'I can handle him.*'

The sailor went – though into the dark night, rather than back to the pub where his pint was waiting for him.

Coutes turned around, the big Prussian knife still in his hand. 'Do you really think you could handle me, Sergeant?' *he asked sneeringly.*

'*There's only one way for both of us to find out, now isn't there?*' *Woodend asked evenly.*

For an instant, it looked as if Coutes were planning to lunge, then he straightened up and slid the knife back into its scabbard.

'*It's not wise of you to cross me, Sergeant Woodend,*' *he said. 'Not wise at all.*'

'*You'll thank me for it in the morning, when you've sobered up, sir,*' *Woodend told him.*

He knew, even as he spoke the words, that Coutes was not drunk, but he said them anyway: to give Coutes an out – an excuse for his bad behaviour.

No, Coutes wasn't drunk. He never was. Alcohol was not his drug – it was power over others which intoxicated him. And that made him more dangerous than even the most violent heavy drinker.

Woodend put the photograph of the knife to one side, and turned his attention to a set of pictures of the shallow grave, with Robert Kineally's skeleton still in it.

'Who took these?' he asked Special Agent Grant. 'Was it the local police force?'

'Yes, it was,' the FBI man replied, then added, almost as if it surprised him, 'and they seem to have made a good job of it.'

They had, Woodend agreed, looking at the collection of bones, some of which must have been disturbed by earth movements over the years, others by the digging which had finally uncovered them.

'The rest of the shots in that pile were taken by our own boys in Washington DC, once the jigsaw had been fitted back together again,' Grant continued.

Woodend grimaced at the Special Agent's choice of words, then found himself wondering why he had reacted in such an uncharacteristic way.

Maybe the problem was that these were not pictures of just any old skeleton to him, he thought. Maybe it was because, in looking down at these bones, he could not help putting flesh and muscle on them.

He had always known he liked Robert Kineally, but until now, he had never realized quite how much affection he had felt for the man – never understood how a confirmation of Kineally's death would bring with it such a great sense of loss.

Doing his best to shrug aside personal feelings, he picked up the batch of photographs taken in Washington, once the 'jigsaw' had been completed.

He remembered Kineally as being around six feet two inches tall, and the ruler which lay beside the reconstructed skeleton proved that his memory had not been playing tricks on him.

Once they had photographed the skeleton as a whole, the FBI photographers had taken close-ups of each distinct part. Woodend examined these now – the skull, grinning obscenely, bereft of Kineally's perfect teeth; the teeth themselves, which had been reassembled separately, in order to match them to the dental records; the fingers; the toes . . .

'Take a look at the ribcage,' Grant suggested, when he noticed what the Chief Inspector was doing.

Woodend flicked through the glossy pack of death shots until he found what he was looking for.

'Is it the third rib down on the left hand side you particularly wanted me to look at?' he asked.

'That's the one,' Grant agreed. 'The bone's chipped.'

'I can see that.'

'And the lab back in DC says there's a perfect match between the injury inflicted and the knife we found in the grave.'

Coutes's knife, Woodend reminded himself.

'If I slice up your stomach in just the right way, it could take you several agonizing hours to die,' Douglas Coutes had told the sailor.

But the wound which had killed Robert Kineally had not been meant to make him suffer. It had been intended to dispatch him with maximum efficiency – to rob him of his life with a minimum of fuss.

There were more shots of bones in the grisly pile – perhaps a hundred or more of them.

Kineally had been a very fit man back in '44, Woodend thought, flicking through them. He could well have lived on to a ripe old age. And who knew what great things he might have achieved if he'd been allowed to?

It didn't seem right that he was dead – and that bastard Douglas Coutes was still alive.

'Do you need our help for anything specific at the moment, or are you happy to plough through this pile of documents on your own for a while, Special Agent Grant?' Woodend asked.

Grant looked shocked. 'You want to *leave*?' he asked.

'If you'd rather we didn't—'

'Oh, I don't mind at all,' Grant assured him. 'Whatever you'd processed yourselves, I'd have double-checked it myself later, anyway. It's just that . . .'

'Yes?'

'It's just that I'm surprised you'd want to go anywhere else, when all the action is here.'

Woodend looked down at the stacks of dusty pages. 'All the action?' he repeated.

'Sure,' Grant reaffirmed. 'Mr Hoover says there's tremendous amounts to be learned from following a paper trail.'

'Does he now?'

'He says that the guys who make the big dramatic gestures out on the streets – like Eliot Ness did in Chicago in the 'thirties – might get all the glory, but it's agents like us who do the real work.'

'Eliot Ness was generally believed to be *quite* effective at enforcing the law,' Woodend said gently.

'Oh, sure, maybe he did OK when it came to tracking down criminals—'

'Which is, after all, what he was supposed—'

73

'—but with his methods, he'd have been no good at finding Communists and radicals, which is what law enforcement is really about.'

'I didn't know that,' Woodend told him, aware, even as he spoke the words, that their import would be completely lost on the special agent.

'Mr Hoover says that when you're hunting Commies, you need to be as cunning as they are,' Grant continued. 'He says it's just plain dumb to follow a suspect around all day, when all you really need to do is tap his phone.'

'Mr Hoover seems to say a great deal,' Woodend said. 'Do you talk to him often?'

Grant actually blushed. 'Talk to him? Gosh, no! The FBI's far too big an operation for Mr Hoover to talk to *all* its operatives. The closest I've ever got to him is seeing him walk down to the corridor – and what a tremendous moment *that* was for me. But even he can't find the time to guide us personally, though he makes sure we all know which way his thinking is going.'

'That's very considerate of him,' Woodend said dryly. 'An' now, if you'll excuse us, we're goin' to make the "dramatic gesture" of visitin' one of the local public houses.'

'You want a drink?' Grant asked.

'Yes, that's the general idea,' Woodend agreed.

'So what's your poison?'

'Mine's a pint of beer, an' my lovely assistant is partial to the odd drop of vodka.'

'Gee, I don't know if we've got any vodka—' Grant began.

'It bein' well-known that's what the goddam Commies drink,' Woodend said to Paniatowski in a soft aside.

'—but if it's beer you want, you'll find crates of the stuff over at the commissary trailer.'

'It's very kind of you, lad, but American beer's a bit too cold an' a bit too gassy for my taste,' Woodend said. 'An' anyway, servin' yourself is no substitute for bein' served by a bad-tempered barmaid.'

'I'm sure it can't be,' Grant said, but the bemusement in his tone showed that Woodend had, once more, lost him.

The two English detectives had reached the trailer door when Grant spoke again.

'Don't you find it a little weird?' the Special Agent asked, completely out of the blue.

'Don't I find *what* a little weird?' Woodend responded.

'The fact that we're here at all.'

'On earth?'

'In Camp Haverton.'

'I'm not sure I'm followin' you,' Woodend admitted.

'Well, say Kineally hadn't been murdered at all. What do you think would have happened to him?'

'I'd say he'd almost definitely have taken part in the Allied Invasion of Normandy.'

'And landed on Omaha Beach?'

'More than likely.'

'And am I right in thinking that the casualty rates on Omaha Beach were absolutely astronomical?'

'You are.'

'Then if he *had* landed in Normandy, he could easily have been one of those killed.'

'Yes?'

'So what we're doing, in point of fact, is pouring vast amounts of resources into the investigation of the death of man who may only have had a few more weeks to live anyway. Don't you find that ironic?'

'Aye, I do,' Woodend said. 'But then life's full of little ironies, don't you find?'

Ten

It had always been one of Woodend's most cherished beliefs that just as a engine needs oil to help it run smoothly, so the brain requires a pint of best bitter if it is to work at its most efficient. Thus, while Special Agent Grant may have been shocked that Woodend would abandon the paperwork in favour of the pub, his sergeant – who knew him considerably better – had only been surprised that it had taken so long for Woodend to feel the need for the necessary lubrication.

By the time they left the camp it was already night, and the narrow country lane, which had looked so picturesque in the daylight, now seemed to Paniatowski to have taken on a slightly menacing air.

'The pub that we're headin' for used to be called the Dun Cow,' Woodend said as they drove through the darkness. 'But if it's still there – if the barbarians who are runnin' the breweries these days haven't pulled it down – it'll probably be goin' by some poncy modern name by now.'

Paniatowski laughed. 'What was it like, living in the Middle Ages?' she asked.

'Cheeky!' Woodend said, without rancour. 'I can't tell you much about the Middle Ages – the older you get, the more your memory goes, so I've all but forgotten my days as King Richard the Lionheart's shield-bearer – but I think I can *just about* remember enough to tell you what Haverton was like in the 'forties.'

'That's as near to the Middle Ages as makes practically no difference,' Paniatowski said.

'I suppose it is, when you're your age,' Woodend agreed dryly. 'Would you like to hear what I've got to say, or are you perfectly happy to just sit there takin' the piss?'

'I'd like to hear what you've got to say,' Paniatowski told him, with mock-contrition in her voice.

'Haverton was a sleepy little place back then,' Woodend said. 'There were only two shops – an' one of *them* had to double up as the local post office. An' I seem to remember that in the middle of the village there was a garage.'

'A garage!' Paniatowski said. 'Just imagine that! How terribly, terribly modern!'

'Aye, but it only had the one petrol pump,' Woodend replied. 'An' while the feller who ran it was willin' enough to work on any cars that might be brought to him, he was much happier – an' much more competent – when he was dealin' with tractors.'

'And the people?' Paniatowski asked. 'Did they all wear agricultural smocks and suck on straws?'

'No, but you're not as far off the mark as you might imagine. They were slow-talkin', slow-thinkin' and slow to take on anything new. Most of them still lived in houses which had been in the same family for generations, an' followed the same callin' as their fathers an' grandfathers before them.' He sighed lightly. 'But I imagine everythin's changed now.'

His suspicions were confirmed as they drew level with the garage – now relocated to the edge of the village – which had a shiny new shop attached to it, and boasted not one, but *three,* petrol pumps on its forecourt.

There was more evidence of change in the village itself. One of the shops had been transformed into a small super-market, and the few people who were out on the street moved more briskly – and dressed more sharply – than any of the inhabitants would have thought of doing twenty years earlier.

'I'm beginnin' to have *serious* concerns about the fate of the dear old Dun Cow,' Woodend said.

The pub was at the other end of the village. It had a thatched roof, and small, leaded windows. There was a beer garden in front – open only during the heady summer days – and a skittle alley at the side.

'The only thing that really seems to have changed is that they've built a car park,' Woodend told Paniatowski. 'They didn't need one in 'forty-four.'

'Petrol rationing?' Paniatowski asked.

'Very few cars,' Woodend replied.

Inside, the pub had low oak beams and a flagstone floor. There was a fire burning in the grate, and the slight smell of wood-smoke hung – not unpleasantly – in the air.

The man behind the bar was very nearly bald, but had compensated for the loss of hair on top by cultivating a set of thick white side-whiskers. He had a red, roundish face. And his belly, which was even rounder, strained valiantly against the buttons on his blue velvet waistcoat.

Woodend ordered a pint for himself and a vodka for Paniatowski, and was slightly surprised – and perhaps a little disappointed – when the landlord seemed to have no difficulty in supplying him with his sergeant's favourite tipple.

'I know you,' the landlord said, as he counted out the money that Woodend had placed on the bar.

'I remember you as well,' Woodend said. 'Your name's Reg, if I'm not mistaken.'

'That's right, it is,' the landlord agreed.

'An' I'm—'

The landlord quickly put up his hand, to cut off any further comment from the visitor.

'Don't tell me,' he said. 'It'll come to me in time. I never forget a face.' He pondered for some seconds, then continued, 'Woodford! No, not Woodford – Woodend! Charlie Woodend!'

The Chief Inspector beamed with obvious pleasure. 'You're spot on!' he agreed.

'And how long is it since you've done us the honour of payin' us a visit, Charlie?'

'Twenty-one years.'

The landlord shook his head slowly from side to side.

'Twenty-one years,' he repeated slowly. '*Twenty-one* years. Doesn't time just seem to fly by, Charlie?'

'It slips through your fingers like sand,' Woodend told him.

'You used to come in with that Coutes bloke, didn't you?' the landlord asked. 'He's in the government now, you know.'

'So I've heard,' Woodend said.

'And that Yank. You used to come in with him, as well. Now what was *his* name?'

'Robert Kineally.'

'That's right. He was a proper credit to his uniform, that Captain Kineally. Which, and I'm sorry to have to tell you this, is more than could be said for that boss of yours.'

'No need to apologize, Reg,' Woodend said. 'I think we were pretty much in agreement about Coutes.'

The landlord's eyes took on a dreamy gloss, as eyes

sometimes do when memories of the past return unexpectedly.

'Do you remember the night that you and Captain Kineally had the argument with those young thugs over the coloured boys?' he asked.

'Indeed I do.'

'I had no idea what was going on in the skittle alley. I'd have tried to put a stop to it if I had, but they'd never have listened to me, and I'd probably have got hammered for interfering. They listened to you, though, didn't they? By God, they did! I have to take my hat off to you for the way you handled it.'

'It was much more Captain Kineally's doing than it was mine,' Woodend said.

'It was both of you that did it,' the landlord said firmly. He stopped counting Woodend's money, and slid it back across the counter. 'Here, have this one on me, Charlie. An' that goes for your lady-friend as well.'

Bob Rutter sat in the guest bedroom of his parents-in-laws' house, looking out at the brightly lit night sky over London, and deciding that he was probably going quietly – but irreversibly – insane.

After Maria's death, he had brought their baby down to stay with her grandparents for a while. It had been the right thing to do, he had argued to himself at the time. They had lost their daughter. They were entitled to whatever solace they could draw from their grandchild's presence.

But it had only ever been intended to be a temporary arrangement – just until he had pulled himself back together sufficiently to be able to look after the baby on his own.

A week.

Two weeks at the most.

Yet the weeks had somehow stretched into months, and he felt no more capable of taking charge now than he had in the first few days following his poor wife's murder.

Was it guilt over his affair with Monika Paniatowski which was holding his recovery back? he wondered.

It shouldn't be. The affair had been over for a long time – and had had nothing to do with Maria's death.

Even his father-in-law did not blame him.

'Men are born into weakness,' Don Antonio had told him gravely, when he'd confessed all, during one drunken evening they had spent together.

'Perhaps they are, but that still doesn't excuse—' Rutter had started to protest.

'It is only natural that a man will stray away from the fold,' Don Antonio interrupted. 'Though I hold my own wife in the greatest of respect, I, myself, have not been entirely immune to that particular failing. But you were a good husband to my daughter. You loved her—'

'I did.'

'—and you married her when she had already gone blind – which many in your place would not have done. You have absolutely nothing to reproach yourself for. Even so,' Don Antonio continued, with a new note of caution entering his voice, 'it would perhaps be unwise of you to be as candid with my wife as you have been with me.'

The confession had not worked the magic that Rutter had hoped it would. For what was the point of confession without the retribution which should follow it? How could he ever cleanse himself, if others refused to accept that he was guilty?

Despite Don Antonio's warning, he felt the urge to tell Doña Pilar the truth, too, and was only held back from doing just that by the thought of how much the revelation might hurt her.

So what *was* he to do? Was he to continue living as he had been – staying in bed until midday, walking the streets aimlessly for hours on end – until he had degenerated enough to be clearly certifiable? Or was he to make one last attempt to regain control of his life.

'I need *work*!' he told the empty room. 'I need to get back to doing the only thing I do well.'

Douglas Coutes lay on the bed of his trailer, thinking about the past and contemplating the future.

He was as superior to most men as the ruthless lion is to the hapless antelope, he thought.

He had grasped the harsh rules in the game of life before most of his contemporaries had even realized there *were* any rules, and – because his nerve had held – he had experienced triumph after triumph.

All the terrible things that had happened to him over the previous few days were as good a case in point. Most men – finding themselves not only accused of murder, but seemingly already convicted by the weight of evidence – would have been completely destroyed. But not he.

True, he had experienced a short period of almost total panic, during which he had felt so desperate that he had actually phoned Charlie Woodend in Whitebridge. But then, in a sudden flash of insight, he had understood just what kind of game was about to be played out in this old American Army camp. And with that insight, calmness had returned.

He had not yet worked out what the resolution to the game would be – there were far too many factors in play for that to be possible – but he was sure that it *would be* resolved.

Charlie Woodend was probably already sifting through the evidence with the same earnest diligence he had shown when he was a sergeant.

But then, Woodend, as had already been established, was a greatly inferior being altogether.

So while Charlie rooted around in the dirt, all he – the superior man – had to do was wait.

Wait while events evolved.

Wait until the moment was right to take action.

He had entered a very dark tunnel, but when he emerged from it again – totally vindicated on all charges – the light would shine on him more brightly than it had ever done.

Eleven

'So what was that all about?' Monika Paniatowski asked, when she and Woodend had taken their drinks over to a corner table in the Dun Cow.

'What was what all about?' Woodend countered.

'All that stuff the landlord was saying. "Argument with young thugs over coloured boys"?' she repeated, in her best Devonshire accent. '"Take my hat off to you for the way you handled it"?'

'Oh that!' Woodend said, unenthusiastically.

'Sounds like a good story to me.'

'It's *not* a good story. As a matter of fact, I find it a thoroughly *depressin'* story.'

'Why?'

'Because in the twenty-one years since that incident occurred, things have only got only a *little* better in the United States – an' they've got a bloody sight worse over here.'

'I'd like to hear the story anyway,' Paniatowski said.

Woodend sighed. 'All right, if you insist,' he agreed reluctantly. 'But if you're to understand it at all, you're goin' to have to endure a bit of a history lesson first.'

'Fair enough,' Paniatowski agreed.

'The American government started sendin' its soldiers over here in 1942,' Woodend said. 'There were both black soldiers *an'* white soldiers. But they were kept separate.'

'Do you mean that they slept in different huts?'

'I mean they were in completely different *regiments* an' usually slept in separate *camps*. The coloured soldiers were never intended to go into battle. I think there was a general belief among the American top brass that they *couldn't* fight – or maybe *wouldn't* fight. They were only there to do the menial work – diggin' latrines an' the like. So, in that way, they were a bit like Victorian servants – never seen at all

82

unless there was a dirty job to be done, an' their white officers had ordered them to do it.'

Paniatowski took a sip of her vodka. 'Interesting,' she said.

'We've had a bit of racial conflict over here in the last few
years, ever since the West Indians started comin' across in
large numbers, but we'd had no problems of that kind *before*
the war. There were less than ten thousand coloured people
livin' in Britain – and most of them were concentrated around
the docklands of two or three major ports. Which meant that
the majority of people livin' in this country had never seen a
black face in their entire lives.'

'So how did they feel about the coloured soldiers?'

'They liked them. As a matter of fact, a lot of folk liked
them more than they liked the *white* American soldiers. It's
true that, in some places, the cinemas and cafés would have
one section for the whites an' another for the coloureds, but
that was more a concession to the white soldiers' sensibilities
than because the locals disliked the idea of rubbin' shoulders
with the coloureds. An' as for the girls, they were very struck
by what they used to call the "tan" Americans.'

'I imagine that some of the white American soldiers can't
have liked that,' Paniatowski said.

'They bloody *hated* it,' Woodend replied. 'Most of them
had been brought up in the belief that the coloured man was
inferior, an' that the races should never – ever – mix. As I
understand it, most of the coloureds who were lynched in the
1930s suffered that fate because they'd been accused of
assaultin' white women. So can you imagine how some of
these white soldiers felt when they saw local girls walkin' out
on the arms of coloured men?'

'Yes, I think I can,' Paniatowski said.

'There was certainly a feelin' among some of the white
soldiers that the coloureds had better be taught a lesson.'

'How did the coloureds react to that?'

'They weren't goin' to take it. For the first time in their
lives, they found themselves in a situation where, if a white
man hit you, you could bloody-well hit him back. An' they
had every intention of doin' just that.'

'Is that what happened in this pub?'

'It might well have done, if they'd been equally matched.'

'But they weren't?'

'No, as things turned out, the coloured lads found themselves outnumbered ten to one.'

There were three of them in the jeep that night. Woodend was driving, and though Kineally would have undoubtedly have preferred to sit next to him, he had decided to follow protocol and travel in the back with Coutes. The real breach between the two captains – the Mary Parkinson breach – was still several days away, but even without that, they had so little to say to each other that they had scarcely exchanged a word on the journey between the camp and the pub.

The moment Woodend pulled the jeep up alongside the Dun Cow's skittle alley, it was obvious that something was seriously wrong. No one played skittles on a cold March evening, under blackout restrictions, yet at least a couple of dozen American soldiers seemed to have gathered in the alley, under the pale light of the half-moon – and were shouting in the harsh tones that men resort to when they have scented blood.

'I don't like the look of that,' Robert Kineally said, worriedly.

'Me neither,' Coutes agreed. 'Riff-raff like them should be confined in barracks, not allowed to roam the countryside disturbing gentlemen's peace.'

'It's not funny,' Kineally told him.

'And I wasn't making a joke,' Coutes replied.

'Look, those are American *soldiers in that alley!' Kineally said, as if he thought that pointing that fact out would be enough to change Coutes's mind about the seriousness of the situation.*

'So they are,' Coutes said. 'Which means that if they're anybody's concern, they're yours.'

'I'm appealing to you, as a brother officer, to help me to . . .' Captain Kineally began.

'If you're so concerned – if you really *feel you have to do something – why don't you just call your MPs?' Coutes suggested.*

'It's over three miles to the camp. You know that as well as I do, Captain. And that means that by the time the MPs get here, whatever's about to happen will probably be all be over.'

'Good point,' Coutes said. 'So perhaps there's no point in

calling in the MPs after all. Can we go and have a drink now? That is, I shouldn't need to remind you, the reason why we're here.'

'You may choose to look the other way, but I'm going to investigate,' Kineally said disgustedly, as he climbed down from the jeep. He took a couple of steps towards the skittle alley, then stopped and turned round. 'Want to give me a hand, Chuck?' he asked.

'Why not?' Woodend asked, ignoring his own captain's meaningful glare and following the American officer.

The soldiers had formed a half-circle around the back wall of the alley, and trapped within that half-circle were two coloured men. Each of the coloured soldiers had acquired a weapon of sorts – one held a bottle in his hand, the other a short plank. The expressions on their faces said they weren't willing to go down without a fight, but they must surely have known that once the white soldiers rushed them, they wouldn't stand a chance.

'Stop this right now!' Kineally bellowed.

The white soldiers, who'd been so absorbed by their own anger that they'd been unaware of the arrival of the two newcomers, turned around. When they saw an officer standing there, they fell silent.

'What's going on here?' Kineally demanded.

One of the white soldiers, a man of middle height, and with a bad case of acne, took a step towards them.

'This has nuthin' to do with you,' he said aggressively.

'This has nothing to do with you, sir,' Kineally countered.

The other man looked down at the ground. 'This has nuthin' to do with you, sir,' he said, in a surly tone.

'What's your name, soldier?' Kineally asked.

'Wallace. Harold Wallace. Private First Class.'

'And what's happened here, Wallace?'

'These two niggers—'

'These two coloured soldiers,' Kineally interrupted. 'These two coloured comrades *of yours.'*

Woodend stood by, watching in amazement and admiration. In the time it had taken the captain to walk from the jeep to the skittle alley, he seemed to have become an entirely different person. The diffident Robert Kineally now seemed a thing of the past. This man who had replaced him was towering and

commanding – this new Kineally would not have been intim-
idated by the devil himself.

Kineally tapped the toe of his shoe on the ground impatiently. 'Start again, soldier!' he said. 'And this time, take
great care to make sure I don't feel the need to interrupt you.'

'These two ni . . . these two coloured soldiers came into
the bar,' Wallace said. 'They just strode up to the counter, as
proud as you please, an' asked for drinks.'

'And why shouldn't they have?'

'You kin see them!' Wallace said. 'Ain't it obvious?'

'Did they do, or say, anything to anger you?' Kineally asked
mildly, as if he were trying to be fair to everyone concerned.
'Did they insult you in any way, Private Wallace?'

'Sure they insulted me. They insulted me by tryin' to order
drinks in a white man's bar.'

'But it's not a white man's bar,' Kineally pointed out. 'In
case you haven't noticed, this is England, and Jim Crow laws
don't apply here.'

'You want these ni . . . these coloured soldiers . . . to go
back home to the States thinkin' that they're as good as we
are?' Wallace demanded.

'We're not talking about them, we're talking about you,' Kineally
told him. 'And what I want you to do is obey the laws of the
country in which you happen to be a guest,' He paused for a
moment, to let the message sink in. 'So what happened next?'

'We invited these boys to come out into the yard with us,'
Wallace said, 'an' we was just about to teach them their place
when you come in like the goddamned US Cavalry.'

'In other words, these soldiers did nothing whatsoever to
provoke you, but you had every intention of hurting them?'

'Yeah. That's right! An' we're still gonna beat the crap out
of them,' Wallace said.

'I think not,' Kineally said calmly. 'What you're actually
going to is to apologize to these soldiers for your behaviour.
And while you're about it, you may as well apologize for
calling them "niggers".'

An angry growl, like that of a wounded and enraged animal,
rose up from the white soldiers standing behind Wallace.

'I ain't gonna do no such thing,' Wallace protested.

'Then I'll personally see to it that you're tried by a court
martial on the charge of treason,' Kineally promised.

86

'Treason! What you talkin' 'bout? I ain't no treasoner. I love my country!'

'If you truly loved it, you wouldn't try to undermine it by taking two of its soldiers out of action.'

'They ain't soldiers. They're ni—'

'You have one minute to make your apology, and after that, whatever you say it will be too late to save you from a court martial,' Kineally said firmly.

Wallace looked down at the ground again.

'You ain't gonna do what he wants, are you, Harry?' a voice from the crowd demanded.

'I don't know, Huey,' Wallace mumbled. 'I just don't know.'

'Thirty seconds left,' Kineally said.

'You cain't do it!' the man in the crowd – Huey – screamed.

Woodend had a fix on him now. He was standing at the very edge of the half-circle. He was a big, ugly-looking bastard, with bad teeth and a rough scar running down his right cheek.

'Fifteen seconds,' Kineally said.

Huey chose that moment to make his move. He broke free of the mob and rushed towards Kineally. He had a brick in his hand, and there was no doubt at all about what he intended to do with it.

Woodend let him get a little closer, then stepped into his path. A look of confusion crossed Huey's face, then it changed to a look of pain, as the sergeant's fist buried itself in his ample gut.

Gasping for air, Huey sank down to his knees. Woodend pushed the fallen man aside, and swung round to ready himself for his next attacker. But having seen their champion felled with comparative ease, none of the other men seemed overly eager to take his place.

'Five seconds,' Kineally said calmly, as if totally unaware of what had just happened only a couple of feet from him.

Harry Wallace swallowed hard. 'I'm sorry, sir,' he said in a croak.

'It's not me you need to apologize to, it's the coloured soldiers,' Kineally told him.

Wallace gulped again. 'I'm sorry, boys,' he said, looking vaguely in the direction of the black men. 'I guess I just got carried away.'

*   *   *

87

'You don't think I handled that very well, do you, Chuck?' Kineally asked Woodend, as they sat together in the bar of the Dun Cow, half an hour later.

'I'm sure those two coloured men appreciated your efforts on their behalf,' Woodend said evasively.

Kineally smiled. *'Give me a straight answer to my question, Chuck,'* he said. *'I can take it.'*

'I think you could have defused the incident without humiliating Wallace quite so much,' Woodend said.

'Don't you think he deserved to be humiliated?'

'I think he deserved to be thrashed to within an inch of his life. But that's not the point.'

'Then what is?'

'In the long term, you've just made matters worse. Wallace won't hate the coloureds any less as a result of what you made him do. If anything, his hatred will only increase, because every time he sees a black man, it will remind him of what happened here. The only difference you've made is that the next time he does something hateful, he'll be much cleverer about it. You haven't taught him to be better – you've taught him not to get caught.'

Kineally sighed. *'I guess you're right,'* he admitted. *'I got angry, and I shouldn't have done. Maybe when this war is over, I'll go into politics. Maybe then I'll be able to help change attitudes.'*

'But he never lived to see the end of the war,' Woodend said to Paniatowski. 'He didn't even live long enough to see any real fightin'. An' it was his brother who eventually ended up in politics.'

He paused, expecting his sergeant to make some comment on the story he had just told her – the story she had been itching to hear – but she said nothing.

'Of course, there's another way of lookin' at it,' Woodend continued. 'Bearin' in mind that Robert was really a robot, put on this earth by bug-eyed aliens intent on world domination, it's probably for the best that it was his brother who ended up with a seat in Senate.'

Paniatowski maintained her silence.

'I'm not borin' you, am I, Monika?' Woodend asked loudly.

The sergeant jumped slightly. 'What was that, sir?'

88

'I asked if I was borin' you.'

'No, I—'

'Or maybe you've simply perfected the art of fallin' asleep with your eyes open.'

'I wasn't asleep,' Paniatowski said defensively. 'I was thinking.'

'Now there's a novelty. An' might I enquire what it was you were thinkin' *about*?'

'I was thinking about your friend, Robert Kineally. I'm starting to see an entirely new side of him.'

'Are you? An' what side might that be?'

'Up until now, the picture that you've been painting has been of a very *nice* man.'

'An' that's just what he was. A grand lad! A lovely feller!'

'But you gave me no idea at all of just how easy he found it to make himself enemies.'

'Come again?'

'He made himself an enemy of Private Harry Wallace that night in the skittle alley, didn't he?'

'I'm not sure I'd put it quite like—'

'You told Kineally that every time Wallace saw a coloured man, it would remind him of how much the captain had humiliated him. But how much more intense that feeling must have been when he actually saw Kineally himself.'

Woodend frowned. 'So you think that Harry Wallace might be the murderer?' he asked.

'It could be him, certainly,' Paniatowski replied. 'But it could be any one of the thousands of other bigots who must have been at Haverton Camp at the same time.'

'Wallace was the one who Kineally forced to apologize to the coloured lads,' Woodend said.

'On *that* occasion,' Paniatowski countered. 'But do you really believe that Wallace was the *only* enlisted man to ever come up against Kineally's almost evangelical zeal and walk away hating him?'

'Probably not,' Woodend said, somewhat gloomily.

'And if one of those enlisted men did decide to kill the captain, wouldn't he have been likely to try and make sure that if the body *was* eventually found, someone else would take the blame for the murder?'

'Yes, but—'

'And who better as the fall guy than a Limey officer?'

'You're forgettin' the bloody fingerprint on the dog tag . . .' Woodend protested.

'Maybe Coutes is right,' Paniatowski argued. 'Maybe that *was* faked somehow! Or maybe – though Special Agent Grant would throw an absolute fit if he heard me say this – the wonderful, super-efficient FBI crime lab made a mistake for once, and it isn't Coutes's fingerprint at all!'

'When you prove me innocent of this murder – and you will prove it – it will be like thrusting a dagger in your own gut,' Coutes had told Woodend. *'And when you see me walk away – more powerful than I've ever been – it will be twisting that dagger round in the wound.'*

'I'd so like it if Douglas Coutes turned out to be the murderer,' Woodend said.

'I know you would,' Paniatowski told him. 'But are you prepared to consider the possibility that he might actually be innocent?'

'Yes,' Woodend replied. 'Unfortunately, I bloody-well am.'

Twelve

It was after eleven o'clock when Woodend and Paniatowski returned to Haverton Camp, and though there were still two MPs on sentry duty at the gate, there was no other sign of life.

'Well, everybody seems to be tucked up safely in his or her own little bed, ' Woodend said, as he parked the Wolseley next to the trailers. 'Do you know what George Bernard Shaw once said about Britain an' America, Monika?'

'Can't say that I do.'

'He said they were two countries divided by a common language.'

'Having talked to Special Agent Grant for a few hours, I think Shaw was probably right,' Paniatowski said.

'So do I. But I also think that he missed one other vital difference, which is that we're divided by our drinkin' habits.'

Paniatowski smiled. 'Go on, I'll buy it,' she said.

'You see, the Americans don't have a closin' time as we know it,' Woodend explained. 'That means that some of their bars close *earlier* than our pubs, an' some of them close *later*.'

'So what?'

'Well, takin' that fact into account, there's no wonder they're confused, is there? Every society needs a clearly defined structure if it's to function properly, an' they haven't got one.'

'What about the American Constitution?' Paniatowski asked, innocently.

'Can't say I've ever looked at that particular document,' Woodend admitted. 'I'm sure it's a wonderful read, but I'd rather wait for the film to come out. Anyway, even allowin' for the fact that it's as fine a piece of work as everybody seems to think it is, there's nothin' gives structure like the "last orders" bell in a boozer. It's the one fixed point in an ever-changin' world, you see. Politicians may argue among

91

themselves, scientists may dispute other scientists' findings, historians may be continually reinterpretin' the past in the light of new findin's, but it's an indisputable fact that at ten minutes to eleven that bell will ring, so you'd better get your last drinks in. An' that one single event provides us with a universal certainty we can build our lives around.'

'Unless you indulge in after-hours drinking, as we so often do,' Paniatowski pointed out.

'Aye, well, you can pick holes in most theories if you're really determined to,' Woodend said, climbing out of the car. 'Do you want me to walk you back to your caravan, Monika?'

'You wouldn't normally make me an offer like that,' Paniatowski said, half-suspicious, half-amused. 'Is there any particular reason for this sudden attack of gallantry?'

'Not really,' Woodend said.

But maybe there was, he thought.

Maybe just talking about Robert Kineally had somehow summoned up the dead American's spirit, and in making the offer, he was only doing what Kineally – a born gentleman if there ever was one – would have done in his place.

'It's a man's natural inclination to want to protect a woman,' he heard himself say.

Paniatowski laughed. 'I've got a black belt in judo,' she reminded him. 'Have you?'

Woodend grinned. 'No, I'm too patriotic to go in for all that foreign stuff. I have to rely on the traditional British martial arts – passed down through the generations – of the fist an' the boot.'

'Besides,' Paniatowski said, suddenly growing more serious and reaching into her handbag, 'I've got this as back-up.'

She held out the knife for him to inspect. The blade was not visible at that moment, but at the touch of a button it would spring out.

'Flick knives like that one are illegal in this country, Monika,' Woodend pointed out.

'I know,' Paniatowski said. 'I've often thought of arresting myself for carrying it around. But since it was *given* to me by a policeman – for my protection, he said – I'd have to arrest him, too.'

This conversation wasn't about the knife at all, Woodend guessed – it was about Chief Inspector Baxter.

'There are times when he's just like a mother hen to me,' Paniatowski continued, confirming his suspicions. 'He clucks, and he fusses, and he treats me like I'm a delicate china doll. And that can sometimes become just a little tiring, you know.'

'Perhaps he *is* a little over-cautious from time to time,' Woodend said, 'but all men are prone to bein' like that as they grow older.'

'You're not,' Paniatowski said. 'You might be older than God yourself, but you can still act like a bull in a china shop when the mood takes you.'

'Aye, an' just look where it's got me,' Woodend said. 'I could have been Chief Constable by now, if I'd learned to practice a little more caution.'

'I sometimes yearn for the dangerous – the unpredictable,' Paniatowski said. 'Is that so wrong?'

Woodend shrugged. 'There's not much point in askin' me, lass. As an agony aunt, I'd make a pretty good hatstand.'

Paniatowski laughed again. 'You're right, of course. Some people are never happy with what they've got – even if what they've got is more than they'd ever dared hope for.' She turned towards her trailer. 'Goodnight, sir.'

'Goodnight, lass,' Woodend said. 'See you in the mornin'.'

Paniatowski had only been inside her trailer for a minute when she heard the knock on the door.

'Have you forgotten something, sir?' she called out.

'It's not Mr Woodend,' the voice outside said. 'It's me. Ed Grant.'

Ed Grant? Paniatowski thought. Not Special Agent Grant, or even Edward Grant, but *Ed* Grant!

She opened the door, and looked out into the night. Earlier, she reminded herself, Grant had been wearing a sober suit and a dark tie. Now he was tie-less and had put on a casual jacket.

'This is something of a surprise,' she said. 'What can I do for you, Special Agent?'

Grant flushed slightly. 'I . . . uh . . . was taking a walk around the camp before turning in for the night, and I happened to see that your light was still on,' he said unconvincingly.

'And so you rushed over here because you thought I might be being burgled?' Paniatowski asked.

93

'No, not exactly. I . . . uh . . . thought you might like a nightcap before you went to bed.'

Paniatowski glanced over her shoulder, at the small fridge in the trailer's kitchen.

'I'm not sure there *is* anything to drink,' she said. 'I haven't actually checked.'

Grant reached into his jacket pocket, and produced a half-bottle of vodka. 'We could always drink this,' he suggested.

'A *Commie* drink?' Paniatowski asked, with mock-incredulity.

Grant shrugged, awkwardly. 'I figured if it was good enough for a fine lady like you to drink, then it was certainly good enough for me.'

'But wherever did you get it?' Paniatowski wondered. 'I thought you told me they wouldn't have any in your commissary.'

'Yeah, that's right,' Grant agreed. 'Thing is, I thought I'd take the opportunity to see something of this wonderful little country of yours, so I went for a drive. I came across this cute little town – Exeter, I think it's called – and that's where I bought the vodka.'

So he had not only managed to drag himself away from his precious documents, but he'd driven all the way to Exeter, Paniatowski thought.

'And when you went on your walk, just now, you took the vodka with you for company?' she asked.

Grant flushed again, deeper, this time. 'I'm not very good at this, am I?' he asked.

'Not very good at what?'

'At being casual. "Casual" isn't something they teach you how to be in the FBI.'

Paniatowski found herself warming to his obvious discomfort. 'Why don't you just say what's really on your mind?' she suggested.

Grant took a deep breath. 'The fact is, I was hoping we'd have the opportunity to spend some time together,' he confessed.

Paniatowski thought of Bob Rutter, her old lover, and Chief Inspector Baxter, her solid, stolid sometimes-part-time current lover. Neither of them could have been truly called a man of the world, but even so, Grant seemed like a stumbling, bumbling boy in comparison to them.

But that didn't necessarily make him unattractive.

'I . . . uh . . . probably shouldn't have intruded on your free time,' Special Agent Grant said.

Paniatowski took a step back inside the trailer. 'Come inside,' she said. 'You open the bottle, and I'll find us some glasses.'

Thirteen

The darkness that had shrouded the earth since the setting of the evening sun was slowly conceding its dominance to the newly-born *morning* sun, already on its slow climb towards its zenith.

At ground level, small, furry nocturnal creatures scurried towards their hiding-place-homes, and small diurnal creatures slowly emerged from their sleepy burrows. In the trees, the birds had already begun their daily song of gratitude at having survived another long cold night. And Woodend, lying in his trailer-bed, reflectively scratched under his armpit.

He was not at all happy to be playing any part in this investigation, he told himself. It wasn't just that the whole situation was fraught with career-busting political possibilities – although it undoubtedly was. It wasn't even that, given the time which had passed, the murder was almost impossible to solve with any degree of certainty – though that was true as well. What really depressed him was that he was being forced to investigate his own past – interrogate his old self – and he was not at all sure that he would like what he might uncover.

Woodend rolled out of bed. He was a bath-taking man by inclination, but there was no bath in the trailer, so a shower would have to do. He wedged himself inside the shower cabinet, and – after just a *moment's* indecision – decided to ignore the inviting hot tap and use only the cold. He emerged from the shower shivering – but feeling virtuous – and after putting on his dressing gown, he decided to reward himself with his first cigarette of the morning.

He allowed the first few inhalations of the blessed nicotine to snake their way around his lungs, then padded over to the trailer's kitchen area. There didn't seem to be a teapot. However, since the caddy did not contain the loose tea he'd expected, but only little bags of the stuff (Tea bags! What *was* the world coming to?) he soon realized that a pot wasn't really necessary.

By using three tea bags in a large mug, he managed to produce a brew which was *almost* as good as the one he would have got at home, and he was just lighting up his second cigarette of the day when the phone rang.

He picked it up.

'Woodend.'

He had expected to find himself talking to either Paniatowski or Grant – but it was neither of them.

'How are you, sir?' asked the thin, uncertain voice at the other end of the line.

'How are *you*, Bob?' Woodend replied.

What a bloody stupid thing to say, Charlie Woodend, he told himself angrily. How do you *think* the lad is? How would you be, if it had been Joan who'd been murdered?

'Forget I even asked you that question,' he told Bob Rutter. 'I know how you must be feelin'. Like shit! But it will get a *little* better, over time. I can promise you that, lad.'

'Well, it's hard to imagine it could get much worse,' Rutter said, chillingly matter-of-factly. 'Listen, sir, I don't know where you are – they wouldn't tell me in Whitebridge, and I had to use a bucketful of favours to even get your number out of them – but I assume that you're working on a case.'

'Yes, I am,' Woodend said cautiously.

'Want to talk it over?'

'I'm not really sure I can.'

'The thing is, I've been to see the police shrink again, and he says I'm not stable enough to return to my normal duties yet.'

'An' he's probably right about that, don't you think? Take your time, Bob. Nobody's rushin' you. Nobody at all. You come back to work when you're good an' ready.'

'I'm ready now,' Rutter said, desperately. 'Whatever the shrink's opinion, I know I am.'

'Well, I wouldn't be too sure . . .'

'If I don't get back to work soon, I'll go crazy. That's why I'm ringing you now.'

'Listen, Bob—'

'I'm not asking for a major part in an investigation. I know that's not possible. I'd be happy just doing a little bit of the background work for the case you're involved in now.'

97

But what kind of 'backroom work' could *anybody* do on a case which was as tightly wrapped up in the Official Secrets Act as this one seemed to be? Woodend wondered.

Still, it must have taken a lot of guts for Bob Rutter to force himself to make this call in the first place, and Woodend just couldn't bring himself to turn the poor feller down flat.

'Where are you, Bob?' he asked.

'London. I've brought the baby down here to be with her grandparents. It's for the best, I suppose. I can't look after her properly myself at the moment, the state I'm in.'

He really *did* need to work, Woodend thought, and quickly racked his brains for something – anything – he could toss to the inspector who he'd come almost to regard as a son.

'Have you still got any of your old contacts from your days in the Met, Bob?' he asked.

'A few. Why?'

'Do you think you could make use of them to do some background checkin' for me?'

'On what?'

On what indeed? Woodend wondered. He was walking through a minefield of officialdom and secrecy here, and if he put a foot wrong, the whole thing would blow up in his face.

'Have you ever heard of a feller called the Right Honourable Douglas Coutes?' he asked.

'Coutes? Isn't he the Minister of Defence?'

'That's right.'

'*He's* not been murdered, has he? Surely if he had been, it would be headline news.'

'No, he's not been murdered.'

'Then what . . . ?'

'He's peripherally involved in the case I'm workin' on,' Woodend lied, 'but, for God's sake, whatever you do, don't tell anybody else that.'

'Understood.'

'An' I was wonderin' if he – or anybody close to him – might have been of especial interest to the Met, recently.'

'It's not likely, is it?' Rutter asked.

No, Woodend thought, it's not likely at all. If Coutes is guilty of a serious crime, it's one he committed twenty years ago.

'My first rule of thumb is collect up as much information as I can, however irrelevant it might turn out to be later,' he said, improvising wildly around the truth. 'Havin' worked with me as closely as you have, you should know that better than anybody.'

'I suppose I do.'

'But you're probably right, Bob. A long-shot like this isn't worth wastin' your time—'

'I'll do it,' Rutter said firmly.

'No, now I've had time to consider it, I think—'

'I *want* to do it.'

'You can't tell your pals in the Met the reason *why* you're interested in Coutes,' Woodend warned.

'No problem there, is there – since I don't actually know myself,' Rutter countered.

'But you're goin' to have to come up with some sort of story to explain away your questions.'

'I'll think of something.'

This was crazy, Woodend thought. If things went wrong, they could both be accused of breaching the Official Secrets Act. If things went wrong, they could both be sunk without trace.

'Well, tread carefully, lad,' he said reluctantly.

'I always do tread carefully in my professional life,' Rutter said. 'It's only in my private life that I bugger things up.'

'You mustn't go heapin' *all* the blame on yourself—' Woodend began – but he was talking to a dead line.

There was an energetic knocking on the trailer door, and when Woodend opened it, he found a bright-eyed and bushy-tailed Special Agent Grant standing there.

'The first of our witnesses arrived at the camp some time in the night,' the Special Agent said.

'Thanks for tellin' me,' Woodend said.

'So I thought we could roll up our sleeves and get started straight away,' Grant said.

Woodend sighed. 'You can die of over-enthusiasm, you know,' he said. 'But fortunately, there is a cure.'

'A cure?' Grant repeated.

'Aye,' Woodend told him. 'It's called "growin' older".'

* * *

99

Woodend had conducted more interrogations in his career than he now cared to remember. And the interview rooms in which he'd conducted them – whether in London, Whitebridge or some other provincial city or town – had all been pretty much-of-a-muchness.

The only window in these rooms would generally be close to the ceiling and rather small, thus ensuring that the man being interrogated could neither be distracted by looking out of it, nor seek to put an end to his ordeal by jumping through it. The walls of the rooms were almost invariably painted in two colours – chocolate brown to waist height, and sickly cream from there to the ceiling. The table and chairs could come in a variety of mismatched styles, but were united by the fact that they had all had a long history of service, and only found their way to this room when no one else – not even the most junior of junior officers – was prepared to tolerate using them any more.

The trailer which Special Agent Grant had set aside for interrogations in this case was – to say the least – from another world. It differed from all the other trailers the Americans had brought with them in that it had no windows, and it bore the sign TC1 on its side in bold black letters.

'Tests have shown that loss of any kind of natural light tends to disorientate the subject under questioning,' Grant said, when Woodend commented on the lack of windows.

'It doesn't do much for me, either,' the Chief Inspector admitted. 'What do you do when it gets hot in there?'

'The same thing you'd do yourself,' Grant said, puzzled he even needed to ask. 'Turn up the air conditioning.'

Turn up the air conditioning! Woodend repeated silently.

As if there was air conditioning *to* turn up in any of the places he'd worked! Even the Chief Constable – who regularly and ruthlessly plundered the police budget in order to enhance his own personal comfort – would never have gone so far as to consider installing *air conditioning* in his office.

'What does "TC1" stand for?' Woodend wondered.

'Truth Centre One.'

Good God! Woodend thought.

'An' is there a Truth Centre Two?' he asked.

'Not yet,' Grant said. 'But we can always fly one in from the States, if the need arises.'

100

Of course they could. These fellers could fly in *anythin'* they decided they needed.

The two men entered the trailer. It contained a table and three chairs, just as an English interview room would have done, but this furniture was brand-spanking new.

Woodend ran his hand across the smooth surface of the table.

'It's rather clinical at the moment,' he commented, 'but I expect it'll feel a bit more like home when its got a few cigarette burns on it.'

'That won't happen,' Grant told him. 'This material was developed for the space programme. It'd take a laser beam to make any impression on it.'

'You certainly do seem to have thought of everything,' Woodend said dryly.

'We like to think so,' Grant replied, with just a hint of complacency in his voice.

The chairs were bolted to the floor. The one on the suspect's/witness's side had been positioned squarely in the middle of the table, but the two interrogators' chairs were fixed at the corners.

'They're like that so that the guy being questioned can't look at both his interrogators at once,' Grant explained. 'Our psychiatrists think that gives us the edge.'

'Good for them,' Woodend said. 'An' where's the bright light, to shine in suspect's face?'

He had been joking, but Grant took the question at face value. 'There's half a dozen different lights in the ceiling,' he said. 'They're activated by a control panel built into the arm of the interrogator's chair.'

'Very clever,' Woodend said. 'Not that we'll be needin' them.'

'Our psychiatrists believe that by varying the light intensity—' Grant began.

'Not that we'll be needin' them,' Woodend repeated firmly.

Grant shrugged. 'Whatever you say.'

Woodend lowered himself into the left-hand interrogator's chair, and thought he would have felt more at ease if it had wobbled a little.

'Right, let's see our first witness of the mornin' now, shall we?' he suggested.

'Sure,' Grant said. 'But there's one more thing you should understand before we begin.'

'An' what might that be?'

'They don't know why they're here.'

'Come again?'

'As far as they're concerned, Captain Robert Kineally disappeared in the spring of 1944, and hasn't been seen – or heard from – since.'

'Are you sayin' the witnesses don't know that his body has been recently discovered?'

'Affirmative. They don't even know there's been a murder of *any kind*.'

'Why?'

'It was decided in Washington DC – at the very highest levels of government, you understand – that until we've completed our investigation, as few details as possible of what actually occurred here should become generally known.'

'So what do all these witnesses of yours *think* they're bein' questioned about?'

'A matter of national importance.'

'Meanin' what, exactly?'

'It doesn't matter what it means. They won't ask that question – and if they did, we wouldn't tell them.'

'Jesus!' Woodend said.

Fourteen

The man standing uncertainly in the doorway of TC1 had once had a mop of thick black curly hair. Now, what hair he had left was pale and limp – and clustered around the bald patch on the top of his head like a petrified forest surrounding a clearing. His body, at one time wiry and hard, had gradually allowed itself to be conquered by fat, and the washboard stomach had become a hill of blubber in constant conflict with the restraints imposed on it by a tightly-buttoned khaki shirt.

In many ways, the years had not treated Abe Birnbaum too kindly, Woodend thought, yet the vital spark – the interest in life and all it involved – was still there, if a little dimmed by age.

'Hello, Abe,' the Chief Inspector said.

'Charlie?' Birnbaum asked. He smiled, and the spark grew brighter. 'Charlie Woodend? *Sergeant* Charlie Woodend. What in the name of blue blazes are you doing here, Sarge?'

'Investigatin' matters of national importance,' Woodend said, repeating Grant's words of earlier – though without the same fervour.

An Englishman would probably have asked what the hell he meant by that, but Grant's earlier assessment of the probable American response proved to be correct, since Birnbaum just smiled wryly and said, 'Well, it's a dirty job, but I guess somebody has to do it.'

Special Agent Grant, looking distinctly unhappy about being excluded from the conversation, cleared his throat and said, 'Would you sit over there, please, Mr Birnbaum?'

'Sure,' Abe Birnbaum agreed, squeezing his paunch between the table and door, and then lowering the rest of himself into the chair.

Grant consulted the notes he had spread out in front of him. 'You are ex-PFC Abraham Birnbaum?' he asked.

103

Birnbaum looked first at Grant, then at Woodend, then back at Grant. 'Is this seating plan designed so that cross-eyed guys can feel right at home?' he wondered whimsically.

'Just answer the question as it has been put to you, please,' Special Agent Grant said firmly.

'Sure, I'm *that* Birnbaum.' He smiled. 'But now I'm Birnbaum the Dry-Cleaner, with outlets all over the tri-state area.' The smile still in place, he turned his attention to Woodend. 'Was that too direct?' he asked. 'My shrink says I should be self-confident enough about my achievements to hold off on that kind of information until people actually ask.'

Woodend grinned. 'Glad to hear you've done well for yourself, Abe. I always knew you would.'

'What you're doing now is of no importance,' Grant said stiffly. 'We are only concerned with the time that you were stationed in this camp, when you were, I believe, the driver assigned to Captain Robert Kineally?'

He had dropped in the last few words into the sentence as casually as he could. But Birnbaum was not fooled – the ex-PFC's sunny smile disappeared instantly, and his eyes hardened.

'Is that what this is all about?' he demanded. 'So the man disappeared! Big deal!'

'It *was* a big deal at the time – or so I've been led to believe,' Special Agent Grant said.

'Listen, a guy goes missing like that, there could be a hundred reasons for it – reasons we can't even guess at,' Birnbaum said. 'But it all happened over twenty years ago, for Pete's sake! Why can't you leave the poor guy alone?'

'Just answer the question,' Grant said sternly.

'I was *kinda* Captain Kineally's driver,' Abe Birnbaum admitted, with some show of reluctance.

'*Kind of* his driver? What does that mean, *exactly*?'

'It means that I was down on the payroll as his driver.'

'But you didn't drive him?'

'Not often. The Captain liked to drive himself most of the time.'

'So what function *did* you fulfil?'

'It wasn't a *function*, exactly, but I guess you could say that as I was as close as an enlisted man could be to being his confidant and buddy.'

'His confidant and *buddy*?'

'Sure. The Captain didn't go in much for social distinctions. He said that we were both citizens of the greatest country in the world, and that's what counted the most.' Birnbaum, seeing the look of growing scepticism in Grant's eyes, turned to Woodend, and said, 'You knew him, Charlie. You tell the Special Agent that I'm right.'

How do you explain the time of your youth to a man who spent his youth in quite another time, Woodend wondered. How do get him to understand what it felt like to know that you might be dead soon – and that history would judge you not on something you might have achieved in the future, but on what you were doing right now?

'American officers tended to be much more informal in their relationships with their men than our British officers were in their relationships with us,' he said, 'but even allowin' for the extra informality, Captain Robert Kineally was still exceptional.'

'Exceptional?' Grant repeated, almost as if he considered it to be a dirty word.

'He once told me that bein' born with a silver spoon in your mouth was no excuse for talkin' like it was still there,' Woodend amplified.

'He seems to have been something of a radical,' Grant said, sounding troubled.

'I suppose you could say he was, in a way,' Woodend agreed.

'But not a Commie?' Grant asked, worriedly.

'No,' Woodend said. 'Not a Commie. Not a Bolshevik, murder-lovin', baby-eater.'

'That's OK then,' Grant said, relieved. He switched his attention back to Birnbaum. 'Captain Kineally disappeared, didn't he?'

'That's right,' Birnbaum said cautiously.

'Tell me about it?'

'What's to tell? One morning I went to his room – like I did every morning in case he had any duties for me – and the guy just wasn't there.'

'What did you think?'

'Think?'

'When you saw that he wasn't there?'

105

'I thought maybe he was hiding in the closet.'

'You did?'

'Course not! I thought he'd gone off to someplace else, and he'd soon be back.'

'And when he *didn't* come back, as you'd expected him to? What did you think then?'

Birnbaum shrugged. 'Not much, I guess.'

'Not much! You must surely have thought *something*,' Grant said, exasperatedly.

'I guess I thought about going over the sea to France,' Birnbaum said. 'I guess I thought that in a few weeks – or maybe a few days, if I was unlucky – I'd probably be dead. That made whatever had happened to Captain Kineally seem kinda unimportant.'

'Were there any indications beforehand that Kineally was going to disappear?'

'What do you mean?'

'Did he seem worried about anything in particular? Was he showing any signs of being nervous?'

'Not especially.'

Abe Birnbaum was lying, Woodend thought.

But the problem was that he had no idea *why* Birnbaum was lying. Or even what he was lying *about*. Perhaps, he decided, it was time to come at the interrogation from another angle.

'Can I ask a couple of questions?' he asked Grant.

'Surely,' the Special Agent agreed, sounding almost relieved at the thought of someone else taking over.

Woodend looked Birnbaum squarely in the eyes. 'Tell me, Abe, do you remember a woman called Mary Parkinson?' he asked.

'Sure,' Birnbaum replied, turning to face Special Agent Grant.

'Is that all you want to say about her?' Woodend wondered. 'That you remember her?'

'I guess I could add that she was Captain Kineally's girl – for a little while, anyway.'

'And *before* she was his girl?'

'What do you mean?' Birnbaum asked.

You know what I mean, Abe, Woodend thought. You know *exactly* what I mean!

'Was she, to your personal knowledge, involved with anybody else?' he asked.

'Not exactly involved,' Birnbaum said. 'Not in the way she was with the Captain. But she was kinda stepping out with another guy. A Brit by the name of Coutes. But why are you asking me about that? You should remember him well enough yourself, Sarge. You were the bastard's go-fer.'

'So Kineally stole this girl from another man – this Captain Coutes!' Grant asked, suddenly interested again.

'It wasn't like that!' Abe said indignantly.

No, Woodend agreed silently. No, it hadn't been like that at all.

It was a typical evening in the Dun Cow, a few nights after Woodend and Kineally had the run-in with Harry Wallace and his big, ugly friend, Huey. It was also the start of the third week of Captain Coutes's concerted campaign to get Mary Parkinson into his bed.

Coutes and Mary were sitting at a table. Woodend was positioned at the bar, in case – so Coutes had informed him – he needed a driver. But whatever the Captain might claim, he wasn't just there as a driver at all, Woodend thought. No, he had quite another – unspoken – function altogether.

For a man like Coutes, success was only real if it was acknowledged as such by others, the sergeant had long ago decided. Thus, he did not only have to seduce Mary, he had to be seen to do it. And that was Woodend's assigned role – the envious observer, the man who not only held a grudging admiration for his captain, but wished he could actually be Coutes himself.

Except that things were not working out quite as planned, Woodend thought with wry amusement. Certainly Mary was being pleasant enough to Coutes, and was likely to see him again if he asked her – but she seemed no nearer being overcome by his charms than she had been at the start of their relationship.

Woodend felt a friendly hand on his shoulder, and turned round to see Captain Robert Kineally standing there.

'Does your mother know you're out on your own?' Woodend asked, good-naturedly.

Kineally grinned. 'I'm not out on my own,' he said. 'I'm

with my good friend, Sergeant Chuck Woodend, who's about to give me further lessons in the English way of life, with special reference to its pub culture.'

'It'll cost you,' Woodend told him.

Kineally's face took on an unnatural expression, a clear indication that he was about to attempt some kind of accent.

'Course it'll cost me,' he agreed. 'So what say I buy you a pint of bitter beer as a down-payment, my old cock sparrow?'

'Is that supposed to be a Cockney accent?' Woodend asked, amused.

'Too right it is. An' why wouldn't it be from a bloke wot was born wivin the sound of Bow Bells?'

'You might fool a passin' Eskimo, but I don't think that you'd have much success with anybody else,' Woodend told him. 'And it's not "bitter beer" – it's just "bitter".'

Kineally's grin widened. 'So much to learn, so little time to learn it before we're sent to France,' he said.

And then he noticed Mary Parkinson for the first time, and his mouth fell wide open.

'I've never seen you look at Captain Coutes like that before,' Woodend said mock-innocently.

'Is she his girl?' Kineally asked. 'I mean, is there anything serious going on between them?'

Keep out of it, Charlie! a voice in Woodend's head warned him. Keep right out of it!

The voice was right, he thought. He'd already crossed Captain Coutes enough, without compounding matters. And Mary Parkinson was a grown woman, easily old enough to make her own decisions. She had not asked to be rescued, and she had no right to expect that she would be. His best course of action, therefore, was to claim complete ignorance.

'I don't think Mary's very keen on Captain Coutes, if you want the truth,' he heard himself say. 'An' Coutes doesn't want her for herself – to him she's just one more potential conquest.'

Kineally nodded gratefully. 'I think I'll just go and say "hi" to my fellow officer,' he told Woodend.

And then he was gone.

Looking back on it later, Woodend would see it all as rather like one of those defining scenes from a Hollywood romantic film.

The young officer walks over to the table, the girl looks up, their eyes meet – and it's love at first sight.

108

Of course, the analogy was not perfect – Kineally was nowhere near handsome enough to play a Hollywood lead, and Mary was sweet rather than beautiful – yet as he took her hand, Woodend could almost hear an orchestra striking up a lush, romantic song in the background.

And the sergeant was not alone in sensing that something special was happening between the two of them.

Captain Coutes – seeing his own carefully mapped-out plans disintegrate before his very eyes – shot Kineally a look which clearly said he wished the other man was dead.

'You told us that Kineally went out with Mary Parkinson *for a while*,' Woodend reminded Birnbaum. 'That would imply, wouldn't it, that they broke up before he went missing?'

'Yeah, I guess it would.'

'So when, exactly, did this occur?'

'It's kinda hard to say, exactly,' Birnbaum replied, his eyes still focussed on Grant, rather than on Woodend.

'I don't think it *is* too hard to say – not if you really put your mind to the problem,' Woodend persisted.

Birnbaum pursed his brow, and made a great show of searching through the darkest corners of his memory.

'Captain Kineally was away in London for a week,' he said finally. 'It was some kind of briefing session with the top brass, I think. I guess he broke up with Mary Parkinson as soon as he got back.'

'Which would have been just a couple of days before he disappeared into thin air?'

'I guess so.'

'There seems to be an awful lot of guessing going on.'

It was very difficult to be certain, with only a side-on view of the man's face, but it seemed to Woodend that Birnbaum was deliberately twisting his features into what could only be called a look of bemused innocence.

'I said, there seems to be an awful lot of guessing going on,' the Chief Inspector repeated.

Birnbaum turned to face him, and Woodend could see his suspicions had been correct – 'bemused innocence' was the look the other man had been striving for, and he'd *almost* got it right.

'But why are you asking *me* all this stuff, Sarge?' the

109

American asked, establishing eye contact – but only briefly. 'You were here yourself when they broke up.'

'No, I wasn't,' Woodend corrected him.

'Oh, that's right,' Birnbaum agreed, making a very poor show of looking as if he'd only just remembered that fact. 'You were shipped out of here shortly before then, weren't you? Where did they send you to, Sarge? You never told us before you left.'

'I couldn't tell you. Any troop movements – even the movements of just one soldier – were top secret at the time.'

'And there was me thinking you were just being unfriendly,' Birnbaum said, with an unconvincing grin.

'Bollocks!' Woodend said. 'You knew as well as I did that I couldn't talk about where I was going.'

'Maybe I did,' Birnbaum agreed. 'Maybe I've just forgotten that I knew. But the war's been over for a long time, Sarge, so why not satisfy my curiosity now. Where *did* they send you?'

'They sent me to the Isle of Wight,' Woodend said, noting that with the change of subject Birnbaum was relaxing a little. 'It was a grand place. A little world all of its own. You should try and visit it while you're over here this time.'

'Maybe I will,' Birnbaum said, now much more at his ease.

'So tell me, Abe,' Woodend continued, in a soft coaxing tone, 'why *did* Robert Kineally and Mary Parkinson break up?'

Birnbaum jerked violently, as if a charge of electricity had been sent through the chair on which he was sitting. 'Who . . . who knows?' he asked.

'Did Mary Parkinson break up with Robert Kineally? Or did Kineally break up with her?'

'Maybe it was a bit of both, Sarge,' Abe Birnbaum suggested. 'You know yourself what wartime romances were like – blazing passion one second, and cold blankets the next.'

Not that wartime romance, Woodend thought. *That* wartime romance was very special.

'You're not under oath at the moment, Abe,' he said, 'but you may well be at some time in the future, so I—'

'Under oath?' Birnbaum interrupted. 'What are you talking about? Why would I be under oath?'

'—so I'm going to give you a second chance to answer my

110

question, and this time, I want you to be completely honest with me. *Do you know why Robert Kineally and Mary Parkinson broke up?*'

'No, I don't know that,' Birnbaum said, with a slightly squeaky wobble in his voice.

'I thought you were supposed to be his buddy,' Special Agent Grant said suspiciously. 'I thought he told you everything.'

'Nobody tells anybody *everything*,' Birnbaum replied.

Woodend's thoughts took him back to that damp night in May 1944 – back to that drab railway station, only a few miles from where he was sitting at that very moment.

He had seen Mary.

He had listened to Mary.

And what she had told him had seared right through his heart.

There'd been a moment, he remembered now, when he had almost decided not to get on the train at all – a moment when he had seriously considered returning to Haverton Camp and hurting someone very badly.

But such heroics were the province of the matinee idols of the silver screen. Ordinary fellers, like Sergeant Charlie Woodend, had responsibilities which made any such dramatic gestures impossible. He had felt for Mary and Robert – felt for them deeply – but he still had his duty to perform for his country, his family and his Joan.

He had climbed on the train, when it pulled into the station, knowing he was doing the right thing. But there was a part of him which had regretted the action – and still did.

If Mary had told Kineally what she had told him that night, he thought – and there was no guarantee that she had – it was more than likely that Kineally had told Birnbaum.

'One last question,' he said to Birnbaum. 'And again, I would caution you to think very carefully before you answer. *Did the break-up have anything to do with Captain Coutes?*'

'Search me,' Birnbaum said.

And this time there was absolutely no question that he was lying.

Fifteen

The map which Monika Paniatowski held in her hands was curling at the corners, and yellowed with age. It had the words 'TOP SECRET' stamped in one corner of it, in bold black capital letters. And she supposed that once, back in the days when this American military camp had played a small – but significant – part in the huge gamble which was the Invasion of Normandy – 'top secret' must have been exactly what it was.

She closed her eyes, and tried to imagine what it must have been like to be stationed in this place in 1944 – to be part of an army which had never once fired a shot in anger, but knew it would soon be facing up to troops who had been hardened by five years of bloody war.

There must have been euphoria and despair, hope and fear, she thought. But it was impossible to conjure up such feelings now – when all that was left was a few decaying huts and the odd strip of crumbling concrete.

She strode quickly over to one of the barrack blocks. This one, according to the map, was where the officers had been billeted. Logically, therefore, this must also have been the one where Robert Kineally spent his last night, before being stabbed to death by a German World War One Army knife, and then hastily buried in a shallow grave.

She studied the map again, and gauged the distance from the hut to the site of the grave. A few hundred yards, at least. And in between the barrack block and the fence had been several other buildings, now long gone – the military stores, the cookhouse, the armoury.

Even in the dead of night, the killer – whether he was Coutes or one of the Americans – had taken a very big chance in making that journey with the body slung over his shoulder.

Unless, of course, Captain Robert Kineally hadn't actually been dead at that point!

Unless the killer had somehow persuaded his victim to accompany him to the chosen spot, and murdered him there! If that *was* what had happened, what excuse had the killer come up with to persuade Kineally to go with him? Whatever it was, Kineally would have had to have trusted the man, or he would never have agreed.

She wondered what Woodend would make of her reasoning, when she talked to him about it later.

And then, frowning without even realizing it, she wondered what Woodend would think if she told him what had happened between her and Grant the previous evening.

She *wouldn't* tell him, she decided.

It was her own business who she saw in her free time – who she *slept with* in her free time. And though she doubted that Woodend would actually express disapproval – *he* probably thought it was her own business, too – she could eliminate even the *possibility* of unpleasantness by keeping the matter to herself.

A couple of men had appeared by the wire, close to the site of the shallow grave. They were not soldiers, and – from their clothes – she guessed that they were not even Americans.

So what the hell were a pair of British civilians doing wandering around close to a crime scene? Paniatowski lit up a cigarette, and began to walk quickly towards them.

The two civilians – one skinny as a rake, the other much inclined towards plumpness – watched Paniatowski's approach with growing appreciation.

'Like it?' the fat one asked.

'Well, let me put it this way, I certainly wouldn't kick it out of bed,' the skinny one replied.

Then they saw the document that the woman was holding in her outstretched hand.

'What do you make of that?' the thin one asked.

'Looks like a warrant card to me,' the fat one said.

'I think you're right,' his friend agreed.

'Bit of a passion killer, really.'

'You can say that again.'

Paniatowski drew level with them, and came to halt. 'I'm Detective Sergeant Paniatowski,' she announced. 'And you are . . . ?'

'I'm Ben Tilley, and my good friend here is Lew Boardman,' the fat man said.

'And what do you think you're doing here?'

'We think we're surveying,' Tilley told her.

'Surveying?'

'It's what we do. We're charted surveyors, so it's become a bit of habit, really. It's how we put food on the table, clothe our young ones and keep a roof over our heads.'

'You are aware that this is a crime scene, aren't you?' Paniatowski asked severely.

'We should be,' Tilley replied. 'We're the unfortunate devils who found the body.'

'Cost us half a day's work, that did, what with answering questions and filling in forms,' Boardman added.

'So you do *know* that you shouldn't be here?' Paniatowski asked.

'Shouldn't be here?' Boardman repeated. 'But we've got permission. In writing!'

'Who from?'

'That American chappie,' Tilley said. 'You know the one I'm talking about. He's around your age. And he never uses a short word when he can find a long one instead.'

'Grant!' Boardman supplied.

'That's right, Grant,' Tilley agreed. 'He said that his team had done all the investigating it needed to—'

'"Had carried out all the necessary investigatorial procedures,"' Boardman corrected him.

'—had carried out all the necessary investigatorial procedures,' Tilley amended, 'and there was no reason why we couldn't get back to doing the job we're paid for.'

It made sense, Paniatowski thought. All the evidence had been bagged and sent back to the States, so there really *was* no reason to keep these men from their work any longer.

'So you found the skeleton, did you?' she asked.

'She's a clever girl to have worked that out, isn't she?' Boardman asked Tilley.

'She didn't need to work it out, Lew,' Tilley replied. 'We just told her ourselves.'

'Still, it was *quite* clever of her to *remember* we'd told her, wasn't it?' Boardman said.

114

Paniatowski sighed. 'Were there just the two of you here at the time?' she asked.

'No, there was another chappie here as well,' Tilley said. 'You see, the developers—'

'New Elizabethan Properties,' Boardman chipped in.

'—are based in London.'

'And they decided they didn't trust local people – people on the ground – to do a decent job.'

'Why should they, when it's well known that down here we all marry our cousins and do unspeakable things to sheep in the dead of night?'

'So they sent somebody from their head office to look over both our shoulders.'

'Full of himself, he was.'

'I should say he was. Thought he knew it all. Thought he could teach his grandmother to suck eggs.'

'He didn't look quite so clever when we uncovered the body, though, did he?'

'He certainly didn't. He turned quite green. Or maybe it was purple.'

'Looked like he was going to throw up.'

'We drove him down to the railway station, didn't we?'

'We did.'

'And we haven't seen hide nor hair of him since.'

'So now it seems that we *can* be trusted to work alone.'

'Which suits us down to the ground. We don't mind finding the odd skeleton.'

'We've come across a lot of worse things than that in our job, we can tell you.'

'Not that we would. We'd never describe any of them to a sweet innocent girl like yourself.'

Paniatowski had abandoned her stern expression a long time ago, and now was finding it hard not to laugh. 'Are you a natural double act?' she asked. 'Or have you had to work on it?'

'Bit of both,' Boardman said.

'If we looked like Kirk Douglas and Tony Curtis, we'd probably be different,' Tilley told her.

'But since we're more like Laurel and Hardy, we just have to play the cards we've been dealt,' Boardman added.

* * *

'Am I speaking to Chuck Woodend?' asked the American voice at the other end of the transatlantic telephone line.

What was this?

A ghost?

A spirit?

A voice from the ether?

Woodend's mouth was suddenly as dry as a desert, and a crazed drummer began to beat out a frenetic tattoo in his head. No one had called him 'Chuck' since 1944, he thought, and even then, only *one* man had ever used the name.

'Hello? Can you hear me?' the American asked.

'Woodend here,' the Chief Inspector croaked.

'I'm Eugene Kineally,' the caller announced.

The desert receded, the drummer ceased his insane attack. No ghost – just a brother.

'Good morning, Senator,' Woodend said.

'It's the middle of the night here,' Kineally told him, and then, as if to answer an unspoken question, he added, 'With all that's going on over there, I just couldn't sleep.'

I'll bet you couldn't, Woodend thought.

'If this is about the inquiry into your brother's death, then the person you should probably speak to is Special Agent Grant,' he said aloud.

'This isn't an official call at all,' Kineally said. 'In the morning, I'll be a senator again. Tonight, I'm just a brother.'

'I see,' Woodend said.

'Have they told you I was the one who insisted the FBI be brought into the case?' Kineally asked.

'Yes, they have.'

'And that the *reason* I insisted was because I didn't trust either the military police or the British police?'

'It may have been mentioned,' Woodend said cautiously.

'I'd never have made that demand if I'd known you were going to be involved with the investigation, Chuck. I want you know that I have absolute confidence in you.'

'You do?' Woodend asked, reeling from the shock. 'Why?'

'Because Robert did.'

'But how do you . . . ?'

'How do I know that? Because Robert wrote to me every day. Even when I was on active service in the Pacific, and he knew I wouldn't get any mail for months – if ever – he never

116

missed writing. I still have those letters, and sometimes, late at night, I . . . I read through a few of them, and it's almost like he's still here. He wrote about everything that happened to him – and he wrote a lot about you.'

'I'm honoured,' Woodend said humbly.

'He told me that if he ever had to put all his trust in just one man, that man would unquestionably be you,' the senator continued. 'He had great faith in you, Chuck – and so do I.'

'I don't know what to say,' Woodend admitted.

'I want to see my brother's death avenged. Even after all this time, I want to see justice done.'

'I'll do whatever I can to see that happens.'

'That's all that any man can promise. That's all I wanted to hear you say.' The senator's voice began to crack. 'It's been a privilege to talk to you, Chuck. Good luck, and may God bless you!'

The line went dead, but for at least half a minute Woodend stood as frozen as a statue.

He had felt the heavy weight of the case pressing down on him before, but the phone call seemed to have made his burden almost unbearable.

Sixteen

Bob Rutter had learned during his years in the Met that there were only two sorts of pubs which were regularly patronized by officers from Scotland Yard, and he had privately christened them 'The Slimes' and 'The Steams'.

'The Slimes' were rough. They invariably had sawdust sprinkled on the floor – so useful for soaking up the blood that would undoubtedly be spilled by closing time! – and brass spittoons within expectorating distance of each table. They drew their clientele from the furthest, darkest fringes of society – burglars and fences, prostitutes and their pimps, bank robbers and would-be bank robbers, bookies and con men. When an officer immersed himself in one of these pubs, it was because he had to – because, if he wanted to talk to his snitches and listen to the current criminal gossip, this was the only place to be.

'The Steams' were a different matter altogether. There was no uniformity of fixtures and fittings about them. They could be smart or shabby – or on the way up or down, from one state to the other. They could be located on one of the broad city streets, or hidden away down a back alley. What gave them their special character – as with 'The Slimes' – was their clientele. They were policemen's boozers – a home from home.

In these pubs, a bobby was sure to come across someone else he knew on the Force, and be able to talk in a language the other man would understand. And if, due to pressure at work, a particular bobby became over-boisterous – or even fairly destructive – the landlord of the boozer had learned to look the other way. After all, they were only letting off steam, he would tell himself, and the police were normally good business. Besides, even if he did decided to report the infraction, who the hell was he going to report it *to*?

The pub outside which Rutter was standing at that moment

– The Thames Waterman – was neither a 'Slime' nor a 'Steam'. Charlie Woodend would instantly have labelled it 'poncy' – by which he would have meant that it was the embodiment of a brewery designer's distorted idea of what traditional pubs had once looked like. It was popular with clerks from the City's merchant banks and brokerage houses, and both policemen and criminals steered well clear of it – which was why, of course, Rutter's old friend, Inspector Tom Wright, had chosen it as the venue for their meeting.

Rutter entered the pub. From the doorway, he looked around the lounge – past the fishermen's nets and the lobster pots – and saw Wright at a table under an artificially aged advertisement for Ogden's Midnight Flake. Wright saw him, too, though he gave no indication that he had. Which meant, Rutter decided as he bought himself a pint, that this was going to be even more difficult than he'd thought it might be.

Rutter took his drink over to the table, and sat down opposite his old colleague.

'Let's make this quick,' Wright said abruptly.

'"How are you, Bob?"' Rutter responded, in a tone which was partly sarcastic and but mostly wounded. '"I was really sorry to hear that your missus got killed, my old mate."'

'If you want us to meet up as old mates, then pick up the blower and just tell me that's what you'd like,' Wright said brusquely. 'When you do that, we'll go out on a bloody good piss up, and I'll let you cry on my shoulder all night, if it'll make you feel any better. But this isn't that kind of meeting at all, is it, Bob? The only reason we're here is because you want information. And not just *any* information. You want information on a bloody *Cabinet Minister*.'

'That's true enough, but as I explained to you over the phone—'

'What you did over the phone was to feed me some complete cock and bull story which I didn't believe for a minute,' Wright said harshly. 'But, to be honest with you, I prefer it that way. I don't know why you want information, and I don't *want* to know. All I *do* want is to get this meeting of ours over and done with as soon as possible.'

'You must have got some real dirt on Douglas Coutes if you're that worried,' Rutter said wonderingly.

'You couldn't be wronger,' Wright told him. 'The man's as clean as a whistle.'

'Then why all the drama?'

'*Because* he's as clean as a whistle, you bloody fool. Because, if I'm asked to justify giving information on Douglas Coutes to a member of another force, I won't be able to.'

'But surely, there's not much chance of that happening, is there?' Rutter asked.

'You never know.'

'London's a big city.'

'Yes, but when you're talking about the people in it who really *matter*, it's a very small world indeed. And ministers don't like it when mere detective inspectors start showin' interest in them. Especially ministers who hold a defence brief. Especially ministers as full of themselves – and as downright bloody ruthless – as Douglas Coutes is.'

'So what *have* you got for me?' Rutter asked.

'Did you know I was on the Burglary Squad now?' Wright asked, with some hostility. 'Is that why you rang me, rather than anybody else?'

'No, I didn't know you were in Burglary,' Rutter said truthfully. 'I rang you because we trained together, because we've covered each other's back more than once, and because I thought we were still good friends.'

'I still don't like it,' Wright grumbled.

'Like what?'

'You wanted to know if anything that's happened to Coutes recently was of interest to the police. Well, apart from the natural interest shown in him by his own protection unit, there's only one thing.'

'And that was?'

'His London flat was burgled – and I was the officer who investigated it. How's that for a coincidence?'

'That's all it is,' Rutter promised him. 'A coincidence. They do happen, you know.'

'Maybe,' Wright said grudgingly.

'When did this burglary take place?' Rutter asked.

'A month or so ago.'

'Was he staying in the flat at the time?'

'No, he was abroad. In America, I think. There was only his housekeeper there – and it scared the hell out of her.'

'Why? Did she catch them in the act?'

'Not exactly. It was half-past two in the morning, so, naturally, she was asleep.'

'If she was asleep, how can you be so precise about the time?'

'The burglars managed to circumvent two of the alarm systems, but they were unlucky – or a little bit careless – with the third. The alarm went off, and even given the state she was probably in, it was loud enough to wake the housekeeper up. But by the time she'd forced herself to get out of bed, the burglars were already well away.'

'The state she was probably in?' Rutter repeated.

'Did I say that?'

'You know you did.'

'Well, I probably shouldn't have.'

'Give me a break,' Rutter pleaded. 'It may turn out not to be relevant, but I'd still like to know.'

Wright sighed heavily. 'Her name's Lily Hanson,' he said. 'She was Coutes's mistress for a long time, but then she started to show her age. When he traded her in for a new model, he gave her two choices: she could collect together her things and get out, or she could stay on in the role of housekeeper. She stayed on, though it's only fair to say that she's not exactly over the moon about the new domestic arrangements.'

'How do you know all this?' Rutter wondered.

'How do you *think* I know? She told me herself.'

'She seems to have been remarkably frank.'

'Drink does that to some women. Makes them talk. Makes them say things they'd never say when they were sober. Lily was floating on a cloud for most of the investigation, and I must have heard her whole life story at least three times.'

'So you think that when the burglary took place, she was probably sleeping off a boozing session?'

'Exactly.'

'I'm surprised Coutes tolerates it.'

'He doesn't have to. She might drink like a fish while he's away, but when he's in London she somehow manages to keep a lid on it. But that won't last. It can't last. Sooner or later, she'll lose what little self-control she's still got left, and she'll be out on the street. Poor bloody woman!'

'What did the burglars take?' Rutter asked.

'Nothing. Not a blind bloody thing.'

'That's probably because they were disturbed, is it?'

'Probably.'

Rutter studied his old friend's face for some seconds. 'But you don't think that *was* the reason, do you?' he said, finally.

'No, I don't,' Wright admitted.

'Why not?'

'It took the burglars a lot of effort to get into the flat. It's true that they eventually tripped the third alarm, but before they could even get to that point, they'd already by-passed the other two – and sprung some of the best security locks the Burglary Squad's ever come across.'

'So they were professionals?'

'They were better than that.'

'Better than *professionals*?'

Wright sighed. 'Look, you know the way we work, Bob,' he said. 'When any job's pulled, one of the first questions that we always ask is who could have pulled it.'

'True,' Rutter agreed.

'So after that break-in, we put our heads together and tried to come up with a few names. And we couldn't! Not a single bloody one! As far as the old hands in the Burglary Squad are concerned, there isn't any villain currently operating in London who could have done that job.'

'So what you're saying is that if they were *that* good – and went to that *much* effort – it's inconceivable that they would have been willing to leave the flat empty-handed?'

'I'm saying it *should be* inconceivable, but it seems to have happened.'

'Is this Hanson woman a solitary drinker, or does she like to have people around her when she's getting smashed out of her head?' Rutter asked.

'Definitely the latter,' Wright replied. 'When Coutes is away, she's in the Duke of Clarence every night until closing time.' He frowned. 'What made you ask that?'

'No real reason at all,' Rutter said casually. 'I was just curious.'

Seventeen

'You were a US Military Policeman, attached to the unit serving in this camp in 1944?' Special Agent Grant asked the bald man sitting opposite them in the interrogation chair.

'Yes, sir!' the man said loudly.

Woodend winced.

Why was it that some ex-soldiers – especially ones who'd held posts of some minor responsibility – never quite seemed able to lose the habit of shouting their answers? he wondered. Surely they should have been able to put the war behind them by now.

Put the war behind them! echoed the malevolent goblin which sometimes seemed to inhabit a dark corner of his brain. How far have you managed to put your war behind you, Charlie?

Not far enough, Woodend readily accepted. Nowhere near far enough. And since that first phone call from Douglas Coutes, it had become closer than it had been for years.

'When did you first realize that Captain Kineally was missing?' Grant asked the MP.

'Not until two days after he went AWOL.'

'Two days? Why did it take so long? Surely someone in authority must have noticed he wasn't going about his normal duties.'

'The Captain didn't have specific duties at Haverton Camp, sir. He'd been given what they called a "roving brief", and he reported directly to a colonel in regional headquarters. So since nobody here knew what he was supposed to be doing, nobody here noticed when he wasn't doing it.'

'I see,' Special Agent Grant said, nodding his head seriously, as if all was clear now.

'Well, I don't,' Woodend admitted. 'Given what you've just told us, why was it only *two* days before you noticed he was missing? Why not five days? Or a week?'

'It wasn't Captain Kineally we missed at first, sir,' the ex-MP said. 'It was the jeep.'

'Come again?'

'The jeep should gone to the motor pool for routine maintenance, and when it didn't, the master sergeant in charge of the pool informed us of the fact.'

'So what happened next?'

'The jeep had been made available for the captain's personal use, but it wasn't signed out to him.'

'Then who was it signed out to?'

'His driver, Private Birnbaum, was directly responsible for it. When we questioned Birnbaum, he admitted he hadn't seen the vehicle for two days. We put him on a charge for negligence, and launched a search for the jeep.'

'But you didn't find it until several days after that, did you?' Special Agent Grant asked.

'No, sir, we did not.'

'And when you did find it, it was hidden in a wood near the local railway station?'

'That is correct.'

If Kineally had actually used it to go AWOL, hiding it would have made sense, Woodend thought. But Kineally *hadn't* used it – because he was already dead by then.

'It wasn't just *hidden*, was it?' Grant asked.

'No, sir, it had been camouflaged. It was practically invisible from the air, and even personnel on the ground would have missed it unless they were very close to it.'

It was the murderer who had driven the jeep, as part of his plan to convince the military authorities that Kineally had deserted, Woodend reminded himself. So why would he hide it *so* well? Why hadn't he left it out in the open, so that the authorities would be set on the false trail as soon as possible?

'Were you able to establish whether or not Captain Kineally had, in fact, boarded a train at the railway station?' Special Agent Grant asked.

'No, sir, we were not. There was a great deal of rail traffic around that time, and the situation was very confused.'

'Did you manage to find any witnesses who had seen Captain Kineally – or anyone else – drive the jeep to the woods?'

'No, sir, we didn't.'

'You didn't hear a rumour that it wasn't Kineally who'd left the jeep there, but a British officer?'

'Absolutely not, sir.'

This was no way to conduct an investigation, Woodend thought.

You didn't solve crimes by sitting behind a desk, questioning witness after witness in the hope that the right answers would just magically fall into your lap. You didn't give witnesses broad hints which just might lead them to confirm your speculations.

What you *did* do was get up off your arse and go out looking for people who didn't want to be witnesses at all. Or for witnesses who didn't even *know* they were witnesses – because they had no idea of how significant the information they were holding might be.

'Do you have any questions for this man, Chief Inspector Woodend?' Grant asked.

'No,' Woodend replied wearily.

'In that case, you can go,' Grant told the ex-MP.

'Sir!' the bald man said, standing up, stamping his foot in the approved manner, and marching out of the trailer.

Grant consulted his notes. 'Our next witness is one of the guys who worked in the cookhouse,' he said.

'An' what particular shaft of the light do you think he'll be able to throw on the investigation?' Woodend wondered.

'We won't know that until we've talked to him, will we?' Grant replied.

The man wasn't a policeman, Woodend thought in disgust – he was a bureaucrat.

Grant saw no need to tease out solutions to crimes. He probably believed that as long as you filled in the correct forms – preferably in triplicate – the solution would be delivered by special courier the following morning.

'What say we take a short break?' Grant suggested, noticing Woodend's lethargic despondency.

'What kind of short break?'

'How about we put on sweats, and do a couple of laps of the camp? That'll get the heart pumping, the lungs opening up, and blood flowing again!'

'You can do that, if you like,' Woodend told him, 'but if I'm goin' to exercise my lungs, I'd rather do it by pullin' on a reflective cigarette.'

Grant clicked his tongue reprovingly. 'You should get some *proper* exercise, you know,' he said. 'It's very well known that a healthy body is the key to a healthy mind.'

'Maybe it is,' Woodend said. 'But I've found that my brain generally works better when it's not bein' bounced up and down.'

'The brain doesn't get *bounced up and down* when you're running,' Grant said, clearly horrified by Woodend's obvious ignorance of anatomy. 'It's held in place by—'

'Paper clips?' Woodend interrupted.

'No, by—'

'Enjoy your run, lad,' the Chief Inspector said. 'An' when you get back, we'll see if this army cook can solve our mystery for us.'

Alone in the interrogation trailer – free at last from Grant's tidy, mundane thinking – Woodend watched the smoke from his cigarette drift towards the roof, and slowly let his mind drift back in time.

He was standing on the railway station platform, watching the big station clock jerkily – and noisily – mark off the passing of another minute.

He was worried about the coming invasion. Not for himself – if he caught a fatal bullet, it would all be over in a second – but for Joan.

He hoped that if he was killed, she would get over it quickly, find herself another young chap, and settle down to a good marriage and a happy life. But there was also a part of him – a small, unworthy part, he was almost sure – which hoped that she wouldn't get over it, that though he would be gone physically, he might live on because she still mourned the loss of him.

His thoughts escaped to the safer subject of Haverton Camp, and he realized, with some surprise, how much he would miss it. Or at least, how much he would miss some of the people he had met there. Robert Kineally, for one. He had grown attached to the American – to his particular brand of idealism which was no doubt naïve and impractical, but was also full of hope and inspiration.

The world could use a good few more people like Robert Kineally, he told himself, and it was a pity that Kineally's briefing session in London had resulted in them being unable to say goodbye properly.

Woodend looked around at the other people waiting for a train which still might be on time, but – if it was anything like many wartime trains – would probably be several hours late.

A group of sailors had gathered near the waiting room, and were standing with their legs wide apart, as if expecting the concrete beneath their feet to suddenly lurch under the assault of an unexpected wave.

Half a dozen Royal Engineers, men who would play an important – and dangerous – part in the coming invasion, were nervously swapping jokes and cigarettes.

And it was not only the military who were on the move that night.

Two men with shabby briefcases – obviously minor civil servants – were conferring gravely, probably over the kinds of matters that minor civil servants always conferred gravely over.

A woman with two small children looked despondently down the track, no doubt wondering how late the train would have to be before the kids grew tired and peevish.

A trio of land girls sat on their suitcases, passing round a bottle which might have contained cheap wine, but could just as easily have been cold tea.

They were all the sorts of characters who his literary hero, the great Charles Dickens, could have made much of, Woodend thought. Indeed, he if he were a writer himself . . .

He would never be a writer, he admitted – he simply did not have the temperament for it. But people did undoubtedly fascinate him, and after the war was over – if he survived it – he would have to find some other kind of occupation which would justify his study of them.

He heard a sudden suppressed sob, and turning, saw the woman huddled down on her haunches, in one of the darker corners of the station.

He walked over to her.

'Is there a problem, Miss?' he asked awkwardly. 'I don't mean to bother you, but if there's anythin' I can do to help, then you've only to ask.'

The woman looked up. 'Charlie?' she said.

He recognized the voice as Mary's. 'Whatever's happened to you, lass?' he asked.

'I . . . I wish I was dead,' she told him.

'There's no point in talkin' like that,' Woodend said, holding out his hand to her. 'Get up, an' we'll go an' see if we can scrounge a cup of tea from the Women's Voluntary Service.'

The two women manning the WVS trolley were only too pleased to provide them with cups of the dark tepid liquid which had passed for tea since rationing had been introduced.

'Now what's this all about?' Woodend asked Mary Parkinson, once they had taken their cups into a quiet corner. 'What are you doin' on this station at this time of night anyway?'

'I was waiting for a train.'

'To where?'

'To wherever it was going. But I've changed my mind about that now. There's absolutely no point in running away when the thing you're running from is yourself.'

'What have you done?' Woodend asked, with growing alarm.

'What have I done? I've let myself down! And even worse – I've let Robert down!'

'You want to tell me about it?'

'I'm too ashamed to.'

'You'll have to tell somebody eventually,' Woodend coaxed, 'an' since I'll be gone from here in an hour or so, you might as well tell me.'

Mary nodded, seeing the sense of the argument. 'Robert has been away in London for over a week,' she began.

'I know that.'

'A couple of days after he left, Dougie Coutes came to see me. He said he had something very important to talk to me about, and why didn't we go out for a drink? So we went to the Dun Cow.'

'Go on,' Woodend said.

Mary swallowed a sob. 'Dougie said he'd known lots of Americans like Robert. Dozens of them! He said they come over to England for the first time, fall in love with the country, and convince themselves they've fallen in love with an English girl, as well.'

The bastard! Woodend thought.

'You didn't believe a word of what he said, though, did you?' he asked.

'Not at first, no. Or, at least, not entirely. I told Dougie that my Robert wasn't like that. He never have said he loved me if there'd been any doubt in his mind about it.'

'Quite right, too.'

'But you see, I'd been worried about Robert – about us – for quite some time before I even spoke to Dougie.'

'Why, for God's sake?'

'I couldn't really understand what he ever saw in me. His family's very rich, you know, and my dad's nothing but a simple Devon farmer. Robert is such a handsome man—'

'Only when viewed through the eyes of love,' Woodend interrupted.

'—and I'm such a Plain Jane,' Mary continued, ignoring his comment. 'Dougie suddenly started to look very uncomfortable. He said he'd been trying to break things to me as gently as he could, but since I wouldn't take the hint, he had no choice but to tell me the plain unvarnished truth.'

'What plain unvarnished truth?'

'That Robert was engaged to a beautiful young lady back in America. And . . . and that she'd come over to London to see him. I didn't want to believe him, but it . . . it all made sense.'

Aye, it would, Woodend thought. Coutes could be a convincing talker when he wanted to be.

'Dougie drove me home,' Mary continued. 'My parents have to get up early in the morning, so they'd already gone to bed. We – Dougie and me – went into the front parlour. And that's . . . that's when it happened.'

'When what happened?' Woodend asked, though he already knew the answer.

'The . . . the physical thing.'

'He raped you!'

Mary shook her head. 'No. He made the first move, but I didn't put up any resistance.'

'But if he'd got you drunk—'

'I wasn't drunk, Charlie. I'd been drinking in the Dun Cow, but I wasn't drunk.'

'Then how . . . ?'

'It's hard to explain. I think I'd probably decided that there

129

was no point in saving my virginity if there was no one I wanted to save it for. If I couldn't have Robert, I might as well have anybody. It sounds mad, doesn't it? But it didn't at the time.'

Coutes hadn't been driven by love to do what he did, Woodend thought.

He'd hadn't even been driven by lust!

Mary had been nothing but a challenge from the very beginning – and how much more of a challenge she'd become once she had fallen for Kineally.

'Robert phoned the very next morning,' Mary sobbed, 'and the moment I heard his voice, I knew that Dougie had been lying to me.'

'Did you tell him what had happened?'

'No.'

'You do know you'll have to tell him when he gets back to Haverton, don't you?'

'I can't! I just can't.'

'You must.'

'Do you think he'll forgive me if I do?'

Would he? Woodend asked himself. It was true that Coutes had tricked her into bed, but shouldn't Mary have had enough faith in Robert for the trick not to work?

'I don't know if he'll forgive you,' Woodend admitted. 'I think he will. But even if he doesn't, you still have to tell him. He has a right to know.'

'I suppose he does,' Mary said gloomily. 'I know he does.'

From somewhere in the dark night, a steam whistle shrieked like a banshee. The train, against the odds, was very nearly on time.

The sailors and soldiers gathered up their kitbags. The land girls stood up – shakily, so it must have been wine they were drinking after all. The civil servants ceased to debate. And the woman with the children placed a protective hand on each of the kid's shoulders, just in case they should feel the urge to rush towards the metal monster which was about to arrive.

'Your train's here,' Mary Parkinson said, dully.

'Aye, it is,' Woodend agreed.

The train steamed into the station, its wheels screaming as the brakes were applied, its boiler hissing furiously at this interruption of its purpose.

'You'd better get on board then,' Mary said, when the loco-motive had finally juddered to a halt.

'Yes, I suppose I better had.'

'After all,' Mary said, laughing unconvincingly, 'you don't want to have to face a court martial, do you, Charlie?'

'No, I certainly don't want that,' Woodend agreed, his laugh as hollow as Mary's had been.

He began to walk towards the locomotive, then stopped and turned around again.

'I'm not so sure I was right,' he said.

'What?'

'Every man who's goin' into battle needs to know he's leaving behind a woman who loves him,' Woodend said. 'So, for God's sake, whatever you do, don't tell Robert what happened.'

'And have him go into battle believing a lie?'

'A lie? What lie? You do love him, don't you?'

'With all my heart. But—'

'Look, you made one mistake – an' it wasn't even really your mistake,' Woodend argued passionately. 'You'd never have done what you did if that bastard Coutes hadn't lied to you.'

'It was still my decision,' Mary said flatly. 'It was still my lack of faith that caused it all.'

'If Robert's got to die, at least let him die knowin' that he's loved,' Woodend said. 'An' if he manages to come back in one piece, marry him!'

'If he asks me to.'

'He'll ask you to. Marry him, an' make him happy for the rest of his life. That'll more than pay him back for one little slip.'

'You make it sound so simple,' Mary said.

'It is – if you just decide that's the way you want it to be.'

The rest of the passengers had already climbed on the train, and the guard was walking along the platform, slamming the doors.

'You'd better go,' the girl told him.

'Remember what I said,' Woodend pleaded. 'Not what I said earlier – what I said just now. Promise me you'll not tell him.'

'The train, Charlie. Get on the train,' Mary said, and he could tell she was crying again.

131

'I'm not goin' before you promise me—' Woodend began.

'We all have to do our duty,' Mary interrupted him. 'And yours is to get on that train.'

She was right. He climbed on to the train, closed the door behind him, and pulled down the window. He'd half-expected that once he'd turned his back on her, she'd have gone, but she was still there, watching him.

'Think about it,' he urged. 'Your future is in your own hands. Mary – an' there's not many of us can say that at the moment.'

She nodded, sadly. 'Goodbye, Charlie,' she said.

'Not goodbye,' Woodend countered, trying his best to sound light-hearted. 'It's more a case of "so long", isn't it?'

'No, it's goodbye,' Mary said firmly. 'I don't think we will ever meet again.'

The guard blew his whistle, and the train slowly began to chug out of the station. The girl did not move, and Woodend only lost sight of her when the train track curved away.

Instructors at police colleges had this annoying teaching trick of stopping training films half-way through, Woodend remembered.

'How many men were there in that scene by the docks?' they would ask their students. 'What colour was the car? Was the man in the bowler hat wearing an overcoat or a macintosh?'

The students would argue among themselves, but eventually agree that there had been four men, the car had been black, and the man in the bowler hat had been wearing an overcoat.

'Are you absolutely – one hundred percent – sure about that?' their instructors would demand.

And the students would say that they were.

The instructors would wind back the film and show that scene again – only to reveal that there were *five* men, the car was *brown*, and the man in the bowler hat wasn't wearing a coat at all.

'How do you account for the discrepancies?' the instructors would ask, in a slightly hectoring tone.

And the students would bow their heads and admit in a mumble that they didn't know.

'You didn't see what actually happened at all, did you?' the instructors would ask.

No, the students would agree, they hadn't.

'What you saw was what you *expected* to happen! Or what you *wanted* to happen! Or what you felt *should have* happened! That's what civilians do all the time. But you're not supposed to be civilians, are you? You're *policemen*. You're supposed to be trained *observers*!'

Sitting alone in the interrogation trailer, lighting up yet another Capstan Full Strength, Woodend softly repeated those instructors' words to himself.

'You're policemen. You're supposed to be trained observers.'

He took a drag on his cigarette, and began to re-wind his own mental film – so that now he was walking backwards along the platform, now turning to Mary, now swallowing the words he had spoken.

Stop!

Rerun!

'You do know you'll have to tell him when he gets back to Haverton, don't you?'

'I can't! I just can't.'

'You must.'

'Do you think he'll forgive me if I do?'

'I don't know if he'll forgive you. I think he will. But even if he doesn't, you still have to tell him. He has a right to know.'

No mistake about it then! He was the one who had delivered the words. They were his – and his alone.

So why had they come as such a surprise to him? How could he have remembered so much about that encounter on the railway station, yet have completely forgotten this crucial part of the conversation?

He hadn't forgotten it, of course. If he had, he could never have recalled now with such accuracy.

What he had actually done, he told himself, was to allow his conscience to keep this part of the exchange between himself and Mary locked away in a shameful – and shaming – room at the back of his mind.

The interrogation trailer door swung open, and Special Agent

133

Grant – positively glowing with health and vigour after his run around the camp – stepped inside.

'OK then, let's get back to the job in hand,' he said enthusiastically. 'Are you ready to begin the next interview, Chief Inspector?' he asked.

'No,' Woodend said.

'No?' Grant asked quizzically.

'I have to make a phone call,' Woodend told him.

'Well go right ahead. There's a phone just by your elbow.'

'It's not the kind of phone call I make with you here,' Woodend told him. 'It's the kind I have to make in private.'

Eighteen

The moment he'd dialled his home telephone number, Woodend felt himself starting to sweat.

This reaction was not something new to him. He'd been suffering from it ever since the holiday in Spain – ever since the doctors had informed him that Joan had a weak heart.

There was nothing to be gained by worrying, he told himself. Living with a heart condition was a bit like fighting a war. In battle, you'd catch a bullet – or you wouldn't. A weak heart would fail – or it would carry on working. You took all the precautions you possibly could, but you knew that, ultimately, the matter was out of your hands. Which meant that fretting over what might happen in the future was worse than pointless – because the fretting only served to sour whatever precious time you actually had left together.

He knew all that. He had explained it to himself a thousand times. Yet still, as he listened to the ringing tone on the other end of the line – as he unconsciously counted off the seconds – he couldn't help picturing Joan lying on the floor of their little cottage, already dead.

And the sweating got worse.

The ringing tone stopped, and a voice said, 'Joan Woodend here. Who am I speaking to, please?'

'It's me,' he said. 'How are you, love?'

'I'm fine,' Joan told. 'Why are you calling? You're not checkin' up on me, are you, Charlie?'

'No, of course I'm not, love,' Woodend protested. 'The doctors told me that with a little care you'd be perfectly all right, an' I always believe what the doctors' tell me.'

'Except when it comes to your own boozin' an' smokin',' his wife said scornfully. 'So why *are* you ringin' me in the middle of a case? You *never* ring me in the middle of a case.'

'I . . . er . . . wanted to consult you about somethin' to do with the investigation,' Woodend said awkwardly.

Joan laughed. 'Now there's a novelty. What does this case involve? Bakin' scones? Or donkey-stonin' the doorstep?'

'It's about the War,' Woodend said. 'Or rather, how people felt durin' the War.'

'Go on,' Joan said.

'Did you ever find yourself attracted to anybody else while I was away fightin'?'

Another woman might have be thrown by such a question, and lapsed into silence. Joan Woodend wasn't.

'I'd be lyin' if I said I hadn't been *attracted* to anybody else,' she replied immediately. 'I was very lonely without you, an' there some good-lookin' lads around. But, I can assure you, Charlie Woodend, it never went any further than just fancyin' them.'

'I know that. But say it *had* gone further.'

'Where's this leadin', Charlie?' Joan asked suspiciously.

'I've been tryin' to get inside somebody's head, an' I've not been havin' much luck.'

'A woman's?'

'Aye.'

'You'd better go on, then.'

'Say you had had a bit of a fling with another feller, an' bitterly regretted it afterwards. Would you have told me about it?'

'That's not an easy question to answer, Charlie, since no such thing ever did happen.'

'I understand that. But just try to put yourself in the place of a woman who it *did* happen to.'

This time there *was* a pause – a long one.

'Not until after the War,' Joan said finally. 'I wouldn't have told you until after the War.'

'Why not?'

'There'd have been no point, would there?'

'Wouldn't there?'

'None at all. I might have felt better in myself for havin' got the whole thing off my chest, but it certainly wouldn't have done you much good to be told, now would it?'

'You don't think that couples should be honest with each other at all times?'

'No! I think couples should be honest with each other *whenever possible*. But there are occasions when it's best to keep your trap firmly shut – and that would have been one of them.'

It was not the answer he would have liked to hear, but he recognized that it was probably the right one.

'Thanks, love, you've been a great help,' he said. 'I'll have to get back to work now.'

'An' so will I, Charlie. Your phone call's put me right behind with all my chores.'

'Don't go doin' too much, now,' Woodend warned, worriedly.

Joan laughed. 'The house doesn't clean itself, you know.'

'I *do* know that, but—'

'I said, it doesn't clean itself,' Joan repeated.

'Of course it doesn't,' Woodend agreed, nodding resignedly. 'I don't know exactly how much longer this case will take, love, but—'

'You never do know how long a case will take. But whenever it's over, I'll be here.'

But would she? Woodend asked himself, as he put down the phone.

Would she?

For a full five minutes after the phone call, Woodend sat immobile. His eyes – almost unseeing – were fixed on the wall of the trailer. His mind had embarked on a guilty journey into its own dark corners and hidden recesses.

He might have stayed like that for much longer, had not his body's craving for nicotine made it necessary for his arm to move, and his eyes to focus. He lit up a Capstan Full Strength, and was not surprised to note that his shaking hand made the match flame dance.

Ever since he'd arrived back at Haverton Camp, he now realized, there had been a goblin of fear squatting in his brain. And this goblin had been whispering incessantly that it was *his* advice – however hastily retracted – which had set off the chain of events which had led to Robert Kineally's death.

By ignoring it – by attempting to push it to one side – he had permitted the goblin to become stronger, so that now its whispers had become a scream.

It was like a disease which had been allowed to grow and

mutate, he thought, and if it was ever to be vanquished, it was first necessary to hold the facts of the situation under the harsh – and unwavering – clinical light.

Was he really to blame for what had happened? he asked himself.

Even though he may have set the ball rolling, could he be held accountable for the final result?

Would it be fair to blame a catalyst, which – after all – only speeds the reaction between two compounds, for the reaction itself?

The goblin screamed no longer. Now it was laughing at him.

He had given Mary *two* pieces of advice, Woodend argued, and it had been her choice, as an adult, to decide which of the two to follow.

And she might well have chosen the second! She might well *never* have told Kineally what had happened between her and Coutes. In which case, he told his goblin, none of what had occurred on the railway station had any relevance to Kineally's murder at all!

True, the goblin agreed. If she didn't tell him, you're off the hook, Charlie. But you don't know whether she told him or not, do you? Because you never bothered to find out!

That was totally beyond dispute. So many of the friends a man made in wartime were little more than ships which passed in the night, and once he had sailed away himself, it was as if Robert Kineally – and Mary Parkinson – had never even existed.

There were plenty of excuses for his behaviour, of course, if he cared to look for them.

There'd been a war going on. A few weeks later he'd been fighting for his own life – and for the survival of the civilization he'd grown up in.

And after that there'd been the invasion of Germany, where he'd seen – with his own disbelieving eyes – the Nazi extermination camps.

The bodies of the dead, and the faces of the dying, were seared into his memory for ever. The images of the inhumanity that man could inflict on man would never leave him.

'*It doesn't take much to see that the problems of three little people don't amount to a hill of beans in this crazy world,*' Rick had said, at the end of *Casablanca*.

And Rick had been right! Compared to tragedy on that scale, the dramas of domestic love affairs shrank to insignificance. Compared to what the Nazis had done in their concentration camps, Coutes's callous seduction of Mary Parkinson had been no more than a harmless dalliance.

Yes, there were lots of excuses he could gather up to imprison his goblin behind, but the stockade he built with them would never be quite high enough – never quite thick enough.

He lit a fresh cigarette from the stub of his old one. It was a long time since he had felt as bad as this.

He would do what he should have done at the very start of the investigation, but had been afraid to, he told himself.

He would go and see Mary Parkinson.

Nineteen

Though Woodend was far from being a slow driver, he did not normally share his sergeant's love for speed – which made it all the more surprising, Monika Paniatowski thought, that he had chosen to treat the road between the camp and the village as if it were a Grand Prix race track.

'Is there some special reason we're in a hurry, sir?' she asked, as he took a sharp bend on two wheels.

'Aye,' Woodend replied, forcing the gears of the Wolseley through a racing change they'd never been designed to endure. 'I'm tryin' to catch up.'

'On who?'

'Not on who! On what! I'm tryin' to catch up twenty-one years!'

'I'm not sure I quite—'

'Shut up, Monika! This requires concentration.'

Woodend did slow down a little as they passed through Haverton, but once they were clear of the centre – once the Dun Cow was in sight – he jammed his foot down on the accelerator again.

'Is it some new lead?' Paniatowski asked.

'No,' Woodend snapped. 'It's an old lead. It's been buried for a long time – I just didn't have the balls to dig it up.'

He drove into the Dun Cow car park and slammed on the brakes. As he climbed out of the Wolseley, the old car was still shuddering from the battering it had been given.

Woodend marched purposefully towards the main entrance of the pub. Paniatowski followed a few seconds later.

Something had happened to her boss, the sergeant thought, as she broke into a trot in order to catch up with him. Something bad!

She had no idea what that something might be. But she *did*

know this was not the same man she had been working closely with for over three years.

It was still early in the evening, and they were the first customers. The barmaid, a pleasant-looking girl of eighteen or nineteen, gave them a welcoming smile.

'Good evening, sir and madam!' she said cheerily.

'Is the landlord anywhere around?' Woodend asked brusquely.

His tone caused the barmaid's smile to fade away, and a look of slight concern to replace it.

'No, I'm awfully sorry, but Mr Halford *isn't* here at the moment, sir,' she said.

'Then where is he?'

'He told me he had a bit of business to do over in Exeter. But he'll definitely be back later.'

'How *much* later?' Woodend asked, and the urgency in his voice only increased Monika Paniatowski's foreboding.

'Don't really know *how* long he'll be,' the barmaid admitted. 'I suppose it could be as little as half an hour. Then again, it might be much longer. Do you want to see him about something important?'

'Important enough,'

'Then would you like to wait? Or would you prefer to leave him a message?'

'I'm not sure yet,' Woodend said. 'Do you know a woman called Mary Parkinson?'

The barmaid pursed her brow. 'Mary Parkinson?' she repeated. 'No, I don't think so. I know a Mary *Parker*, but that's not—'

'In that case, we'll wait for Reg to get back from Exeter,' Woodend interrupted her.

'Would you like to order any drinks?' the barmaid said tentatively, as if half-expecting that Woodend would tell her to mind her own business.

'Aye, we would,' the Chief Inspector replied. 'We'll have a vodka with ice – an' a whisky on its own.'

'Are you sure about that, sir?' Paniatowski asked, her concern deepening by the minute.

'Am I *what*?' Woodend demanded.

'Are you sure you want a whisky,' Paniatowski said, holding her ground. 'You normally stick to pints at this time of day.'

'Tell me, Sergeant, has there been a new law passed which says that you're the only member of the team who's allowed to drink spirits?' Woodend said sarcastically.

'No, but—'

'Well, that is nice to know,' Woodend told her. He turned back to the barmaid. 'Make that whisky a double, will you?'

He paid for the drinks, and they took them over to a table which was out of earshot of the barmaid. The moment they had sat down, Woodend knocked back at least half his whisky.

'What's bothering you, sir?' Paniatowski said, in a voice which was almost pleading.

'Nothin's botherin' me,' Woodend said. 'Why should anythin' be *botherin'* me?'

'I don't know, but—'

'Then we'll let the matter drop, shall we?' Woodend gulped down the rest of the whisky, and signalled to the barmaid that he'd like another one. 'So tell me, Sergeant, what have *you* been doin' all while I've been cooped up in a tin box all day with Young Mr America?'

'This morning, I talked to two of the surveyors who found the body,' Paniatowski told him. 'I rang the company's main office in London as well, to see if I could possibly talk to the third one. But the person who I spoke to seemed very vague – *deliberately* vague, I think – about exactly where the third surveyor is at the moment.'

'Hmm,' Woodend said, abstractly.

The barmaid arrived with Woodend's second drink. He gave her a ten shilling note, and told her to keep the change.

'Then, this afternoon, I started ploughing my way through one of the mountains of documents that Special Agent Grant has had sent from the States,' Paniatowski continued, not sure that Woodend was hearing a single word she'd said. 'It's a very impressive collection, on the face of things, But when you actually get down to the details, there doesn't seem to be a great deal there that will be of much use to this case.'

'You may be right,' Woodend said.

'Right? About what?'

'Right that, at this stage of the investigation, we certainly can't afford to rule anythin' out.'

'I don't think that's *exactly* what I was saying,' Paniatowski told him.

But she was wasting her breath, because the landlord had chosen that moment, to enter the bar – and now Woodend no longer had interest in anything but him.

'Could you spare me a couple of minutes of your time, Reg?' the Chief Inspector asked.

'Be glad to, Charlie,' the landlord replied. He walked over to the table and planted his ample backside on the chair next to Paniatowski's. 'Now what I can do for you?' he asked with a smile. 'I'll bet I know. You've heard about Old Joshua's famous rough cider, haven't you? It's a fine drink, and I can get you a barrel if you want one. But since no duty's been paid on it, it is just a little *bit* illegal, so I'll have to insist on payment in cash.'

'I need to know about Mary Parkinson,' Woodend said.

The landlord's joviality melted away, and he began to look distinctly troubled. '*What* about her?' he asked warily.

'Does she still live in this village? Or has she moved away?'

'Charlie, she's—'

'And if she *has* moved away, do you happen to have an address I can contact her at?'

The landlord shook his head, slowly and mournfully, from side to side. 'You don't know, do you?' he asked.

'Know what?'

'Mary's dead!'

'Dead?' Woodend repeated. 'She can't be.'

'She is.'

'But if she was nineteen when I knew her, that would only make her – what? – only forty or forty-one now.'

'Something like that,' the landlord agreed.

'So when *did* she die?'

'In May 1944.'

'Good God! An' what did she die *of?*'

'They said it was pneumonia. Well, they would, wouldn't they? But if it was that, it caught her awful quick, because one minute she was walking around as healthy-looking as you please, and the next minute she was gone.'

'What do *you* think killed her?' Woodend asked, though he was dreading the answer.

'Are you sure you really want to know?'

'Yes, I do. It's very *important* that I know.'

'The day after she died, her dad lit a big fire in the farm-yard,' the landlord said darkly. 'And once it was going properly, he brought out her mattress and all her bedding – and he burned them. Now why do you think he would have done that, Charlie?'

'Because they were soaked in blood?' Woodend guessed.

'We'll probably never know for sure,' the landlord confirmed, 'but that certainly seems to be the general opinion round here. Whatever the doctor put on her death certificate, we don't think she died from natural causes. We think she slit her own wrists.'

The woman perched precariously on the tall stool in the saloon bar of the Duke of Clarence was probably in her middle to late thirties. She had a firm bosom, shapely legs – tantalizingly revealed by the split in her skirt – and a mane of long blonde hair. From a distance, she looked stunning.

Closer to, her imperfections were immediately apparent. The hair was dyed – badly, and some time ago. Both the skirt and top were sloppily pressed, and none too clean. And as for the shapely legs, they were disfigured by a good number of broken veins.

But it was her face which showed most clearly how Lily Hanson's lifestyle had ravaged her, Bob Rutter thought. It must once have been very pretty, but now it was a wreck, and even the layers of hastily applied make-up could not disguise the fact that this woman drank far too much.

He had been following her ever since she left the luxury apartment block in which she had once reigned as Coutes's mistress – and now served only as his humble housekeeper. He had thought of approaching the moment she had entered the pub, but had then decided to wait until she had two or three drinks inside her. That had been less than half an hour earlier, and since she was already on her third gin and tonic, he judged the time ripe.

Rutter sat on the stool next to hers, and ordered a whisky and soda. Lily Hanson seemed to be totally unaware of his presence until he contrived to knock her drink over.

The gin and tonic spilled over the bar, soaking the woman's

cigarettes. She shrank back to avoid the spillage, and almost fell off her stool.

'You want to look what you're doing, you clumsy oaf,' she said, once she'd re-established her balance.

The voice had a refined quality which didn't quite mask the coarser speech patterns which lay beneath it, Rutter thought.

Like the woman herself, it had made a long ascent – and was now on the decline again.

'I really am most awfully sorry,' Rutter said.

'So you should be,' Lily Hanson retorted, though not quite so aggressively now that she'd got a good look at him.

'Let me clean up this mess I've made, and then buy you another drink,' Rutter suggested.

He picked up a napkin, and wiped down the bar. He reached for a second napkin, and dabbed her naked thigh with it. She did not object to this almost intimate contact, though she must have been as aware as he was that none of the gin and tonic had spilled on to her leg. And Rutter knew that the first – and probably most difficult – obstacle had been overcome.

They chatted for over an hour, during which time she gave him a potted autobiography which was only loosely based on the truth, and he returned the favour by telling her one which was a complete bloody lie.

She worked as the chief advisor to 'a very important politician', she told Rutter.

'Of course, I can't reveal his name, for reasons of security,' she added, in a confidential whisper.

Of course she couldn't, Rutter accepted.

Her work was very high pressured, she continued, and sometimes the strain got so much that it was necessary to leave it all behind her, and go out for a couple of drinks. But that was only normal, wasn't it?

Absolutely, Rutter agreed. He found the same in his work with the international bank.

Still, as hard as it was, the job did have its compensations, she was willing to admit.

Like what? Rutter wondered.

Well, for example, it did mean that she was able to afford an extremely nice flat, quite close to this very pub.

Interesting she should say that, Rutter replied. He had been thinking of moving into the area himself.

Oh yes?

But he was still not quite sure in his own mind whether or not it would suit him.

Well, why didn't he come up and see *her* flat, just to see how he liked it? Lily Hanson suggested.

That *did* seem like a good idea, if it wouldn't be too much of an imposition, Rutter agreed.

No imposition at all, Lily assured him.

Ignoring the barman's knowing leer, Rutter ordered another round of drinks. When they had finished them, he helped Lily Hanson on with her coat and escorted her to the door.

Twenty

Woodend had parked the Wolseley in the driveway to the Parkinson's Farm, and was just reaching for the door handle when he felt Paniatowski's restraining hand on his arm.

'Best you stay here, sir,' the sergeant said softly.

'What?'

'I think it would be better, all round, if you left this particular interview to me.'

'Oh, so *you're* runnin' the show now, are you, Sergeant Paniatowski?' Woodend demanded.

'Not at all,' Paniatowski countered. 'You're the boss. I've never argued with that.'

'Well, then?'

'But of the two of us, I'm more equipped to deal with the grieving. We both know that's true.'

'The grievin'!' Woodend repeated disdainfully. 'Why should they still be grievin', for God's sake? It's been over *twenty years* since their daughter died, you know.'

'Do you think *you'd* have got over your own daughter's death in only twenty years?' Paniatowski asked.

Woodend's head jerked back, as if she'd just slapped him.

For perhaps half a minute, he remained silent, then he said, 'You're right about the grievin', Monika. If Annie died, I don't think I'd ever get over it.' He paused again. 'But you're wrong about the other thing. It's because I'm a parent – and you're not – that *I'd* be the best person to talk to the Parkinsons.'

'No, you wouldn't,' Paniatowski contradicted him. 'You're too involved to do a good job.'

'Am I now?' Woodend asked, with a hint of his belligerency rising to the surface again. 'An' would you mind tellin' me just exactly *how* an' *why* I'm too involved?'

'I don't know the answer to that,' Paniatowski admitted.

'Well, then?'

'But I do know it's true. I've never been so sure of anything in my entire life.'

Another silence followed, and when Woodend spoke again there was a catch in his throat. 'I really need a result on this one, Monika,' he said. 'I'm *desperate* for a result.'

'I can see that for myself,' Paniatowski confirmed. 'And that's why I think you should stay in the car.'

Paniatowski sat in the Parkinsons' farm kitchen, facing Mary's parents. She knew, given the time which had elapsed, that the couple had to be quite old by now, but they looked positively *ancient* – as though, despite still drawing breath, they had both been dead a long, long time.

'You wanted us to talk about our Mary,' Mr Parkinson said.

'That's right.'

'She was the apple of both our eyes, you know. She was a lovely, lovely girl.'

'That's what I've heard. That's what everybody else I've talked to says about her,' Paniatowski agreed.

'It was a terrible tragedy that she should lose her life so young,' the old man continued.

'It wasn't her fault,' Paniatowski told him.

'Of course it wasn't her fault! How could it be her fault? She died of pneumonia.'

'Nobody in the village really believes that, you know,' Paniatowski said gently.

'I don't care what them evil-minded people think,' the old man said bitterly. 'They can say whatever they like about her, but they're wrong. Our Mary caught pneumonia. That's what she died of – and that's what it says on the her death certificate.'

'The doctor who signed it was a friend of yours, wasn't he?' Paniatowski asked.

'Who told you that?'

'Wasn't he?'

'Yes, we'd known old Doc Adams for years.'

'And he'd have written anything on the death certificate that you'd asked him to, wouldn't he?'

'I want you to leave!' the old man said, as fiercely as his weak voice would still allow. 'I want you to go right now.'

'There's no shame in what she did,' Paniatowski said. 'Your

148

friends will all understand. They won't think any less of her because of it.'

The old man raised a shaky hand, and pointed it across the room. 'There's the door, Miss,' he said. 'If I still had the strength to throw you out through it myself, I'd do it.'

'There were two great wrongs done back then,' Paniatowski said desperately. 'One was to your daughter, and the other was to someone else. We can't do anything to help Mary any more, but at least we can still right that second wrong. And if you helped me to do that, by telling me the truth, I'm sure Mary would sleep more peacefully in her grave.'

'What are you talking about?' the old man asked. 'I've no idea what you're talking about.'

'I'm not allowed to give you any more details about that second wrong,' Paniatowski said. 'You'll just have to trust me on it.'

'Why *should* I trust you?' the old man asked. 'Why should I help you, if it means blackening my darling daughter's name?'

To hell with the Official Secrets' Act! Paniatowski thought. To hell with all the politics and red tape!

'Did you know an American Army captain called Robert Kineally, Mr Parkinson?' she asked.

'Yes, we knew Robert. He was a wonderful young man. He was in love with our Mary, you know.'

'He disappeared shortly after she died,' old Mrs Parkinson said, speaking for the first time. 'I don't think he could bear to stay around here after our Mary was gone.'

'He didn't disappear,' Paniatowski told them. 'He was murdered.'

'Murdered!' Mrs Parkinson gasped.

'I don't believe you,' her husband said. 'If he'd been murdered, somebody would have told us.'

'Nobody knew,' Paniatowski explained. 'They've only just found his body –buried at the old camp. And now we need to find his killer.'

'Poor Robert,' the old woman said mournfully.

'It's a terrible thing to have happened,' her husband agreed. 'But how will talking about our Mary help you to find the murderer?'

'I wish I could give you a clear answer to that, but I can't,' Paniatowski admitted. 'We're blundering around in the dark here, and even if you can shed only a little light, it might help us to find our way.'

'It's very painful for us to talk about it,' the old man said, as tears began to run down his sunken cheeks.

'You owe it to Mary,' Paniatowski said, hating herself for putting them through so much suffering, but knowing she had no choice. 'You have to do what she would have wanted you to do.'

The old couple exchanged agonized glances, then the father said, 'Before Mary died – before Mary *killed* herself – she wrote two letters. The first one was to me and her mother. She . . . she said she was sorry for all the pain she knew she'd cause us by going like that, but she was so desperately unhappy, and she didn't see any other way out.'

'Did you keep the note?' Paniatowski asked.

The old man feebly shook his head. 'No, we didn't keep it. We couldn't bear to. So when I'd lit the bonfire, I burned it, along with all the . . . the blood-soaked bedding.'

'And what about the other letter?' Paniatowski asked. 'What did she say in that?'

'We don't know. It was in a sealed envelope.'

'And you didn't open it?'

'No.'

'Why not?'

'If Mary had wanted us to read it, she wouldn't have sealed it in the first place. Anyway, it wasn't addressed to us.'

'So what *did* you do with it?'

'In her letter to us, she asked us to post it for her. She'd even put a stamp on it. It was her last wish. It seemed . . . it seemed that the least we could do was to respect it.'

'Do you remember who you posted it to?' Paniatowski asked.

Just a hint of anger appeared in the old man's watery eyes. 'I may be old and I may be frail – but I'm not quite senile yet,' he said. 'Of course I remember who I posted it to.'

'I'm sorry,' Paniatowski said. 'I never meant to imply—'

'Yes, you did,' the old man told her. 'But it doesn't matter. Nothing much matters now.'

'So it was addressed to . . . ?'

'It was addressed to *Robert*. Who else would our Mary have written to in the last few precious moments of her life?'

Twenty-One

Inspector Tom Wright had been no more than accurate when he'd talked about the excellence of the security system which was installed Douglas Coutes's flat, Bob Rutter thought.

The front door was made of a hardwood – possibly mahogany – which would have made it a formidable obstacle even without the steel plate that was probably embedded in it. The locks, with which Lily Hanson was drunkenly fumbling at the moment, would not have looked out of place on the strong-room door of a major bank. The average burglar would have taken one look at this door, and then moved on. Even the expert cracksman – and there were few enough of those about – would have thought twice before taking it on.

Lily, after more fumbling, finally got the door open. 'Just wait here for a minute, will you, Sweetie?' she said.

'Have you changed your mind about inviting me in?' Rutter asked, in a flirtatious voice that sounded nothing like his own.

'Changed my mind? No, not for a minute,' Lily assured him. 'Only an idiot would slam the door in the face of a good-looking boy like you.'

'Then why keep me waiting out here?'

'Because I've got to disable the security system before you can come in.'

'Really?'

'Really! If I don't do that, the sensors will detect more than one person in the hallway, and the alarms will go off.'

'And we wouldn't want that,' Rutter said.

Lily giggled. 'No, we wouldn't,' she said. 'Not just when we're getting really close to the interesting bit.'

Lily disappeared into the flat, leaving Rutter with a moment to himself for reflection.

This kind of behaviour wasn't like him at all, he thought. He didn't make up stories about himself, and then feed them to people he was investigating. He *never* pretended to be something he wasn't. That was the sort of thing that only the wonderful – irrepressible – Monika Paniatowski could get away with.

And yet despite all his qualms – despite the odd prick of conscience – he was, for the first time since he'd been told about his wife's death, actually beginning to enjoy himself.

Lily appeared in the doorway again.

'It's safe to come in, now,' she said. She threw her arms out in an expansive gesture. 'Welcome to my humble home.'

Rutter followed her into the flat. She led him down the corridor, and from there to a large, luxurious living room.

'At last!' Lily said. 'We're finally in my little home, and now we can really start to get comfortable.'

But almost as soon as the words were out, she began to look very *un*comfortable in herself.

'Excuse me for a moment,' she continued, speaking through a mouth which she was keeping almost entirely closed.

She turned, and staggered back into the corridor. Rutter heard another door open, then close again, and guessed it led into a bathroom. He waited for a few moments, then followed her out on tiptoe.

The second he entered the corridor, he could hear the sound of the woman vomiting her heart up into the toilet bowl. Which meant, he estimated, that he had at least five minutes to look around.

Still walking on tiptoe – though given that Lily Hanson was retching so loudly, he doubted she'd have heard an elephant stampede – he began opening the other doors.

There was a large, palatial bedroom, which Douglas Coutes must have shared with Lily before her fall from favour – and to which he now, no doubt, took his newer conquests, with little regard for how it must make his poor neglected house-keeper feel.

There was a second bedroom, which had so few personal touches in it that he assumed it was reserved for guests.

And there was a third bedroom – much smaller and meaner than the others – which stank of alcohol, and served not only as a refuge for the inebriated Lily, but also as a constant reminder of the rejection and humiliation she had been made to endure at the hands of Douglas Coutes.

He continued checking out the rooms, keeping one ear cocked for signs that the housekeeper had recovered enough to emerge from the bathroom.

There was a large kitchen, and a small sitting room. There was a second bathroom.

It was all so ordinary, he told himself – so opulent, yet conventional – that he was beginning to think the whole expedition was nothing but a complete waste of time.

And then, he reached the room at the far end of the corridor. It was the biggest one in the entire apartment – and easily the most interesting and self-indulgent.

This was Coutes's study. There was no doubt about that. There was a huge teak desk at one end of it, and a full-sized snooker table at the other. Two pieces of modern sculpture flanked the big window which looked out on to the street, and the expanse of polished parquet between the desk and snooker table was broken up by several expensive oriental carpets.

But it was the walls which immediately attracted Rutter's interest. Almost every inch of available space on them had been taken up with glass-fronted display cases.

The cases were works of art in themselves, delicately constructed from the finest woods, by the most skilled of craftsmen. And they were full of knives. Hundreds of them!

Some of the knives, Rutter recognized – a Fairbairn-Sykes Commando knife, a Bowie knife, an Indian Khukri dagger.

Others were new to him, though he could make an informed guess as to their origins – that one a Bronze Age dagger, that one a Medieval dagger, and the one in the corner something Japanese.

But that still left a fair number of exhibits about which he had no clue whatsoever.

He heard the toilet flush, and hurriedly returned to the lounge. By the time Lily appeared again, he was standing by one of the bookcases, studying the titles with apparent fascination.

'Had a bit of tummy trouble,' Lily Hanson said weakly. 'Hope that won't put you off.'

'No,' Rutter said, setting his face into a mask of interest and concern, and turning to look at her. 'It won't put me off at all. That kind of thing can could happen to anybody.'

She looked less green than she had earlier, and, after puking up her load, had obviously made some effort to repair her make-up.

'A drink,' she said. 'That's what we could both do with now. A good stiff drink.'

'Are you sure that's such a good idea?' Rutter asked.

'Why wouldn't it be?' Lily asked, exhibiting a flash of that aggression that habitual drunks are often prone to.

'Well, I just don't think it's entirely wise, given your tummy trouble,' Rutter said.

'A little drink is *exactly* what I need,' Lily Hanson told him. 'A little drink will just set me up for the frolics that we've been promising each other ever since we left the pub.'

She walked across to a large cabinet set into the wall. She seemed a little less shaky than she had been earlier.

'Are you sticking to whisky?' she asked.

'Might as well,' Rutter replied. He waited until she was concentrating on mixing the drinks, then added, 'I have to say that with all the security you've got installed here, it must have taken some very determined burglars indeed to even *consider* breaking in.'

Lily froze. 'Burglars?' she asked warily. 'Who said anything about burglars?'

'You did,' Rutter told her. 'Don't you remember?'

'No, I'm not sure that I do.'

'When you were disabling the alarms, you told me that you'd been broken into.'

'I said that?' Lily asked doubtfully. She shook her head, as if attempting to clear it. 'Suppose I must have done, if you know all about it.'

'You said the burglars got past two of the alarms, but were caught out by the third,' Rutter said, pushing his luck.

'That's right, I did say that,' Lily agreed.

'So where was the third alarm situated? It can't have been with the others, can it?'

'No. It's attached to display cases in Douglas's . . . in my . . . study,' Lily said. 'Don't want to talk about burglars any more. Upsets me.'

'Then we won't,' Rutter promised.

'Drinks are done,' Lily said. 'Take a seat.'

Rutter considered the sofa for a second, then selected the

armchair opposite. Lily looked disappointed, but made no comment.

They took a preliminary sip of their drinks, then Lily said, 'You are going to take me to bed later, aren't you?'

After all the loneliness – all the despair – it was tempting to say that he would, but Rutter found himself shaking his head.

'You're not?' Lily asked.

'No, I'm not,' Rutter agreed.

Lily's jaw quivered, and tears appeared in her eyes. 'It's because I'm ugly, isn't it?' she wailed.

'You're not ugly at all,' Rutter replied.

And he meant it. Somewhere, beneath all that make-up and all the excesses, there lay a pretty face – a face it was still possible to salvage.

'Then, if you don't think I'm ugly, why *won't* you sleep with me?' Lily demanded.

'It wouldn't be fair to take advantage of you, not when you're not feeling well.'

'I'll tell you what's fair and what isn't,' Lily said, almost screaming the words. 'I'm the one who decides what's fair!'

Rutter stood. 'I really think I'd better go,' he said.

Lily looked up at him pathetically. 'Please don't leave me!' she implored him.

'My staying wouldn't be good for either of us,' Rutter told her as he walked towards the door.

'You're just like Douglas!' Lily screeched after him, as he stepped into the corridor. 'You're just like all the men I've ever known. You're nothing but a complete bloody bastard!'

Perhaps she was right, Rutter thought, as he headed towards the lift. Or perhaps, by walking away as he had done, he had at last begun his own long climb back to decency and honour.

Twenty-Two

A be Birnbaum – ex-GI driver and now major player in the tri-state dry-cleaning world – was about to get ready for bed when he heard a loud pounding on his trailer door.

'Who's there?' he asked.

'Woodend,' replied the furious voice from outside.

Birnbaum unlocked the door. Looking down at his visitor, the thought came to him that although he'd always thought of Woodend as a big man, he'd never known quite *how* big he could be when he was angry.

'Is there a problem, Charlie?' he asked.

'Don't "Charlie" me,' Woodend said, pushing Birnbaum back into the trailer, and immediately following him. 'Sit down, you bastard. I want some answers, and I want them now. An' you're goin' to give them to me – even if I have to break every bone in your body to get them.'

Birnbaum sat, and realized he hadn't been quite as frightened as this for a long while – that the last time his bowels had turned to water, as they were doing now, was during the Normandy Landings.

'Why did Robert Kineally and Mary Parkinson break up?' Woodend demanded.

'They didn't,' Birnbaum confessed. 'Everything was fine before he went to London – and by time he came back, she was dead.'

'But he got a letter from her, didn't he?'

'Yes, he got a letter.'

'An' what did she say in it?'

'She told him she'd slept with Coutes. She said she was so ashamed of herself that she couldn't bear to go on living any more.'

'And what did Kineally do when he'd read it?'

'What would you have expected him to do? What would you have done yourself, in his place? He went out looking for Coutes.'

Kineally confronts Coutes in the Dun Cow's skittle alley.
'Mary's dead!' he says.
'I heard,' Coutes replies. 'I'm very sorry.'
'It's all your fault.'
'My fault?'
'You seduced her – you son-of-a-bitch – and she couldn't live with the shame of it.'
Coutes laughs. 'I assure you, there was no seduction involved. She was at least as willing as I was. And if every woman I'd slept with killed herself because of it, the countryside would be strewn with dead bodies.'
This is too much to take, and Kineally lunges at him. And it is only when it is already too late to stop himself that he sees the short iron bar in Coutes's hands, and realizes that this is exactly what Coutes wanted him to do – what all the taunting was designed to make *him do.*
The first blow strikes him on the arm, and knocks him off balance. Two more blows hit home – one to the side and one to the leg – as he is going down. And then he is lying on the ground.
In incredible pain!
Fighting for breath!
And through the pain, he can still hear Coutes's voice.
'As soon as I learned that Mary had topped herself, I knew it would come to this,' Coutes is saying. 'Anybody else would have shrugged it off – would have said that if she'd been sleeping around, she wasn't worth grieving over. But not you, you stupid bastard. You'll keep coming back at me as long as you're able to. So I'm just going to have to make sure you're not *able to, aren't I?'*
There is no mistaking what the words mean – no possibility of misinterpretation. Even through the pain, Kineally realizes that Coutes intends to kill him.
And there is nothing he can do about it!
He hears a new voice. Not as near as Coutes's voice, but not that far away, either.

157

'Captain Kineally? Captain Kineally? Where are you, sir?
Are you in the goddam skittle alley?'
And suddenly Coutes is no longer there.

'He was in one hell of a state when I found him in that skittle alley,' Birnbaum said. 'I didn't know how to deal with him myself, so I put him into the jeep and brought him back to the camp for the paramedics to take a look at him. They did their best to patch him up, but it wasn't an easy job, because his shoulder was dislocated and three of his ribs were broken.'

'What a touching story,' Woodend said, in a voice as menacing as a cut-throat razor. 'Truly touching. And do you know, I'd almost be inclined to believe it – if I hadn't spent more than an hour this morning listening to you feed me an entirely different load of horse shit!'

'Believe me, this isn't horse shit!' Abe Birnbaum pleaded. 'Believe me, because – I promise you, Charlie – this time I'm telling you the truth.'

'Special Agent Grant has had a whole vault full of documents shipped out from the States. Did you know that?'

'I . . . I guess I saw some cardboard boxes being—'

'And among those documents are all the medical records for Haverton Camp – so they should contain the details of the treatment given to Robert Kineally, after he was attacked, shouldn't they?'

'I—'

'I'm goin' to ask you a question, Abe, an' I want you to think very carefully before you answer it. An' the question is this – if I look for those records, will I find them?'

Birnbaum looked down at the floor of the trailer. 'No, you won't,' he mumbled.

'And *why* won't I?'

'Because nothing went through the official channels. The paramedics were buddies of mine, and they didn't make any record of the treatment.'

'How very convenient!' Woodend said. 'An' would you like to tell me why you did things that way?'

'Because that's what Captain Kineally wanted.'

'Because that's what Captain Kineally wanted! Of course that was the reason! It's common sense, when you think about it!' Woodend paused. 'Tell me, Abe, just how stupid do you think I am?'

'It's all true, Charlie! I promise you it is. The Captain said that if it got to be common knowledge that he'd been fighting with a British officer, both him and Coutes would be arrested. And that was the last thing he wanted.'

'I can understand him not wanting to be arrested himself, but after what Coutes had done to him, he surely wanted to see that bastard behind bars.'

'You don't understand him,' Birnbaum said.

'Then explain him to me, so I will.'

'He said he didn't want Coutes to be punished by anybody else. He said he wanted them to be both to remain at liberty, so he could get a second crack at Coutes himself – and this time he wasn't going to take no sucker punches.'

'So what was the point of all the lies that you told to me an' Special Agent Grant?' Woodend asked sceptically.

'I lied because I loved the guy,' Abe Birnbaum said. 'I loved him like a brother. I loved him like I loved my own father. And I didn't want nobody thinking he was a coward – even if he was.'

'Hang on, you've lost me there completely,' Woodend admitted.

'When I got up the next morning, the jeep was missing,' Abe Birnbaum explained. 'I should have reported it, but I didn't.'

'Why not?'

'Because I didn't want anybody to know that he'd taken it.'

'He *didn't* take it!'

'Yes, he did,' Abe Birnbaum said sadly. 'He sounded brave enough while the paramedics were patching him up – and maybe he *was* feeling brave then. But later, when he was all alone, he must have realized that he'd never have the nerve to face down Coutes again. So what did he do? He took the jeep and drove to the railway station! Then he caught the first train he could out of here. And nobody's ever seen him since – because he's too ashamed to show his face.'

'No, he—'

'That's what he did, Charlie. I *know*, because I went out looking for the jeep, and found it where he'd left it. It wasn't the Captain who drove the jeep deeper into the woods, and covered it with camouflage. I did that! I did it because I wanted to buy him more time to get away!'

'You've got the wrong end of the—'

'Let me finish,' Abe Birnbaum said, and there were tears pouring from his eyes now. 'I've held it all back for over twenty years, Charlie, so now please *let me finish*!'

'All right,' Woodend agreed.

'Everybody who knew him – from his own parents right down to the enlisted men on the base – knows that he disappeared. But they don't know *why* he disappeared. They can guess – but they don't *know*. And there's some comfort in that, because it's their choice whether to believe good things about him or to believe bad ones. So they can *choose* to believe that he fell in the sea, and was drowned. Or they can *choose* to believe that he was sent on a top-secret mission to Germany, and was killed in action. But if they knew the truth, Charlie – that he ran away because he was scared to death of Douglas Coutes – then they'd have no choice at all.'

'The truth is that Robert Kineally never took that jeep,' Woodend said. 'The truth is, he was murdered during the night and buried in a shallow grave at the edge of the camp.'

Birnbaum looked as if he had been hit in the face with a rock. For several moments he said nothing at all, then his mouth began to move frantically, like that of a landed fish.

'Take it easy,' Woodend said softly.

'B . . . but if he didn't take the jeep,' Birnbaum stuttered, 'that means . . . that means . . .'

'Yes,' Woodend agreed grimly. 'We all know what *that* means.'

Twenty-Three

Woodend closed the door of Abe Birnbaum's trailer behind him, and stepped out into the night. The air had been mild – almost spring-like – during the day, but now that darkness had descended, the heavy frost which accompanied it had made that same air as cold and sharp as a knife.

As he walked along the line of trailers, Woodend wondered if it had been as cold as this on the night that Douglas Coutes had attacked Robert Kineally with an iron bar – the night when, but for Birnbaum's sudden appearance on the scene, the English captain would probably not have walked away until he had made sure that his enemy was dead.

He had almost reached Coutes's trailer. Earlier in the day, there had been two American MPs guarding it from a discreet distance, but now there was no sign of them at all.

Now why *was* that? Had the wintry conditions made them decide to go temporarily AWOL? Or was it that Special Agent Grant had decided that Coutes no longer posed a flight risk?

Woodend knocked on the trailer door, and Coutes answered the knock almost immediately.

The Minister was wearing a dressing gown of shot-silk, and smoking a long fat cigar. He looked down at Woodend with what could only have been called amused disdain.

'Do you mind if I come in?' the Chief Inspector asked.

'Do you have a warrant?'

'Do I need one?'

Coates smirked. 'Of course not. Even in these days of doctored statements and cunningly fabricated evidence, the truly innocent man very rarely has anything to fear from the authorities.'

Woodend entered the trailer, and looked around him. Though all the units on this site were of the same basic design, the fixtures and fittings in this one were far superior to those in either his own or Abe Birnbaum's, he noted. But he should not really have been surprised by that, he thought. Even when they were under suspicion of committing a capital crime, the élite were *still* the élite.

'Would you care for a drink?' Coutes asked, with mock-graciousness. 'I'm afraid I can't offer you the pint of "wallop" that you're probably used to. But if you think it wouldn't be *entirely* wasted on you, I can provide you with a glass of fine malt whisky from my private stock.'

Patronizing bastard, Woodend thought.

'I didn't come here for a drink,' he said. 'This isn't in the nature of a social visit at all.'

'No, of course it isn't,' Coutes agreed. 'Why *would* it be? Indeed, given our respective backgrounds, how *could* it be? We're like oil and water, you and I. Or perhaps fine brandy and bathtub gin would be nearer the mark. Still, the fact that you decline a drink is no reason for my not indulging myself, now is it?'

'No, it isn't,' Woodend agreed. 'Especially since, from what I know of you, I'd say that indulgin' yourself is what you do best.'

Coutes gave a short, unamused, laugh. 'Very good,' he said. 'Almost witty – in a crude, proletarian sort of way. Did they teach you how to do that at police college, or is it a natural gift?'

Woodend said nothing, and Coutes, not expecting an answer, went over to the cupboard and poured himself a drink.

'So how's the investigation going, Sergeant?' the Minister asked, with only mild interest.

'I've told you before, Mr Coutes, I'm a Chief Inspector now,' Woodend replied. 'An' since you're askin', I'd have to say that the investigation's goin' rather well.'

'Rather well,' Coutes repeated, rolling the words around in his mouth. 'Rather well. Am I to take it then, *Chief Inspector*, that you now know who killed Robert Kineally?'

'Yes.'

'Then please don't keep me in suspense any longer. Tell me who the murderer was.'

'It was you.'

'Really?' Coutes said, as casually as if a matter under

discussion was of only marginal interest to him. 'And what has led you to this astounding – and rather far-fetched – conclusion?'

'I've got a motive – a really strong motive.'

'That I didn't like Kineally, and Kineally didn't like me? But you've always known that.'

'That's true,' Woodend agreed. 'But what I didn't know was just how bad it had got.'

'Ah, you must have learned about our little contretemps in the skittle alley of the Dun Cow!'

'I've learned that you took an iron bar with you, and beat the shit out of him. And that if Abe Birnbaum hadn't turned up when he did, you'd probably have killed him, then an' there.'

'You're exaggerating what was, in truth, a very minor incident,' Coutes said easily.

'A minor incident in which Robert Kineally happened to get three of his ribs broken.'

'If you're too weak and feeble to play in the big boys' games, then you stay away from them.'

'There was no other way out, was there?' Woodend continued. 'Kineally was goin' to come after you again, as soon as he was strong enough. And this time, he'd know what to expect. This time, he'd be ready for you. An' you simply couldn't have allowed that to happen.'

'I could have taken him any time, anyhow, anywhere.'

'Maybe you could. But he'd have made sure there were witnesses the next time, an' even if you won, you'd lose.'

'Would I?'

'You know you would. You might have wriggled your way out of goin' to gaol if you'd hurt him badly – or even if you'd killed him – but it would have damaged your military career beyond repair. An' not just your military career – there was no way you'd ever make your mark in politics with that kind of dark stain on your character.'

'I can see that you don't know much about the world of politics,' Coutes told him. 'Any stains which I might – or might not – have on my character are nothing to the huge black blotches which cover some of my esteemed colleagues from head to foot.'

'I wonder if anybody saw you with the jeep?' Woodend mused.

Coutes blinked, and turned a shade paler. 'What jeep?' he asked, unconvincingly.

'Robert Kineally's jeep. You see, since it was found in the woods, the military police assumed that he'd dumped it there himself, an' gone the rest of the way on foot. So the one thing they *won't* have asked the people they questioned is whether they saw anybody drive the jeep to the railway station.'

'And why should they have?'

'Because somebody – an' by somebody, I mean *you* – did just that. You hoped the military police would find the jeep at the station, an' assume that Kineally had taken a train.'

'And why would I have wanted them to assume that?'

'Don't try playin' me for the fool,' Woodend said. 'You wanted the American military police to think he'd already left the area, so they wouldn't start lookin' for him closer to home. An' it would have worked, too. When they did finally find the jeep, more than a week later, that's *exactly* the conclusion they reached. It was only because they *couldn't* find it initially that they did the very thing you didn't want them to do – search the whole area with a fine-tooth comb.'

'It was amazing the efforts they went to,' Douglas Coutes said. 'If I hadn't seen it with my own eyes, I'd never have believed that – with a war going on – they'd waste so many resources searching for just one man.'

Woodend chuckled. 'I'll bet you wouldn't. An' I'll bet you crapped yourself every time you saw anybody walkin' near the perimeter fence. Because if they had found the body then, so soon after what had happened in the Dun Cow skittle alley, you would have been the Number One suspect – even without the knife an' the fingerprints.'

Douglas Coutes drew heavily on his cigar. 'This is all pure speculation,' he said.

He suddenly seemed much calmer, Woodend thought. *Why* did he suddenly seem calmer?

'It will only take one witness to place you at the railway station with Kineally's jeep, an' we'll have a cast-iron case against you,' he said.

Coutes laughed. 'One witness?' he repeated.

'That's what I said.'

'You think you'll be able to find a witness who – after twenty-one years – will be willing to swear under oath that he saw *me* drive up to the railway station on that particular day and in that particular vehicle?'

'You'd be amazed at the odd things people *do* remember.'

'You're clutching at straws,' Coutes told him. 'And I must say, I'm really disappointed in you.'

'Why? Because you thought I'd be so impressed at workin' for an important government minister that I'd manufacture the evidence necessary to get you off, even though I knew you were guilty?'

'No, it's not that at all. I'm disappointed because you've let your personal animosity cloud your professional judgement. I knew you didn't like me when I first asked you to investigate the case, but I assumed you'd be more interested in serving justice than in settling old scores.'

'I *am* servin' justice,' Woodend told him. 'You murdered Robert Kineally. How can you keep on denyin' it like this, when there's so much evidence stackin' up against you?'

'Since you appear to be a particular dense and stubborn individual, I will repeat this one more time,' Coutes said. 'My knife was stolen from me at least a week before the murder. I did not use it to kill that man, nor did I use any other method to kill him. I did not bury his body in a shallow grave. I have been framed. I don't know by whom, and I don't know why – but I *have* been framed. And I expect you to prove it, because that's your *job*.'

Woodend shook his head in wonder. 'You still think you're goin' to get away with it, don't you?' he asked. 'Even at this late stage of the game, you're still convinced you'll find a way to cheat fate.'

'I've said all I intend to say,' Coutes told him haughtily, 'except that I'm very much looking forward to hearing your grovelling apology when you realize just how wrong you've been.'

Monika Paniatowski stretched out luxuriantly on the bed in her trailer. She felt good – like the cat who'd got the cream, or a hungry bear which had suddenly come across a gourmet picnic basket.

She took a drag on her cigarette, and then turned her head to look at the lean, hard back of the man who was lying next to her.

Ed Grant was full of surprises, she thought.

Who would ever have guessed that the mild-mannered American would not only have decided that he wanted to sleep with her, but would have aggressively pursued that desire, as he had the night before?

Who could have imagined that a man with such a pedestrian, bureaucratic attitude to the business of crime detection could ever turn out to be so amazingly inventive in bed?

'Are you asleep?' she asked.

'The FBI never sleeps,' Grant replied – predictably.

'How much longer do you think this case is going to last?'

'Now why would you want to know that, Little Monika? Is it perhaps because you've realized that once the investigation's all over, I'll be on my way back home *tout de suite*? Are you already starting to worry about how much you're gonna miss me when I'm gone?'

She could only see the back of his head, but she was sure, from the tone of his voice, that there was an arrogant grin plastered over the front of it.

'Miss you!' she repeated. 'Miss you? To tell you the truth, I don't think I'll miss you at all.'

She was not lying. She felt no particular affection for the man. Or even any affection at all! The plain fact was that, on a purely social level, his company bored her.

'You'll miss the sex, though, won't you?' Grant said. 'They don't call us Special Agents for nothing.'

He was right about that. She hated to admit it – but he was right. She had slept with plenty of men in her time, but never one who had roused her to the heights that Grant had.

'The sex *has* been good,' she admitted, 'but what you should never forget, Special Agent, is that it takes two to tango.'

They both fell silent for a while, then Grant said, 'Since you seem so interested in the progress of the investigation, how much longer do *you* think it's gonna last?'

'Not long.'

'Is that right? And what do you base this belief of yours on? Woman's intuition?'

'Not at all,' she said, resisting the temptation to turn him over and knee him – as hard as she possibly could – in his FBI-approved testicles. 'It's based on something much more substantial.'

166

'And what might that be? You haven't been reading the entrails again, have you?'

He was insufferable, she thought. Really insufferable. Even for the best sex in the world, it wasn't worth putting up with this.

'We've found evidence,' she said. 'Do you know what that means – "finding evidence"? It means going out and looking for it, rather than just sitting behind your big FBI desk, and waiting for it to come to you.'

'And what does this evidence you've uncovered – by going out and looking for it – actually show?' Grant asked.

This wasn't going to be an easy thing to say, Monika Paniatowski thought. Admitting to this insufferable prig that he'd been right all along wasn't going to be easy at all.

'It would seem to support all the previous evidence,' she said, through gritted teeth.

'And what does that mean exactly, Detective Sergeant? That you think Coutes is our killer?'

'Yes.'

'Now that *is* interesting,' Grant said thoughtfully.

'What is?'

'That just as you two English bumpkins have started to see the investigation through my eyes, I've done a complete back-flip and – much to my surprise – have started seeing it through yours.'

'You don't think he *is* the killer?'

'Nope!'

'But you must agree that all the evidence points to—'

'All the evidence is far too neat – far too clean. Coutes always claimed he was set up by somebody else, back in 1944, and the more I think about it, the more I'm inclined to believe him.'

167

Twenty-Four

*W*oodend was standing on the platform at Coxton Halt Railway Station, worrying about the way he was dressed. He was in the army – he was sure of that – so why the bloody hell was he wearing a hairy sports jacket and cavalry twill trousers, rather than a khaki uniform?

He smiled with relief when he saw the girl approaching him, because he knew that even if the uniform dilemma could not be resolved, here, at least, was one problem he could handle.

'I phoned my wife yesterday,' he told Mary Parkinson.

The girl frowned. 'How could you have done that? You're not married, Charlie.'

He suspected she was right about that, but he wasn't going to let a little thing like reality deflect him from his purpose.

'I asked her about your little problem,' he ploughed on. 'You know what I'm talking about, don't you?'

'Yes, Charlie. Of course I know what you're talking about.'

'And do you know what she said? She said that under no circumstances are you tell Robert anything about what happened between you and Coutes until the war's over. Have you got that? Until the war's over, you're not to say a word!'

Mary Parkinson smiled, and Woodend noticed for the first time that not only was her face a deathly pale, but there was blood dribbling out of the corner of her mouth.

'It's too late to say that now, Charlie,' she told him, lifting up her hands so he could see her lacerated wrists. 'Far too late!'

In shock, he turned quickly away from her, only to have fresh horrors revealed to him a little further down the platform, where Kineally and Coutes were standing.

Kineally was holding himself stiffly and awkwardly, as was only to be expected from a man who had just been beaten up.

Coutes was much more relaxed, and had his big Prussian knife in his hand.

Coutes saw that Woodend was looking at them, and held out the big knife to him.

'Do you want to do it, Sergeant?' he asked.

'No!' Woodend heard himself gasp. 'No!'

Coutes looked perplexed. 'Really?' he asked. 'I must say, I can't understand your refusing. After all, Sergeant, you're the one who's made all this necessary!'

The train steamed into the station, a huge angry monster with its whistle ringing deafeningly.

Ringing? Woodend thought hazily. Why would it ring? Whistles whistled. That's how they got their name.

'Come on, Sergeant,' Coutes urged. 'Be a man! Take responsibility for your actions.'

The ringing would simply not go away, and Woodend reached groggily for the bedside phone.

'Yes?' he croaked.

'It's me, sir,' said the voice on the other end of the line.

The guilty calling the guilty, on a phone line of deep regret, Woodend thought.

Except that Bob didn't *sound* particularly guilty. There was new life to his voice that morning – a whole new enthusiasm – as if he were finally emerging from a long deep tunnel.

'Since you're ringin' me at the crack of dawn, I assume that you've got somethin' really interestin' to report,' Woodend said, groping around on the bedside cabinet for his cigarettes.

'I don't know how interesting it is,' Bob Rutter admitted chirpily. 'How could I know, when you've kept me so much in the dark? But I certainly do have *something* to report.'

'Fire away,' Woodend said, striking a match and lighting his first Capstan Full Strength of the day.

'I was in Coutes's London flat last night,' Rutter said, just as the Chief Inspector had inhaled.

Woodend choked.

Had it been a mistake to give the lad this job, he wondered, as a coughing fit wracked his body.

Had he pushed him too far, too soon?

'Are you all right, sir?' Rutter asked.

'I'm fine,' Woodend rasped. 'But I'm not so sure about you. You didn't *break* in, did you?'

Rutter laughed. 'No, I didn't. If you'd seen the security system protecting the flat for yourself, you'd soon have realized that it would have taken a better man than me to *break* in.'

'So how *did* you manage to get your foot through the door?'

'I was invited in.'

'An' are you goin' to tell me *who* invited you in? Or would you prefer me to guess?'

'I could certainly tell you, if you absolutely insisted on it,' Rutter said, obviously still enjoying himself, 'but I rather think you'd be much better off not doing that.'

'Maybe you're right,' Woodend agreed. 'So, however you managed to talk your way in, what did you find out once you were there?'

'I'll have to give you a little of the background, first,' Rutter said, milking the story for all it was worth.

'Fair enough,' Woodend said.

'A few weeks ago, there was an attempted burglary at Douglas Coutes's flat. It was a really professional job. The burglars eventually triggered one of the alarms and fled the scene, but the interesting thing is that *when* they set it off, they were in the process of examining the display cases – which contain Coutes's collection of knives.'

'Knives!' Woodend repeated, suddenly feeling much more awake.

'Knives,' Rutter reaffirmed, 'He's got hundreds of the things.'

Professional burglars?

Examinin' Coutes's knife collection?

It was more than just interestin', Woodend thought – it was bloody fascinatin'.

But that was not the same as saying that it had any connection at all with this investigation, now was it?

'You're sure the burglars didn't take any of the knives away with them?' he said, searching for some kind of connection, however tenuous.

'I'm absolutely certain they didn't. They couldn't have – not without damaging the display cases.'

'I see,' Woodend said, disappointedly – though he was not quite clear what he was being disappointed *about*.

'I wouldn't be at all surprised if they hadn't been planning to take some of them *before* the alarm went off,' Rutter said encouragingly.

Well, that was something, at least.

'You didn't happen to see a World War One German Army dagger in one of the cases, did you?' Woodend asked.

'I don't know. What would it have looked like?'

'It'd be a big bugger, with a channel runnin' down the middle of it to drain off the victim's blood.'

'No, I'm sure I didn't see one like that.'

And neither had Coutes, or so he claimed. At least, not since late in April 1944.

'You've done well, Bob,' Woodend said.

'But have I been of any *use*?' Rutter asked hopefully.

'Definitely,' Woodend lied. 'If nothing else, you helped us to eliminate certain possibilities.'

'Will you be needing me to do anything else in connection with this investigation?'

That was unlikely, Woodend thought. Highly unlikely.

'I don't know,' he said aloud. 'I'll ring you if I do.' Then he added, to give the statement verisimilitude, 'If you're going to be away from your parents-in-laws' house for any length of time, make sure you leave them a number where I can contact you.'

'I'll do that,' Rutter said happily. 'It's great to be back on the job with you, sir.'

'It's great to *have* you back,' Woodend told him.

The first of the morning's 'witnesses' to be brought to the interrogation trailer was a big man in his middle forties, with a rough – though ancient – scar running down his cheek.

He arrived under an escort of two military policemen, and was wearing handcuffs. Woodend thought he looked vaguely familiar, though he couldn't actually put a name to the man's face.

'Sit down over there, Bascombe,' Special Agent Grant said, indicating the chair at the opposite side of the table.

Bascombe! Woodend let the name roll around his mind, but it still didn't ring any bells.

As Bascombe took his seat, the Chief Inspector watched him with interest. In his own experience of handling prisoners, Woodend had found that they tended to be very self-conscious about wearing cuffs, and usually kept their hands on their laps. Bascombe showed no such inclination to hide his shackles, and instead placed his hands squarely on the table.

A hardened criminal, the Chief Inspector thought. But where *had* he seen the bloody man before?

And then it came to him!

The last time they had met had been in the skittle alley of the Dun Cow, when Bascombe had tried to attack Kineally with a brick, and Woodend had dropped the bastard with a powerful punch to his stomach.

'Your name is Huey Clarence Bascombe,' Special Agent Grant asked, reading the name off the sheet in front of him.

'Yeah,' the man agreed.

'And what is your current address in the United States?'

'A sweet little place what goes by the name of Fulsom Prison, Fulsom, California.'

'Are you an inmate of that prison?' Grant asked.

Bascombe looked down at his manacled wrist, and grinned. 'What do you think, Special Agent?'

'Just answer the question,' Grant said sternly.

'Yeah, I'm an inmate.'

'You were imprisoned for carrying out an armed robbery on a drug store? Is that correct?'

'No.'

'No? Then why *were* you imprisoned?'

'Cuz I got caught.'

'How long a sentence were you given?'

'Ten years.'

'And how many of those years have you now served?'

'Eight.'

'Which means you still have two years left to do?'

'That's what the math says.'

'You won't be getting any time off for good behaviour?' Special Agent Grant asked.

Bascombe smiled unpleasantly. 'Good behaviour's for faggots,' he said. 'I'm a man.'

'A man who still has two full years behind bars to look forward to,' Grant pointed out.

'I can do the time if I have to,' Huey Bascombe told him.

'I can do it easy. But maybe there's no need to. Maybe I can squeeze some kinda deal out of you two guys.'

'And why should we give you a deal?'

'For helpin' you out.'

Grant smiled, almost benignly. 'You appear to have completely the wrong impression of the position that you find yourself in, Mr Bascombe,' he said. 'You seem to think, if I'm reading what you've just said correctly, that you hold all the cards. Is that right?'

'Maybe.'

'Well, you don't,' Grant said, switching from the benign to the harsh in the flickering of an eye. '*We* hold them. The whole deck belongs to *us*. And you'll help us to the best of your ability – not to improve your own situation, but in order to prevent that situation from becoming any worse.'

Bascombe grinned. 'You got me scared now.'

'And so you should be. Because if we're not happy – and I mean *completely* happy – about the way you've co-operated with us, we'll send you to Fulsom with a report which states that you attacked us. And the two years you've got left to serve will very quickly become five or six. Maybe even more.'

Bascombe grinned again. 'Yeah, sure,' he said. He shifted his weight slightly. 'I think I know pretty much what this is all about.'

'Do you? And what *is* it all about?'

'You're investigatin' the disappearance of a nigger-lovin' captain called Robert Kineally, ain't you?'

Grant rocked in his chair, then tried his best to look as if he hadn't.

'Who told you that?' he demanded.

'*Ain't* you?'

'We are investigating a matter of national importance. The exact details of it are no concern of yours.'

'Only we both know that the nigger-lover didn't *disappear* at all, don't we, Special Agent?'

'Do we?'

'Yeah, I reckon so.'

'If you are involved in – or know of – any crime which relates to Captain Kineally, and if you conceal that fact from us, then you have yourself committed a criminal act,' Grant said stiffly.

173

'So maybe I *don't* know nothin',' Bascombe countered. 'Maybe I just got a theory.'

'Then we'd like to hear it.'

'I think he was kidnapped.'

'And *who* do you think kidnapped him?'

'Them big old bug-eyed monsters from outer space. Way I figure it, they beamed him up to their flying saucer.'

'You're yanking my chain,' Grant said angrily. 'And that's a very, very, foolish thing for you to do.'

'You don't like that theory?' Bascombe asked easily. 'OK, I got another one you'll prob'ly be happier with.'

'If you're still wasting our time—'

'I ain't wastin' your time. You're *really* gonna like this one.'

'Then let's hear it,' Grant said.

'Not yet awhile,' Bascombe told him. ''Fore I tell you my second theory, I gotta talk to a lawyer.'

Twenty-Five

Two hours had passed since Huey Bascombe had dropped heavy hints that he knew a great deal more about what had happened to Robert Kineally than he was saying – two hours in which frantic phone calls had been made, and urgent meetings convened. And as a result of all those phone calls and meetings, the three original participants were back in the interrogation trailer, though now they had two additional men for company.

The two newcomers, who flanked Bascombe like the guardian angels they had, in fact, been assigned to be, were a middle-aged English solicitor in a tweed suit and a younger American army captain who had been originally slated to play a role in the anticipated court martial.

'Before we begin, I would like my client's position made completely clear,' the English solicitor said. 'He agrees to tell you what he knows about the disappearance of Captain Robert Kineally in May 1944, and in return for that information, you agree to commute the remainder of his prison sentence for armed robbery.'

'Fine,' Special Agent Grant said, with just a touch of petulance.

'You will also agree to grant my client full immunity for any part which he himself might have played in the events surrounding the disappearance of the said Captain Kineally,' the solicitor continued.

'Provided he didn't play any direct part in the murder,' Special Agent Grant cautioned.

'As far as I can recall, we have not yet mentioned any murder of any kind,' the solicitor continued, smoothly. 'But should we do so in the course of our discussion, I am assuming that unless my client actually struck a blow himself, or restrained the victim of the attack while such a blow was delivered, he is covered by any and all immunities already stipulated.'

'He's covered,' Grant said wearily.

'Very well then, that being the case, I am happy to proceed,' the solicitor said.

'I ain't,' Bascombe said.

The solicitor raised a quizzical eyebrow. 'My dear chap, why ever not? Is there a problem of some kind?'

'Yeah! What's this guy doin' here?' Bascombe asked, jerking his thumb in the direction of the captain sitting next to him.

The solicitor sighed. 'As I've already explained, Mr Bascombe, I am not licensed to practice law in the United States—'

'We ain't *in* the United States!'

'For the purposes of these proceedings, I can assure you that we are. At least temporarily, this camp has been designated as American soil. And taking that as a given, it is necessary for the captain – as an American *lawyer* – to provide you with additional representation.'

'But he's in the army!'

'That doesn't matter in the slightest. Since he has agreed to accept you as his client, your interest has become his primary concern.'

'An' he can't welsh on the deal?'

'Nobody can "welsh" on the deal, Mr Bascombe,' the solicitor said, wrinkling his nose at the inelegant language he had just been obliged to use. 'Welshing is simply not an option.'

'Well, all right!' Bascombe whooped triumphantly.

'Can we proceed now?' Special Agent Grant asked.

'Sure,' Bascombe agreed. 'What do you wanna know?'

'We want to know who killed Robert Kineally,' Grant said.

'Hell, that's an easy one to answer. That liberal piece of shit was stuck by a good ole boy called Harry Wallace.'

'Why did Wallace kill him?'

'Cuz Kineally showed him up in front of a couple of niggers. Harry said no white man should do that to another white man, an' he was just gonna have to be punished for it.'

'So he decided to kill him?' Grant asked.

'Not first off, no. First off, he was just gonna beat the crap outta the Yankee son-of-a-bitch. But then he saw the problem.'

'What problem?'

'Kineally was an officer. If you beat up an officer, they lock you in the stockade, an' throw away the key. So whatever he did to Kineally, Harry had got to make sure Kineally couldn't talk about it afterwards.'

'So *then* he decided to kill him?'

'Yeah! He didn't have no choice, did he?'

'*How* did he kill him?'

'A couple o' weeks earlier, Harry had stole this big old knife from a dipstick Limey officer called Coutes, an'—'

'Why had he stolen it?'

'Cuz he liked the look of it, and cuz Coutes had left it around where it could be stole. Anyways, once he'd decided to kill Kineally, he thought it'd be real smart to use that knife to do it with.'

'Why would it be "real smart"?'

'Cuz if the stiff was ever found, they'd blame the whole thing on this Coutes guy.'

'How did Coutes's bloody fingerprints come to be on Kineally's dog tags?' Woodend asked.

'How in hell would I know that?' Bascombe demanded.

'Quite,' Grant agreed dryly. 'Now the next thing I want to know is the exact location—'

'Just hold your horses a minute!' Bascombe said.

'Yes?'

'I think I got an answer to that dog tag question.'

'You have?'

'Sure. A couple o' hours before Harry killed him, that son-of-a-bitch Kineally got into a fight with this Coutes guy over at the Dun Cow. Maybe Coutes grabbed his dog tags *then*.'

'Maybe he did,' Grant agreed. 'I'd now like you to tell me *where* Wallace killed Kineally.'

'He done it over on that piece o' land where they used to keep all the military vehicles.'

'How did Wallace persuade Kineally to go there?'

'Dunno. Musta fed him some kinda yarn about wantin' to show him somethin'.'

'Why did he choose that spot?'

'Cuz it was well away from the main camp. An' cuz that's where we were gonna bury the body.'

'Did you actually *see* Wallace kill Kineally?'

177

'Oh yeah! Not from close to, cuz I was keepin' watch. But I seen it, right enough. Drove that knife into him like he was stickin' a hog. Kineally didn't hardly make no sound at all.'

'What about the jeep?' Woodend asked.

For the first time since he'd begun his story, Bascombe looked uncertain of himself. 'What jeep?'

'Captain Kineally's jeep. It was driven to the railway station and abandoned.'

'Don't know nuthin' about no jeep,' Bascombe said. 'Maybe Wallace took it later.'

'Once Wallace had killed Captain Kineally, the two of you buried the body?' Grant asked.

'Right.'

'Where?'

'Under one of them ole armoured cars. See, we figured the tracks would soon cover what we done.'

'Where's Wallace now?' Grant asked.

Bascombe shrugged. 'Don't rightly know. Ran into him in a bar in Montgomery once – must have been round about 'forty-eight or 'forty-nine – but I ain't seen him since.'

'What made you decide to run the risk of helping Wallace in the first place?' Woodend asked.

'The guy was a buddy of mine, an' you always help your buddies out,' Bascombe said.

'An' that was the *only* reason you helped him?'

Bascombe turned to his solicitor. 'Can they get me for somethin' I *didn't* do – somethin' I only *planned* to do?' he asked.

'Not if you took no actual steps to put the act into commission,' the solicitor said.

'Say what?'

'Not if you did no more than think about it.'

Bascombe nodded. 'The other reason I helped Harry out was cuz Harry had promised he was gonna help me right back,' he said.

'Help you with what?' Grant wondered.

'Harry wasn't the only one who'd been showed up in front of them two niggers,' Bascombe said.

'Who else was?' Grant asked.

Bascombe ignored him, and turned to Woodend, instead. 'Remember it?' he asked.

'I'll never forget it,' Woodend told him. 'When my fist hit your gut, it felt like I was punching an overstuffed bag of sand.'

'Yeah, I was a real hard man back in them days,' Bascombe agreed complacently.

'But when you went down, you went down like the bag of *shit* that you really were,' Woodend added.

'I wish I'd got you, like I wanted to,' Bascombe said angrily. 'I wish I'd stuck you like Harry stuck Kineally.'

'But I'd been transferred by then, hadn't I?' Woodend said.

'Yeah, you had, you Limey bastard,' Bascombe agreed, 'an' I was *real* sorry about that.'

Woodend sat in the 'operational command module', smoking a cigarette and watching Special Agent Grant transfer files from the table to boxes labelled, 'FBI documents in transit'.

'So what happens now?' he asked. 'Will you give Douglas Coutes a clean bill of health, and release him?'

'The Minister was never *officially* under arrest,' Grant said, closing one full box, and then immediately opening an empty one. 'Even so, I think that to state unequivocally that he's been completely exonerated on all charges would be a tad premature.'

But from the speed with which he was packing away his files, it was plain that he didn't consider it *that much* premature, Woodend thought.

'You'll start looking for Harry Wallace now, will you?' the Chief Inspector asked.

'We're *already* looking for him. There are agents all over the States following up leads, even as we speak.'

'An' d'you think you'll find him?'

Grant nodded. 'I don't want to sound in any way disrespectful to you or any of the rest of the wonderful British bobbies, Chuck,' he said, 'but I don't think you have any real concept of just how *effective* the Bureau can be once it's got its teeth into a case.'

'Robert Kineally called me "Chuck",' Woodend told him.

'Is that right?'

'Which means I'd rather you didn't.'

Grant looked troubled. 'You've never really liked me, have you, *Charlie*?' he asked.

A wave of guilt swept over Woodend. Though he could not put his finger on *why* it had happened, he had begun to experience a feeling of vague discontent from the moment Bascombe had made his confession. And rather than starting to abate, as he'd expected it to, the feeling had got worse – like a sting which only really begins to itch some time after it's been inflicted. But even so, that was no excuse for being deliberately unpleasant to Grant.

'I'm sorry, Ed,' he said. 'I don't think it's that I dislike you so much as that I don't *understand* you. We're two very different kinds of policemen. You see the big picture – the Communist menace, and the spread of organized crime – while I just look at a dead body and wonder who-dun-it. But I think there's room in the world for both kinds.'

Special Agent Grant smiled gratefully. 'That's what I think, too,' he said. 'It's what I've always thought. But it's still a great pleasure to hear those words coming from you.'

'What happens if you *can't* find Wallace?' Woodend asked.

'We'll find him.'

'But what if he's dead?'

'That would be a pity,' Grant conceded. 'The Senator would dearly love to see his brother's murderer stand trial for his terrible crime. But the really important thing is that we've solved the case.'

'So you do believe Bascombe?'

'That depends exactly what you mean by your question. Do I believe that he had no part in the actual murder? I'm not sure about that. But even if we hadn't granted him immunity, we'd never have been able to put together a case against him. As for the rest of what he told us, I'm pretty confident it happened in just the way he described it.'

'Bascombe had a great deal to gain by lying,' Woodend pointed out, playing devil's advocate. 'Less than two hours ago, he still had a couple of years of a prison sentence left to serve. Now, he's going to walk away from Haverton Camp a free man.'

'Sure, he had a lot to gain from the situation,' Grant conceded. 'But the only way he was ever going to gain it was by telling us the *truth*. And that's just what he did, didn't he?'

'Maybe,' Woodend said, reluctantly.

'Look, most people thought that Kineally had simply

disappeared, but Bascombe knew that he'd been murdered. He also knew which particular knife had been used to do the killing. And to top it all, he knew exactly where Kineally's body was buried.'

'Maybe somebody else fed him some of those details,' Woodend said, still doubtful.

'Who?' Grant asked.

'I don't know.'

'When he arrived here, he was a convict with time yet to serve, so he's been housed here under what were essentially prison conditions. He's been under guard even when he took his exercise.'

'So maybe those guards told him—'

'There wasn't much they *could* tell him. They're not directly involved in the investigation, so they know as little about what's been going on here as the electricians or the guys who work in the commissary.'

'Which is the same as saying that they knew nothing at all?' Woodend asked.

'Which is the same as saying that they knew nothing at all,' Grant agreed. 'Face the facts, Charlie. Bascombe might have made a lucky guess about one particular detail of the crime, but he couldn't possibly have guessed it all. He had to have been there. He had to have seen it all with his own eyes.'

'That's true enough,' Woodend agreed reluctantly.

But his feeling of discontent – the irritating itch – still refused to go away.

Twenty-Six

Woodend and Paniatowski were the first customers of the day to cross the threshold of the Dun Cow, but this would not normally have bothered the Chief Inspector. He didn't need other drinkers around him to help him to relax. It was enough for him to be inside a pub – the welcome refuge of the true-born Englishmen over the centuries, in which the very walls oozed a feeling of benign well-being. Yet that morning, the Dun Cow's public bar was failing to have its usual healing effect on him, and the pint of best bitter, within easy reach of his right hand, was refusing to work its usual magic.

Woodend gazed moodily out of the window at the wall, beyond which lay the skittle alley where Harry Wallace and Huey Bascombe had once intended to teach two black soldiers a lesson they'd never forget, and Captain Douglas Coutes had beaten the living daylights out of Captain Robert Kineally.

'It makes perfect sense that Harry Wallace should be the killer, you know,' Monika Paniatowski said. 'He was a racist – and a violent one, at that.'

'Hmm,' Woodend said.

'For a man like him, being humiliated in front of those two black men must have been like his worst nightmare come true,' Paniatowski argued. 'Being made to *apologize* to them was a depth he'd never thought he would sink to. Is it any wonder, then, that he couldn't rest until he got his revenge?'

'No wonder at all,' Woodend said – but with a lack of conviction in his voice which belied his actual words.

'So, given everything I've just laid out for you – all of which you seem to agree with – just what *is* your problem, sir?' Paniatowski asked, impatiently.

'My problem?' Woodend replied. 'My problem is that it's all too neat an' tidy.'

182

'Ed Grant used almost exactly the same words,' Paniatowski said. 'Only he wasn't referring to the case against Wallace, he was talking about the one against Coutes.'

Woodend's eyes flickered with a sudden interest. 'An' when did Grant say this?'

'Last night,' Paniatowski said vaguely.

'That doesn't sound at all like the Special Agent I know,' Woodend mused. 'Right from the start of this investigation, he was absolutely convinced Coutes was our man. Of course, he's changed his mind about that now. He didn't have much choice in the face of the fresh evidence that's turned up, did he?'

'No, I suppose he didn't.'

'But until this mornin', there *was* no fresh evidence. An' yet you're tellin' he said this *last night*?'

'That's right,' Paniatowski said, starting to wish she'd never begun this conversation. 'Shall I order us some more drinks?'

'We've hardly touched the ones we've got,' Woodend replied. 'Now, what would make a man who was so sure he was right about every single aspect of the case suddenly back down like you say he did last night?'

'Doesn't really matter, does it, sir?' Paniatowski asked. 'The case is officially closed.'

'Didn't he realize that, by backing down in that way, he was makin' himself look a complete bloody fool?' Woodend said, refusing to let go.

Paniatowski sighed, and gave in to the inevitable.

'Perhaps he said it without really believing it,' she suggested. 'Perhaps he was just teasing me.'

'*Teasing* you?' Woodend repeated. 'Teasing *you*?'

'Yes.'

'How could sayin' somethin' like that have been seen as *teasin'* you?'

There really was no way out of it, Paniatowski thought.

'I'd told him that, as a result of our investigations, we were coming round to the view that Coutes was guilty,' she said. 'And then Ed . . . then Special Agent Grant . . . said that because the evidence was so neat and tidy, he was starting to think that Coutes had been framed.'

'An' that was teasin' you?' Woodend said, as if he still hadn't grasped the point.

'He was showing off,' Paniatowski said, exasperatedly. 'Asserting himself by taking a contrary opinion to mine. It's what a certain kind of man will do when he finds himself in a certain kind of situation.'

'Where, exactly, did this conversation take place?' Woodend asked.

'In bed!' Paniatowski said angrily. 'All right? We were in bed! Do you have any objections to that?'

'No objections at all,' Woodend told her, though he was shaking his head sadly. 'It's none of my business what you do in your free time. But, I have to say, Monika, you really can pick 'em, can't you?'

'Yes, I suppose I can,' Paniatowski agreed wistfully. 'But that still doesn't mean that I appreciate you sitting in judgement on the quality of the men I choose to sleep with,' she continued, her anger returning. 'If I make mistakes, then at least they're *my* mistakes, as an adult, I'm entitled . . .'

She stopped, not because she had run out of either steam or righteous indignation, but because there wasn't any point in going on when it was plain that Woodend was no longer listening to her.

'Grant didn't look all that shocked when Huey Bascombe confessed,' Woodend muttered, almost to himself. 'He saw his own rock-solid certainties collapse around him, and it didn't bother him at all – or at least, nowhere near as much as it should have done.'

'I *am* still here,' Paniatowski said, annoyed. 'And I am *still* trying to make a point.'

'Finish up your drink, Monika,' Woodend said. 'We need to get back to the camp.'

If Special Agent Grant had still been occupying the 'operational command module', Woodend would have invented some pretext to take him somewhere else, and left Monika Paniatowski to do the search. But Grant wasn't there. Having packed away most of the files in their FBI transit boxes, he had probably returned to his own trailer to do something equally neat and efficient there, and the two English detectives had the place to themselves.

Woodend opened the first of the boxes with great care. 'We don't want Grant to know we've been rooting around in here,' he explained. 'At least, we don't want him to know quite *yet*.'

'Would you mind telling me what you're looking for, sir?' Paniatowski asked, for the fourth or fifth time.

'I'm lookin' for photographs!' Woodend replied. 'Eight by ten glossy photographs! Of the corpse!'

'Well, that is nice for you,' Paniatowski said sarcastically. 'And is it your intention, sir, at some point in the distant future, to tell me *why* you're looking for them?'

'If I'm right about them, that should be very obvious to you,' Woodend said, opening a third box. 'An' if I'm wrong, then we might as well just pack our bags an' go home.'

'Which is what I thought we were planning to do anyway,' Paniatowski commented.

Woodend opened a fourth box, looked inside, and let out a low whoop of triumph.

'If I'd have been in Special Agent Grant's shoes – which is to say, workin' from Special Agent Grant's *brief* – I wouldn't have left these pictures around for just anybody to see them,' he said.

'You wouldn't have?'

'I most definitely would not.' Woodend spread out the photographs on the table top. 'Of course, to be fair to the man, he can't really have been expected to see the need to get rid of them. An' why is that?'

Monika Paniatowski sighed. 'I don't know, sir,' she said, resignedly. 'Why *is* it?'

'Because he wasn't privy to my little chat with Abe Birnbaum last night. So he doesn't know everythin' that I know. None of them do.'

'None of *who* do?'

'Just as I thought!' Woodend said, ignoring the question and devoting his whole attention to examining the photographs. 'Just as I remember them!'

The excitement in his voice was so evident – and so intense – that Paniatowski began to wonder if perhaps the strain of an investigation in which he'd been so personally involved hadn't been too much for him.

'Take a look at these four shots in particular, Monika,' Woodend urged. 'Take a *close* look, and tell me exactly what you see.'

185

Paniatowski did as she'd been instructed. 'I see the recon-structed torso,' she said.

'Look again!'

She did. But the rib cage had not suddenly rearranged itself to give her a vital clue, and what she was looking at was still just bones.

'I don't know what you're expecting me to say,' she confessed.

'An' you call yourself a detective sergeant,' Woodend said, with a good-natured exasperation which had been sadly missing since the start of this case. 'Do you notice anythin' special about this torso, Monika?'

'No. I'm sorry, sir, but I can't say that I do.'

'Well, exactly!' Woodend said. 'There *is* nothin' special about it. *Now* do you see what I'm on about?'

The perplexed expression slowly left Paniatowski's face, and a look of excitement – almost equal to Woodend's own – replaced it.

'Yes!' she said. 'Now I *do* see!'

Twenty-Seven

The nearest public telephone phone box to Haverton Camp was on the edge of Haverton Village, and as luck would have it, it was neither occupied nor had it been vandalized.

'You really think that the telephone lines back at the camp might be tapped?' Paniatowski asked Woodend, as they climbed out of the Wolseley.

'I'm almost *certain* they're bloody tapped,' Woodend told her. 'Grant will have wanted to know the way our minds were workin' at every stage of the investigation, an' a tap on both our phones was one of the ways he could have found out.'

And another way was to come to my caravan in the middle of the night, and climb into bed with me, Paniatowski thought bitterly.

'He won't have learned much which will have caused him serious concern,' Woodend continued. 'He'll know Bob Rutter went to Coutes's flat, but he'll probably assume that was a waste of effort – which is what *I* thought it was, until all the other pieces of the puzzle started to fit together.'

'The whole thing still sounds just incredible to me,' Monika Paniatowski confessed.

'Aye, to me an' all, if I'm honest,' Woodend admitted, 'but as Sherlock Holmes once said, when you've eliminated the impossible, then whatever remains – however improbable – must be the truth.'

He reached into the voluminous pocket of his hairy sports coat, and brought out a handful of loose coins which, if he'd been at home, Joan would long ago have removed for the sake of the coat's shape.

'You make the first call,' he told Paniatowski. 'An' do all you can to be persuasive.'

'Would you like me to tell him I'm making the phone call stark naked?' Paniatowski asked tartly.

'Aye – if it'll help,' Woodend replied. 'In fact, if you think a bit of method actin' will make your performance any more convincin', you could strip off before you even begin to dial the number.'

Paniatowski gave him a look which would have frozen most men in their tracks, but she was not in the least surprised when Woodend didn't even seem to notice.

When he was like this, she thought – when he had the scent of the chase in his nostrils – the rest of the world did not really exist for him.

She stepped into the booth, dialled Dunethorpe CID, and asked to be connected to Detective Chief Inspector Baxter.

'Monika!' Baxter exclaimed, when he came on to the line. 'Where are you? I've been ringing and ringing, but nobody at your headquarters seems to know how to get in touch with you. And, apparently, *you* felt absolutely no desire at all to get in touch with *me*.'

He sounded hurt, Paniatowski thought. But how much more wounded would he have been if he'd known about what had gone on between her and Special Agent Grant?

It would be his own fault if he *did* get hurt, she told herself. He'd been the one who'd pursued her, not the other way around. And she made no promises to him – given no commitments. So he simply didn't have the right to think he had any sort of hold over her.

'Monika?' Baxter said, worriedly.

'I've been working on a case down south,' she said.

'*Where* down south?'

'I'm sorry, but I can't tell you that. It's all very hush-hush, you see. But I should be back in Whitebridge in a couple of days, three days at the most, and – if you like – we can get together then.'

'You sound like you're doing no more than throwing me a bone,' Baxter told her.

Yes, I do, don't I? Paniatowski thought.

'I didn't mean it to come out like that at all,' she said. 'I'm really looking forward to seeing you. But before I can come home, I need to get shut of this bloody awful case. And that's precisely why I ringing you now – because I need a favour from you to *help me* close it.'

'I see,' Baxter said.

'You don't sound very enthusiastic about the idea of helping me,' Paniatowski said.

'Of course I'm enthusiastic,' Baxter replied, without much conviction. 'Why wouldn't I be?

'You just didn't seem—'

'I'm absolutely over the moon about it! I feel as if all my birthdays have come at once!'

'There's no need to overdo it,' Paniatowski said.

'Just tell me what the favour is,' Baxter told her.

'It's nothing, really. Remember you told me that you'd done some training with the FBI in Washington?'

'Of course I remember.'

'And did you get on well with the people you met over there?'

'Yes, as matter of fact, I did.'

'Well enough to persuade one of them to do you a similar kind of favour to the one you'll be doing for me?'

'Probably,' Baxter said. 'Of course, I've not actually slept with any of *them*, but I suppose it is just conceivable that they'll do it because they like me just for myself.'

Woodend paced up and down outside the phone box, puffing furiously on a Capstan Full Strength.

He should have thought of all this earlier, he fretted. He should have made the mental connections the night before, while he was talking to Abe Birnbaum. Now, with the Americans already starting to prepare for their return to the States, he might come up with the answer too late.

Which wouldn't be a bad thing, Charlie, a nagging voice in the back of his head said.

Wouldn't it? he wondered.

No, the voice said. Because even if you *find* the answer, you've still no idea what you're going to do with it.

Monika Paniatowski stepped out of the phone booth, and Woodend took her place.

'Sometimes, the things you get me to do make me feel like a real bitch,' Monika said, over her shoulder – and with a hint of bitterness. 'But perhaps I shouldn't blame you for that. Perhaps being a real bitch is just what comes naturally to me.'

We'll sort it out later, Monika, Woodend thought. Whatever your problem is, I promise you we'll sort it out later.

189

He picked up the phone and dialled a London number.

'I thought I might be hearing from you, sir, but I never expected it would be so soon,' Bob Rutter said.

'Aye, well, neither did I, but events have been movin' at the speed of an express train down here,' Woodend told him. 'Have you ever heard of a firm called New Elizabethan Properties?'

'They're a construction company, aren't they?' Rutter asked. 'I've seen their signs on some office blocks and public buildings in the centre of London, but I think they mainly concentrate on building houses for the moderately prosperous. What made you ask about them?'

'Their head office is somewhere in London, isn't it?'

'Yes, I believe it is.'

'Well, I'd like you to pay it a visit.'

Twenty-Eight

The man in the pinstriped suit had reached that stage in his life when he was about to shed the mantle of youth, yet was not quite ready to assume the cloak of middle age. He had introduced himself to Bob Rutter as the senior project manager for New Elizabethan Properties, and then – almost as an afterthought – had added that his name was Brian Bosworth. He had shaken Rutter's hand with practised firmness and invited him to sit down. That had all been five minutes ago, and since then he had not stopped talking.

'Quality, that's the key,' Bosworth was saying. 'New Elizabethan is committed to bringing *quality* housing to all parts of the country. The old Haverton Camp is just *one* of our many exciting new projects which are aimed at making London-style sophistication available to everyone.'

He was nervous, Bob Rutter thought. The man was definitely *very* nervous.

'I was asking about your surveyor,' he prompted.

'I beg your pardon?' Bosworth said.

'You used three surveyors on the Haverton Camp job – but only one of them was actually from this office. When I phoned, I told you he was the one who I wanted to talk about.'

'You're quite right about where the surveyors came from,' Bosworth gabbled. 'We like to use local people whenever we can, you see. Gives them a sense of participating in the project. Makes them aware that we really do care about their interests and desires.' He paused, and grinned weakly. 'Got rather carried away there, didn't I? Sort of missionary zeal, I suppose.'

'Yes, I suppose it is,' Rutter agreed sourly. 'And as long as you're talking about the company in general terms, you don't need to talk about the surveyor in particular, do you?'

'I hope you don't think that I—'

'What's his name?' Rutter snapped.

191

'Nicholas Bosworth.'

'Really? That's the same surname as yours. Is it a coincidence? Or is he, perhaps, a relation of yours?'

'He's my younger brother.'

'And where will I find your younger brother?'

'I'd rather he wasn't disturbed.'

'I'll bet you'd rather he wasn't. But you see, what you want or don't want is of no particular interest to me. You've already wasted nearly half an hour of valuable police time – and that's a prosecutable offence. So why not tell me where I can find him, and save yourself any future trouble?'

'He'll probably be at his flat,' Bosworth said, defeatedly.

'At his flat? At this time of the day? What's the reason for that? Is he on holiday or something?'

'Not exactly.'

'Then why?'

'He's . . . er . . . on sick leave.'

'Is he now? And what's his problem? Has he broken his leg? Or has he been struck down with the bubonic plague?'

'His problems are more of a psychological nature. It came as quite a shock to him, discovering a body at Haverton Camp like that. It was such a pity. He'd been doing so well before then, and it set him right back.'

It was clear from the expression on Brian Bosworth's face that the moment he'd uttered that last sentence of his, he bitterly regretted it. But it was already too late.

'Set him back to *what*?' Rutter demanded.

'Nick's . . . er . . . had a few problems?'

'What kind of problems?'

'I'd prefer not to—'

'Women? Drink? Drugs?'

'No, nothing as extreme as that. He likes to have the odd flutter on the horses.'

'What you're trying to say is that he's a compulsive gambler.'

'*Was* a compulsive gambler. He hasn't placed a bet for months,' Brian Bosworth said, unconvincingly.

'How did he happen to be given the surveying job at Haverton Camp?' Rutter wondered.

'He . . . er . . . asked for it.'

'Did he now? Isn't that interesting!'

'But there's a perfectly reasonable explanation for his asking to be sent there.'

'Then I'd certainly like to hear it.'

'The company gives quite a generous allowance to staff whose work takes them outside London, and if you live frugally while you're away, you can save most of it. Nick built up quite a lot of debts when he was gambling, and this was one way of helping to pay them off.'

'As convincing fairy tales go, I rate that somewhere between Snow White and the Seven Dwarfs and the Three Little Pigs,' Rutter said. 'He's told you all about it, hasn't he?'

'All about what?'

'*Hasn't he?*'

Brian Bosworth nodded his head mournfully. 'He had to tell someone,' he said. 'He just *had* to. And who else would he choose to confide in but his big brother?'

'*When* did he tell you? Was it before he went to the camp? Or did he leave it until after he came back?'

'It was after he came back. If he'd told me what he was planning to do before he left, I'd never have let him go.'

'I'd like his address,' Rutter said.

'I don't think—'

'If you don't give it to me, somebody else will.'

'You're right,' Bosworth said defeatedly, writing out the address on a slip of paper. 'You won't be too rough on him, will you?'

'That's up to him,' Rutter said. 'And here's a word of warning. If you ring and let him know him that I'm on the way – and if, because of that, he does a runner before I arrive – I'll have the local bobbies swarming all over this building within the hour. And your bosses wouldn't like that, would they?'

'No,' Bosworth agreed gloomily. 'I'm sure they wouldn't.'

The Rt. Hon. Douglas Coutes was looking across the table at Jack Braithwaite, his chief political aide. They were in the trailer which, for the previous few days, had officially been listed as Coutes's 'accommodation', though, in reality, it had been no more than a luxury, unbarred, prison cell.

It was fascinating to observe how rapidly situations could change, the Minister thought. Only a few hours earlier, there had been a couple of grim-faced American military policemen standing guard outside this trailer, but now there was no sign of them at all. Less than *one* hour previously, the whole 'trailer city' had been intact, but now it was being broken up, as several of the trailers were loaded on to big trucks on the first stage of their journey back to the USA.

But the changes in Coutes's own standing were even more interesting. The Prime Minister, previously too busy to talk to him, had sent a message which said that, after his ordeal, he must go down to Chequers for a weekend's relaxation. Cabinet colleagues, who had been impossible to contact for several days, had begun to ring him up to offer their congratulations. And Jack Braithwaite, conveniently confined to his bed for the last seventy-two hours with a virulent case of flu, had made a sudden dramatic recovery, and driven straight down to the camp.

'Will you travel back to London with me, Minister?' Braithwaite asked. 'Or should I have a car and driver sent down to pick you up?'

'Neither,' Coutes told him. 'I'll drive myself back. I'll probably do it overnight. I like driving in the dark.'

'Are you sure, Minister?' Braithwaite said, apparently almost overcome with concern for his beloved master.

'Why wouldn't I be sure?' Coutes asked.

'Well, you've been under considerable stress.'

'I'm *always* under stress. Stress is built into my job. And I positively thrive on it.'

'That's true. But you've never been under this *particular* kind of stress before. There seemed, it has to be said, to be a great deal of damning evidence against you, and—'

'Tell me, Braithwaite, did you think I'd actually be charged with the murder?' Coutes interrupted.

The other man flushed. 'Of course not, Minister.'

'The truth, Braithwaite,' Coutes said sternly. 'I want the truth.'

The aide's flush deepened. 'I'm afraid I thought it was almost inevitable, Minister.'

'And so you, as one of my most loyal civil servants – perhaps even the *most* loyal – were greatly stressed at the thought of losing your master?'

'Naturally, Minister.'

194

'I, on the other hand, knowing myself to be completely innocent, had no such worries. I was sure I would be vindicated – as indeed, I was.' Coutes paused. 'Do you think we might talk about the tasks ahead of us, now?'

'Of course, Minister.'

'I want you to arrange for the talks on the American military bases to resume the day after tomorrow. Let the General know – informally – that I am open to further compromise.'

'But . . . but . . .' Braithwaite spluttered, astonished.

'But what?'

'But by falsely accusing you of murder, they have so weakened their own position that—'

'That *they* should be the ones to back down?'

'Well, yes.'

Coutes laughed. 'How little you know about power, Braithwaite,' he said. 'The very worst time to make people back down is when they are already feeling weak. They will never forgive you for it. On the other hand, if *you* are in the strong position, and *you* choose to back down, they will be eternally grateful. We will give the Americans *a little* of what they want in this particular negotiation, and they will give us a *great deal* of what we want in future conflicts of interest.'

'But your Cabinet colleagues will never—'

'Sanction such an agreement?'

'Yes.'

'My Cabinet colleagues are experiencing an emotion hitherto almost entirely unknown to them. Can you guess what it is?'

'No, I—'

'Guilt! They abandoned me, and they are feeling *guilty* about it. In a month or so, they will have persuaded themselves that they behaved entirely properly in the circumstances, but at the moment they will give me anything I want.' Coutes paused. 'I know what you're thinking, Braithwaite.'

'Do you, Minister?'

'I believe so. Now I have explained my own thought process to you, you are thinking that it's little wonder that I am a minister of the crown, while you are a mere aide.'

And, indeed, Braithwaite had been thinking *exactly* that.

* * *

Nicholas Bosworth looked like a weaker, more watered-down, version of his older brother. He hadn't seemed exactly happy when he answered the door, but once Rutter had identified himself, the unhappiness had rapidly transformed itself into a look of pure panic.

'You're . . . you're a policeman,' he gasped.

Rutter made a show of examining his own warrant card. 'Yes, that's what it appears to say here,' he agreed.

'Who . . . who told you where I live?'

'Your brother, as a matter of fact. But that doesn't really matter, does it? The only important thing, as far as you're concerned, is that I'm here now – and I want to talk to you.'

'W . . . well, I don't want to talk to *you*,' Bosworth said, with a sudden show of defiance.

'Please yourself,' Rutter replied, turning to go. 'After all, it's your funeral, not mine.'

'My *f . . . funeral*? What do you mean?'

'Sooner or later, you'll have to talk to somebody about what you did at Haverton Camp,' Rutter told him. 'And my main worry is that the next person they send might not be anything like as friendly and understanding as I am. I'm told that Special Branch, for example, can be really quite rough.'

'Why would Special Branch want to talk to me? I haven't done anything,' Bosworth whined.

Rutter put his hand on the other man's shoulder, and looked him in the eye. 'I believe you,' he said.

'You do?' Bosworth asked, hardly able to believe his own luck.

'Or rather, I believe that you didn't know just *how* serious the thing you got yourself involved in was,' Rutter said, tightening his grip on Bosworth's shoulder ever so slightly.

'I didn't know,' Bosworth moaned. 'I swear on my mother's grave that I didn't.'

'Then why don't we go inside, where you can tell me all about how you were duped?' Rutter suggested. 'That sounds like a good idea, doesn't it?'

Bosworth nodded his head weakly in agreement.

Twenty-Nine

As Monika Paniatowski picked up the phone in the box at the edge of Haverton Village and dialled the number of Dunethorpe CID, she noticed that her pulse was racing.

It's the excitement that's making it do that, she told herself – the excitement and the tension.

But there was a part of her which suspected that it probably had much more to do with shame.

'I've done what you asked me to,' DCI Baxter said, from the other end of the line.

'Good, I'm very—'

'But before I tell you what I've found out, I want to make it quite clear that there are no strings attached to my giving you the information.'

'Strings?'

'If you still want to see me when I've given it to you, that's fine. And if you don't – well, I'll get over it.'

'I *do* want to see you,' Paniatowski said.

And she meant it. Baxter might not be the handsomest man or most exciting lover in the world, but he was kind and gentle – and he would never have used her as Special Agent Grant had tried to.

'Are you sure that when you gave me the name of the man you'd wanted me to ask about, you got it exactly right?' Baxter asked.

'Yes.'

'It wasn't "Brant" or "Grantham", or anything like that?'

'It was Grant.'

'And his first name is definitely "Edward"?'

'Yes. Why are you asking me these questions? Are you about to tell me that there *isn't* anybody working for the Federal Bureau of Investigation called Edward Grant?'

'No, I'm not,' Baxter assured her. 'There certainly *is* an Edward Grant on the FBI payroll.'

'Well, then?'

'It's just I'm surprised, given what *you* do for a living and what *he* does for a living, that your paths have ever crossed.'

Nicholas Bosworth's living room was a shrine to apathy and neglect. The sofa and easy chairs were shabby, the table dust-covered, the windows streaked with dirt. The only item on which any care had been lavished was the large television that the rest of the room seemed to be centred around – and even that was probably only ever switched on for the horse racing.

'Tell me how it all started,' Rutter suggested.

'I'm not sure I know where to—'

'Begin with whoever it was who first put the idea into your head. You do know who that was, don't you?'

Nicholas Bosworth nodded miserably. 'It was a girl,' he said. 'A very *pretty* girl.'

Well, isn't that amazing? Rutter thought wryly. Whoever would have thought that a girl – and a pretty one at that – would have been involved?

He had no idea he was being followed when he came out of the betting shop, Nicholas Bosworth said, but looking back on it, he supposed that he must have been.

He went straight to the nearest pub. He wasn't much of a drinker under normal circumstances, but after the implications of the loss he'd just suffered had sunk in – after he'd really begun to appreciate that he'd dug himself into an even deeper hole than he'd been in already – he needed a shot of whisky to give him the courage to keep on going.

He knew he wasn't looking anything like his best – and that even at his best, he wasn't exactly great – so he'd been more than surprised when the attractive young woman sitting at the bar had given him a broad, inviting smile. And his surprise had only increased when she'd climbed down off her stool, come over to his table and asked if she could join him.

'You look a bit down in the mouth,' she said. 'Why don't you tell me what's bothering you?'

He hadn't needed a second invitation. He poured out his woes in a great torrent. And she just sat there, giving him all

198

her attention and occasionally nodding her head sympathet-
ically.

'Do you know what you need?' she asked, when even he
had finally grown tired of hearing himself rail against his
place in the universe in general, and his place in the book-
makers' account books in particular.

'No,' he said. 'What do *I need?'*

'You need to make yourself one big killing. You need to hit
the jackpot just once, so you can tell yourself you're walking
away a winner.'

'But how would I do that?' he wondered.

'There's lots of ways, if you just stop and think about it.
But the one that comes to mind at the moment is that you
could find something valuable – something that everyone else
is looking for.'

'Like what?'

'Oh, it could anything. An infallible betting system—'

'I've been trying to find one of those for years.'

'—a cure for cancer, a way to make cars run on something
much less expensive than petrol—'

'You have to be very clever to come up with something like
that. And the problem is, I'm not.'

The girl smiled. 'I suppose I was getting a bit carried away
there,' she admitted. 'Let's think about something more ordi-
nary – something much more down to earth. A big jewellery
robbery, for example.'

'What!'

'The insurance companies hate paying out the full amount,
so they usually offer a ten per cent finder's fee – no questions
asked. And in the case of really big jewellery thefts, even ten
percent can be a lot *of money.'*

'Go on,' he said, intrigued.

'Say this particular gang of robbers we're talking about
had buried their stash somewhere. Say that one of the robbers
had a girlfriend who was tired of the relationship and wanted
to leave him – but wasn't prepared to go away empty-handed.
And say that she knew where the jewels were buried. What
do you think she should do?'

'I suppose she could dig the jewels up herself – or else tell
the insurance company where they were buried,' Nicholas
Bosworth suggested.

The girl laughed. 'Not if she wanted to go on living, she couldn't. These are very bad people we're talking about here. Very violent people. If there was to be even the slightest suspicion she'd double-crossed them, they'd kill her without thinking twice.'

Nicholas Bosworth shuddered. 'Yes, I suppose they might,' he said.

'There's no might *about it,' the girl assured him. 'But say the jewels were discovered in a way which looked totally random and accidental. The robbers wouldn't suspect the girl, would they? And she would be free to split the reward with her new accomplice. So all she would need, to make things work out beautifully, is to meet a man who had an excuse for digging things up.'*

'And you actually *fell* for that?' Rutter asked incredulously.

'Yes.'

'You actually *believed* she was a gangster's moll?'

'I'd never met one before, so how would I know what they look like? And it wasn't as crude as I know I'm making it sound. She didn't rush things, like I have when I've been telling you about it. And she smiled a lot.'

'She smiled a lot. So she *must* have been genuine!'

'You had to be there,' Beresford said sadly.

'Well, I wasn't. What happened next?

'She said she'd been thinking about how to get her hands on the reward for a long time, and when she noticed the New Elizabethan Properties sign go up close to where they'd buried the loot, she saw it as the answer to her prayers. It all seemed so plausible.'

Yes, Rutter thought, to a man who – against all the evidence – believed he could make a fortune by backing horses, most get-rich-quick schemes probably *would* seem plausible.

'What instructions did she give you?' he asked.

'She told me exactly where we should dig. All I had to do was to persuade the other surveyors to go along with it. I was expecting to find a box, but what I found was a b . . . body.'

'A skeleton, anyway,' Rutter said, unsympathetically. 'Did the girl speak to you again, after you'd done what she *really* wanted?'

'No.'

'But somebody else did?'

'A man phoned me. He said that I could go to prison for a very long time for what I'd done. He said my best plan was to keep quiet about it. But that didn't work, did it? You're here, and I'm doomed. How long will I get?'

It was on the tip of Bob Rutter's tongue to tell him he'd probably get no more and no less than he deserved. And then he found himself asking exactly what he *did* deserve.

Bosworth was a weak man – there was no doubt about that – but he wasn't necessarily a very *bad* man.

He had thought that the only people he would be stealing from were criminals.

And he wasn't the first person in the entire world to do something which was both wrong and stupid, because there was a pretty young woman involved, now was he?

To be honest, he wasn't even the only person in that *room*!

'I promise I'll do my best to keep your name out of the whole affair,' Rutter heard himself say.

'You . . . you will?' Bosworth asked, incredulously.

'But in return, you've got to promise me to try and beat this gambling addiction of yours.'

'I will! I have been—'

'Because if you don't, it'll ruin your life even more than it has already,' Rutter concluded.

And as he was saying the words, it occurred to him that though they came out of his mouth, they could just as easily have been spoken by Charlie Woodend.

The bright red ex-Post Office van was standing on the forecourt of the village garage, with a 'for sale' sign slashed across its window.

If it had been a horse, it would probably have been taken to the knackers' yard by now, Monika Paniatowski thought, but Charlie Woodend had said it was probably the best thing available, and she supposed herself that beggars couldn't be choosers.

Not when they were stuck out in the arse-end of nowhere.

Not when they were working desperately against the clock.

There was no one in evidence around the petrol pumps, but she heard a banging sound from the back of the garage, and when she went there to investigate, she found herself in the repair shop.

A pair of legs, clad in greasy blue overalls, were projecting from underneath a dilapidated Ford Prefect.

'Excuse me!' Paniatowski said loudly.

The man slid out from under the old banger, giving her lower half a thorough inspection as he did so.

He was about her age, she guessed, but his hair was thinning and his weak chin suggested he had already experienced more than his fair share of life's disappointments.

'Can I help you?' he asked, completing his inspection of her by running his eyes up and down her torso.

'I saw that old van outside,' Paniatowski said. 'Are you the one who's selling it?'

'I am,' the mechanic agreed.

'And have you had any offers for it yet?'

'No,' the mechanic admitted, 'not yet.'

'I wonder why that could be?' Paniatowski asked innocently.

'Don't be fooled by the appearance of the old girl,' the mechanic said. 'She might look a bit clapped out—'

'She does!'

'—but she's got a fine little engine in her, and she goes like a bomb. Why are you asking, anyway? Are you interested in buying her?'

'I may be,' Paniatowski said. 'But only if you can give it a complete re-spray for me.'

The mechanic grinned. 'That's no problem at all. I'm very good with my spraying. People bring their cars from miles away to have them sprayed by me.'

'I'm sure you're the Leonardo da Vinci of the paint spray-gun,' Paniatowski said.

'Pardon?'

'But it's speed, not beauty, that I'm interested in. I'll want it done by six o'clock tonight.

'Now that *is* a problem,' the mechanic admitted. 'I've got a lot of work on at the moment, you see.'

'It has to be by six o'clock,' Paniatowski said firmly. 'It's no good to me if it isn't done by then.'

'Well . . .'

Hating herself for doing it, Paniatowski put her hands on her hips and favoured him with her sexiest smile.

'I know it's a big job,' she said, 'but then you're a big man and I'm sure you can handle it.'

The mechanic, who – in point of fact – wasn't that big at all, melted almost immediately.

'Like I told you, it'll mean putting other jobs off,' he'd said, 'but if you say it's important—'

'It's *very* important!'

'—then I can probably just about do it in time.'

'Wonderful,' Paniatowski said, giving him another flash of that sensual promise which would never be his to enjoy.

'What colour would you like it?' the mechanic asked. 'Red, like it is now? Or would you prefer a nice electric blue?'

'Neither of those,' Paniatowski told him. 'I'd like it to be South Western Electricity Board yellow.'

'That's not a very attractive colour, you know,' the mechanic said doubtfully.

'Perhaps you're right about that—'

'I've got charts I could show you—'

'—but it's the colour I want.'

'Thing is, you'll probably be having people mistaking you *for* the electricity board,' the mechanic pointed out.

'Perfect!'

'Perfect?'

'That's what I said, and that's what I meant. And just to complete the illusion, I'd appreciate it if you'd paint the electricity company's name on the sides of the van.'

Thirty

Darkness had already fallen over Haverton Camp, but under the glare of several powerful searchlights, the work of completely dismantling 'Hoover City' continued unabated.

There was an almost unseemly haste about it, Woodend thought, as he made his way towards the trailer of the man whose name he could no longer pronounce without putting mental inverted commas around it.

By the following afternoon – at the very latest – everything belonging to the Americans would be gone. The trailers and their generators, the jeeps and the trucks, would all be on their way back to the United States, and the only evidence they had ever been at Haverton Camp would be a few indentations in the ground, and the odd piece of rubbish which the clean-up team had somehow missed. And then, within another day or two more, the bulldozers from New Elizabethan Properties would arrive and plough up the earth with callous indifference to whatever life it had had before.

Case closed! Crime scene gone!

Woodend knocked on the trailer door, and Grant opened it.

'Oh, hi!' the Special Agent said, without much warmth. 'What can I do for you, Chief Inspector?'

'Charlie,' Woodend corrected him. 'Or you can even call me "Chuck", if you're happier with that.'

'What can I do for you, *Charlie*?' Grant said.

'There's a tradition that us English bobbies like to maintain,' Woodend told him. 'When we have a result, we like to get together over a few drinks and sort of wind down.'

Grant frowned. 'As you can see for yourself, Charlie, I'm really rather busy and—'

'Too busy to give me half an hour of your time?' Woodend asked, sounding surprised – and not a little hurt. 'Too busy to have a quick drink with one of your colleagues? I thought that in the Agency they taught you to respect the traditions of the country in which you're operating.'

'In the *what*?' Grant asked.

'Sorry, did I say the *Agency*?' Woodend apologized. 'What I meant to say was the *Bureau*! So what do you think? Shall we have a drink together, and chew over the fat?'

'I . . . er . . . I'm afraid that I don't have any kind of alcohol in the trailer,' Grant said.

'No problem there, my old mate,' Woodend replied, reaching into his pocket and producing a square bottle. 'I've brought my own booze with me. An' look, Ed, in your honour I made sure that it was the finest Kentucky bourbon. Now you wouldn't want to turn that down, would you? It'd be a bit like insultin' the Stars an' Stripes, don't you think?'

Grant sighed, and gave in to the inevitable.

'But we'll have keep it strictly to the half hour limit,' he said. 'I can't possibly spare any more time than that.'

'Fine,' Woodend agreed. 'Half an hour should be all I need.'

Monika Paniatowski parked Woodend's Wolseley on the garage forecourt, and walked around the side of the building, towards the repair shop.

The van was standing just inside the door. It was no longer the Post Office red which it had been only a few hours earlier. Now it was a bright yellow colour, and the words 'South Eastern Electricity Board' had been sprayed on both its sides and bonnet.

It had been a rush job, Paniatowski thought, and it showed. Once she was close to it, she could see imperfections almost too numerous to count. But in the dark – and from a distance – it would probably pass muster.

'Well, what do you think?' the mechanic asked.

'Lovely,' Paniatowski said.

'It's not dry to the touch yet.'

'That doesn't matter. I'm not a cat.'

'I beg your pardon?'

'I don't have any intention of rubbing my body all over it.'

The mechanic blinked several times, as if he'd just been blessed with a vision of Paniatowski's completely naked body covered in the South West Electricity Board yellow paint.

'And you're sure painting the van in the electricity board's colours is legal?' he asked.

205

Was it? Paniatowski wondered.

Probably.

If you had the permission of the company involved.

Which she and Woodend didn't!

'I'm a detective police sergeant,' she said, as if that answered his question. 'You know that for a fact, because I showed you my warrant card when I wrote out the cheque.'

'That's true,' the mechanic agreed. He hesitated for a moment. 'I was wondering . . .'

'Yes?'

'There's a dance in Exeter tomorrow night, and I was . . . well, I got to thinking that if you're still around . . .'

'I'd love to,' Paniatowski said.

'You would?'

'But my husband's always been an awfully jealous kind of man, and ever since he's taken up heavyweight boxing, he seems to have no control of his temper at all.'

'You didn't say you were married,' the mechanic grumbled.

'Didn't I?' Paniatowski asked. 'It must have slipped my mind. But I'll tell you what – if you're prepared to take the risk of getting on the wrong side of the Bone-Crusher, then so am I.'

'The Bone-Crusher?' the mechanic repeated.

'That's my husband's nickname,' Paniatowski said. 'Can't imagine where he got it from, but everybody calls him that – even the people who duck down alleys and hide behind cars when they see him coming. Anyway, as I was saying, if you're willing to take the risk—'

'I'm sorry, I've just remembered that I'm doing something else tomorrow night,' the mechanic said hastily.

That was the trouble with men, Paniatowski told herself, as she drove the van out of the repair shop. They wanted you – but they didn't want the pain that having you might involve.

She laughed. She had quite enjoyed her amusing little interchange with the mechanic, she thought.

Which was just as well, because there wouldn't be a great deal to laugh at from now on. In fact, if Woodend was right, everything was just about to turn very nasty indeed.

*　*　*

206

'Have you ever heard of an English writer called E. M. Forster?' Woodend asked Grant, when the drinks had been poured, and they were sitting, facing each other, across the table.

'Sure,' Grant agreed. 'I studied him at college. He was worth half a credit, if I remember correctly. What about him?'

'He once wrote, "If I had to choose between betrayin' my country and betrayin' my friend, I hope I should have the guts to betray my country",' Woodend told him.

'I'm not sure I could subscribe to that idea at all,' Grant said.

'No, I suspect you couldn't,' Woodend agreed. 'I don't think Abe Birnbaum could, either, although – without havin' any real idea of what was goin' on – that's exactly what he did.'

'*Birnbaum* betrayed his country?'

'In a manner of speakin'. What Birnbaum actually did was to inadvertently put a spanner in the works of an operation run by an agency *representin'* his country,' Woodend explained. 'Tell me, Ed, my old mate, what's the secret of your eternal youth?'

'Say again?'

'Accordin' to FBI records, you're fifty-seven years old, but you don't look a day over thirty.'

'What is this?' Grant demanded.

'Also accordin' to FBI records, the last assignment you had before this one was cleanin' out the toilets in the Department of Justice,' Woodend continued. 'So this particular job is a real promotion for you, isn't it?'

'You've got your facts wrong!' Grant protested.

'I don't think so,' Woodend said. 'My source is right there in the FBI payroll department.'

'You misunderstand me,' Grant said, shifting his ground. 'FBI agents will often use an alias when they're out on assignment.'

'Bollocks!' Woodend said mildly. 'FBI agents are just ordinary bobbies with guns an' an unnatural fear of anybody mildly liberal. Now the CIA's an entirely different matter.'

'You think I'm CIA?'

'I've absolutely no doubt about it.'

'And could you explain to me how the Company would get itself involved in a criminal investigation?'

'Ah, that's an easy one,' Woodend said. 'It's *not* involved in a criminal investigation, because there hasn't actually been any crime – at least, not at Haverton Camp.'

'This is crazy talk,' Grant told him.

'Let me tell you what I've pieced together, an' then you can tell me where I've gone wrong,' Woodend continued, unperturbed. 'Your government wanted the Right Honourable Douglas Coutes, MP, to do somethin' for it. I don't what that *somethin'* was, but the details don't really matter. Anyway, whatever it was, Coutes absolutely refused to play along. So somebody – possibly in the State Department, but more likely in the CIA – decided that what you really needed to do was to get some leverage on him.'

'The CIA would never—' Coutes began.

'Never involve itself in dirty tricks?' Woodend interrupted. 'We're talkin' here about an organization that planned to kill Fidel Castro, by either givin' him an explodin' cigar or a fatal disease. In comparison to that, what the Company's done to Douglas Coutes is no more than a harmless jape.'

'Castro's a Commie,' Grant said. 'The Company would never think of using dirty tricks against a British politician. Britain is our ally!'

'But even allies need to be strong-armed now an' again, if only for their own good,' Woodend countered. 'Would you like me to go on, or should I just write down everythin' I know an' post it to the Prime Minister?'

'I suppose I should hear the rest of the story, if only so I can point out how deluded you've been,' Grant said.

'You started out by examin' Coutes's recent history, but you didn't have much luck there. It's true that the man has the morals of a tom-cat – which looked promisin' at first – but the problem is, he doesn't care who knows it. How can you shame a man who abandons his mistress because she's the wrong side of thirty and then – totally indifferent to how much pain an' sufferin' it might cause her – employs her as a servant?'

'It would ruin an American politician,' Grant said.

'But not a British one,' Woodend pointed out. 'John Profumo, who used to be our Minister for War, didn't lose his job because he was consortin' with prostitutes – he lost it because he *lied to Parliament* about consortin' with prostitutes. An' Coutes isn't even married, so nobody in the government would give a hang about what he does in his private life.'

'You're so decadent over here,' Grant said in disgust.

'Now you *are* talkin' like an FBI agent,' Woodend told him, 'but I still don't believe you are one. Anyway, after you failed to turn up any sex scandal you could use, you probably turned your attention to Coutes's financial dealin's. But you didn't find anythin' there, either. Coutes isn't really interested in money. Never has been. I realized myself, over twenty years ago, that *power* is his drug – an' not power as a means of gettin' somethin' else, but power for its own sake. So, havin' failed on two fronts to get the goods on him, what were you to do next?'

'You tell me,' Grant said.

'You started diggin' back even deeper into his past. An' it was probably at that point that some bright spark in Langley came across the disappearance of Robert Kineally. That was a truly wonderful discovery, wasn't it? Because Robert just happened to be the brother of Senator Kineally. An' Senator Kineally, without him havin' any real idea of what was goin' on, could be manipulated into lendin' all of his considerable political weight to your scheme.'

'You really are a remarkable case study in paranoia, Chief Inspector,' Grant said.

'It's hard *not* to be paranoiac when everybody's out to get you,' Woodend told him, with a grin.

'Nobody's out to get you.'

'Aren't they? Ten minutes ago, I was your mate, Charlie. Now I'm "Chief Inspector" again. But I digress.'

'This whole story of yours is just one *big* digression.'

'I'm bettin' that things really started to gel when you tracked down Huey Bascombe in Fulsom Prison,' Woodend continued, ignoring the comment. 'Because, you see, what Huey was able to tell you filled in a lot of the larger gaps in your initial plan.'

'And what *did* Bascombe allegedly tell us?'

'For a start, he told you that Coutes an' Kineally had a big fight, just before Kineally disappeared. So there's your motive, handed to you on a platter. Then he told you that his mate, Harry Wallace, had stolen Coutes's knife – which gave you a murder weapon.'

'So you believe the part about Wallace taking the knife, do you?'

209

'Aye, I believe it, right enough. Why wouldn't I, when it's what actually happened?'

'And how can you be so sure that it *did* happen?'

'We'll get to that in a minute,' Woodend promised. 'The next step in your little scheme was to track down Harry Wallace. But either you didn't find him, or he was already dead. Whatever the case, you didn't have Coutes's knife, which was a pity. But then you decided that didn't really matter. You were already workin' on producin' a duplicate set of Kineally's dog tags, so why not make a duplicate of Coutes's knife as well?'

Grant shook his head. 'I don't know where you get it all from,' he said. 'I really don't.'

'Of course, neither the knife nor the dog tags would stand up to a thorough examination in our labs at Scotland Yard, but since our labs were never goin' to get to see them – since they were supposedly goin' to be sent back to *your* labs – that didn't matter either.'

'Are you claiming that the knife and the dog tags *didn't* go back to our labs?'

'I don't know about that, one way or the other. But if they did, they certainly weren't tested thoroughly, because the results of the tests – includin' the one which revealed it was Coutes's bloody fingerprint on the dog tag – had been written weeks earlier, possibly even before the "evidence" itself had been manufactured.' Woodend paused. 'But not findin' the knife did cause you *one* problem.'

'And what problem was that?'

'You couldn't be sure Huey Bascombe was tellin' the truth. He said Harry Wallace had stolen the knife, but what if he hadn't? What if you planted the duplicate knife, an' then Coutes could produce the genuine one? Now that would have been embarrassin', wouldn't it? So you had to make sure Coutes really *didn't* have the knife any more. That's why, despite the risks of trippin' off a very sophisticated alarm system, you broke into Coutes's flat – because you needed to take a close look at his weapon collection. And when your operatives reported back to you that what should have been one of the prize pieces in the collection wasn't there in the case, you knew that Huey Bascombe had been completely straight with you, an' you were ready to start the final stage of the operation.'

'Which was?'

'You conned a surveyor from New Elizabethan Properties into makin' certain that the skeleton was discovered.' Woodend paused. 'I was wonderin' how you made it look as if the ground hadn't been disturbed for years, when, in fact, you must have been tinkerin' with it only a few days earlier.'

'I have no idea what you're talking about,' Grant said.

'Did you have to lay new turf when you'd finished? Or did you take the old turf up with such care that you could put it back without anybody noticin'? Were chemicals involved? I'm told you can do marvellous things with chemicals.'

'This is beyond fantasy!'

'So you won't tell me, eh?' Woodend asked philosophically. 'Doesn't matter. It's only technical details – an' as you've been pointin' out all along, one thing you Yanks do have is the technology.' He lit up a cigarette, and inhaled with relish. 'Anyway, the next thing you did was to have Coutes brought down here, an' let him sweat for a couple of days while the so-called "evidence" was buildin' up against him. An' then you made him an offer.'

'What kind of offer?'

'You said that if Coutes agreed to do whatever it was your government had been wantin' him to do all along, you'd get him off the hook by producin' somebody else to take the rap for killin' Kineally. An' you did. With the help of Bascombe, you produced Harry Wallace.'

'Are you saying that Wallace *didn't* kill Kineally?' Grant asked.

'Definitely,' Woodend told him. 'An' not only didn't he kill Kineally, he didn't kill the man whose skeleton you dug up from the shallow grave near the perimeter fence, either.'

'What are you talking about now?' Grant demanded.

'I don't exactly know how you got your hands on that skeleton. It could have come from a teaching hospital. You might have filleted some dead tramp you'd picked up off the street. Knowing the lengths you seem willing to go, you might even have dug it up in a graveyard. But the source isn't important. The simple fact is, that skeleton *isn't* Robert Kineally's.'

* * *

211

Monika Paniatowski stood in the shadows by one of the remaining trailers. She was feeling nervous, and desperately wanted a smoke – but she was only too aware that if the flare of the match didn't give away her position, the glow from the cigarette which followed it undoubtedly would.

So far, the Target had shown absolutely no sign of wishing to go anywhere at all. So perhaps Woodend was wrong about him. Perhaps he was wrong about the whole case.

Cloggin'-it Charlie *had* been wrong before, she reminded herself.

But not often. And not as wrong as that.

Besides, the way he had explained things this time had made perfect sense. In fact, his explanation was the *only* one which made *any sense* at all.

The door of the trailer opened, and the Target stepped out. She'd been expecting him to be holding some kind of travelling bag, but he wasn't. Instead, he was carrying something long and thin, wrapped up in a blanket.

'I'll never doubt you again, Charlie Woodend,' Paniatowski said softly to herself. 'From now on, I'll take everything you say – however outlandish it might seem – as gospel.'

The Target got into the car parked next to his trailer, and turned the ignition key. The engine refused to fire.

He would try at least a couple more times, then wait to allow his carburettor to dry out, Paniatowski thought.

Then he'd try again, and when the engine still wouldn't start, he'd decide that his spark plugs had probably come loose. And he'd be right, because they were loose. She'd made sure of that herself.

Once the Target had discovered the problem, it would only take him two or three minutes to fix it, and he'd be ready to go.

But by then, they'd be ready too.

Thirty-One

Glancing down at his watch, Woodend saw that exactly two minutes had passed since he had told Grant that Harry Wallace had been responsible neither for Robert Kineally's death nor the death of the man 'found' in the shallow grave.

Two minutes!

One hundred and twenty seconds!

And in those two minutes, Grant had not spoken, looked directly at him, or even seemed to move a muscle.

It was like sitting opposite a cardboard cut-out, Woodend thought. But then that came as no real surprise. Special Agent Grant – earnest, enthusiastic, naïve Special Agent Grant – had *always* been a cardboard cut-out, a fresh-faced front used to conceal the dark machinations of the CIA officer who had assumed his persona.

Now, Grant – or whatever the bloody man's real name was – finally seemed to be coming back to life, and the worried frown which had been frozen on to his face was slowly transforming itself into something resembling a confident grin.

'You think you've found a way out, don't you?' Woodend asked, conversationally. 'You think you've discovered a loophole that you might just be able to slip through and save your own skin?'

'I've never been concerned for myself,' Grant told him. 'My only concern – and, I admit, it *did* concern me – was that this crazy theory of yours might be just *credible enough* for one or two of our more disreputable journalists to take an interest in it.'

'You're full of shit,' Woodend said.

'Of course, even if that had happened, it wouldn't have taken us long to expose the story as no more than the ravings of a madman,' Grant continued. 'But we'd much rather not

213

do that unless we absolutely have to – because even "crazy" mud sticks a little.'

'An' now you don't think you *will* have to expose it?'

'I'm sure I won't. Because this story of yours has such a huge flaw through it that even the sleaziest of tabloids won't touch it.'

'An' that flaw is . . . ?'

'That the cornerstone of your whole theory is that body in the shallow grave isn't Robert Kineally's. Take that away, and your argument collapses like a house of cards.'

'True,' Woodend agreed. 'But why would I *want* to take it away?'

'Because your argument's unsustainable. And I can demonstrate that by asking you one simple question.'

'Then, by all means, ask it.'

'What actually happened to Kineally, if Wallace didn't kill him back in 'forty-four? If it wasn't his body lying in that shallow grave, then what has he been doing for the last twenty-one years?'

'I don't know – yet,' Woodend admitted.

'Of course you don't! How could you? Let me tell you something, Chief Inspector – men like Robert Kineally don't just disappear into thin air! He comes from a good family. An important family. I don't know what happened to him back in 1944 – no one in my government does – but—'

Grant clamped his mouth tightly shut, as if he were still hoping against hope that there was a chance to bite back the words.

'No one in your government knows what happened to him in 1944?' Woodend repeated. 'I thought you thought you did. I thought you thought you'd found his body in a shallow grave near the perimeter fence.'

'You're deliberately misinterpreting my words again,' Grant said, making something of a recovery. 'I meant we don't know the *exact* details of what happened. We don't know whether or not Huey Bascombe played a direct part in the murder, and we don't know—'

'Give it up, Ed,' Woodend said. 'The gaff's blown. The game's over.'

'For God's sake, if Kineally was still alive, don't you think we'd have found him by now?' Grant asked, exasperatedly.

'I never claimed he was still alive,' Woodend said quietly.

'And even if you were right about the body not being his – and I'm not conceding for a second that you are – there's absolutely no way on God's green earth that you'll ever be able to prove it.'

'You might well have been right about that – if it hadn't been for what Abe Birnbaum told me,' Woodend countered.

'Huh?'

'Remember what I said earlier about betrayin' your country rather than betray your friend? Well, that's what Birnbaum's done. Without even intendin' to, he told me somethin' that will blow this whole, sordid operation of yours wide open.'

'What was the unpleasant word you used to me earlier?' Grant asked. 'Bollocks?'

'Bollocks,' Woodend agreed.

'Then I have to say that you're talking bollocks, *Chuck*. Birnbaum's a mere dry-cleaner—'

'The biggest in the tri-state area,' Woodend interrupted.

'Birnbaum *is* nothing, and Birnbaum *knows* nothing,' Grant continued, ignoring him.

'He knows about the fight Douglas Coutes and Robert Kineally had,' Woodend pointed out.

'Hell, *everybody* knows about that!'

'But what everybody *doesn't* know is that Coutes broke three of Kineally's ribs.'

'What?'

Woodend chuckled. 'I thought that would take you by surprise. It's not in the records, is it? It was never recorded because Kineally, for reasons of his own, didn't *want* it recorded. Which is why you didn't know about it. Which is also why the skeleton you used might have been perfect as far as the height an' build goes, but is missin' the magic ingredient – those broken ribs.'

'I . . . I . . .' Grant said, in a strangled voice.

'You're lost for words?' Woodend suggested helpfully.

'Birnbaum's mistaken,' Grant managed to gasp.

'He isn't, you know,' Woodend said. 'An' the paramedics who treated Robert Kineally unofficially will confirm that he isn't.'

There was a knock of the trailer door, and Monika Paniatowski appeared. 'He's on the move,' she said to Woodend, with some urgency.

'Good,' Woodend replied. He turned to Grant. 'You'll have to excuse me now, "Special Agent",' he said, 'because as interestin' as our conversation is turnin' out to be, I need to go an' catch a *real* murderer.'

There was no difficulty at all in following the car down the narrow country lanes, because even when they lost sight of it – which they frequently did – they could always see its lights in the distance.

'If we'd been in the Wolseley, he'd have known we were on to him long before now,' Paniatowski said, changing gear to take a bend. 'But who'd ever suspect an electric company van, out on a mission of mercy to some outlying farm which has lost its power? It was a brilliant idea of yours, sir.'

'Aye, it wasn't bad,' Woodend replied, almost absently.

'Out with it!' Paniatowski ordered him.

'Out with what?'

'Whatever's on your mind. Whatever's dragging you down at a time when the adrenaline rush should have you climbing the walls of the van.'

'I keep thinkin' it's all my fault,' Woodend admitted.

'You shouldn't blame yourself.'

'How can I *not* blame myself? If I'd chosen my words a bit more carefully, back in May 1944 – if I hadn't told Mary she couldn't keep what she'd done a secret from Robert – then two people who've been a long time dead might very well still be alive.'

'You can't possibly know that's true,' Paniatowski said. 'At least,' she amended, 'not with any degree of certainty.'

'Which is another way of sayin' that I can't possibly know it *isn't* true with any degree of certainty, either,' Woodend said miserably. 'It only took me a few seconds to speak those words, Monika, but the weight of them will be pressin' down on me until the day I die.'

Paniatowski took her right hand off the wheel, and placed it on Woodend's arm. 'I wish I could help you, Charlie,' she said softly. 'I wish there was something I could do to take away a little of the pain.'

'I know you do, lass,' Woodend said. 'An' I want you to know that I appreciate it.'

A small sign at the side of the lane advised them that there was a major road ahead.

'What happens when we get to a crossroads?' Paniatowski asked, suddenly concerned. 'If we turn the same way as he does, won't he start to suspect that we're following him?'

'Not if we only have to do it the once,' Woodend reassured her. 'After all, why shouldn't the electrician's van be goin' the same way as he is?'

'And if we have to do it *twice*?'

'That could be trickier,' Woodend admitted. 'But once we turn, we'll be on the main road to Coxton Halt Railway Station now, so I don't think that there *will* be any more turns after that.'

'You don't *think* there will be – or you *hope* there won't?' Paniatowski asked him.

'A bit of both,' Woodend admitted. 'But I'm almost sure that I'm right. You see, I think this is the route that Robert Kineally's jeep took on that night in May 1944.'

'Why?'

'Because the driver had *two* tasks he needed to complete – an' I don't think he'd have risked makin' two separate trips to do them.'

'In other words, what we're looking for is somewhere between here and the railway station?' Paniatowski asked.

'Exactly,' Woodend agreed.

The car reached the crossroads, and turned towards the railway station. The van, a hundred yards or so behind it, did the same.

It was less than a mile to the point at which the road ran through the woods, and the moment the driver of the car had trees on either side of him, he indicated that he was about to pull in.

'What do I do now?' Paniatowski asked, whispering, even though there was no actual need to.

'Keep drivin',' Woodend said, sinking lower down into his seat. 'An' keep your eyes firmly on the road ahead. I don't want him thinkin' we've been lookin' at him – even for a second – or he'll probably decide it's safer to leave what he has to do until another night. An' that will bugger up everythin'.'

Neither speeding up nor slowing down, Paniatowski drove past the now-parked car.

'How much further along the road do you want me to go?' she asked, when they were well clear of the other vehicle.

'Just to be on the safe side, you'd better make it at least a mile,' Woodend told her.

'A mile!' Paniatowski repeated. 'That's much too far.'

'No, it isn't,' Woodend assured her. 'He's got a lot to do in that wood, an' even on foot, I'll be back there well before he's finished.'

'*You'll* be back there?' Paniatowski repeated.

'That's what I said.'

'I'm coming with you!'

'No, you're not, lass. This is by way of bein' personal business. I have a very old score to settle.'

Thirty-Two

Even from some distance down the road, Woodend could hear the sound of a shovel slicing through the earth.

The Target was making no effort to be quiet, he thought. But then why should he, out here in the middle of nowhere?

He reached the parked car, and stood there for perhaps a minute, calculating exactly where the noise was coming from.

The moonlight was bright that night, and it suddenly struck Woodend that all the significant events in this case – the incident with the coloured soldiers, the fight between Coutes and Kineally, and Kineally's murder itself – had all happened under a bright moon.

It was time to make a move. Feeling along the ground with his feet – searching for any irregularities or loose twigs – he entered the woods.

He had only gone a few steps when he saw the paraffin lamp glowing in the darkness, four or five yards ahead. A few *more* steps, and he could see all there was to see – the hole, the man inside it, and the blanket spread out on the ground to collect the earth.

This was a much deeper grave than the one at Haverton Camp, he thought, but then, unlike the one at the camp, this grave had never been *meant* to be discovered.

'You should have dug him up years ago, when most people hardly even remembered his name,' the Chief Inspector said.

The man in the hole froze.

'Woodend?' he asked.

'Failin' that, you should have left him where he was. I'd never have found him if you hadn't led me to him. But I knew you *couldn't* just leave him here, could you – because you'd already had one shock to your system, an' you weren't prepared to risk another.'

'Listen, Sergeant—' the man in the hole said.

'As I seem to keep havin' to remind you, Mr Coutes, I'm a Chief Inspector now,' Woodend said.

'And why stop there?' Coutes wondered. 'With my help, you could soon be a Superintendent. Maybe even a Chief Constable. The possibilities are endless, if you'll just turn round and walk away now.'

'Even if I trusted you, you couldn't tempt me,' Woodend said. 'An, as it is, you're the *last* person on earth I'd be likely to trust. So tell me, Mr Coutes, why *did* you kill Robert Kineally?'

Coutes laughed. 'Why are you even asking that question, when you already know the answer? I killed him, as you so clearly explained to me last night, because I had to.'

'Because you knew he wouldn't rest until he'd done somethin' to avenge Mary Parkinson's death?'

'Exactly. Very neatly put. The next time he'd come after me, he might have had a knife or a gun. And even if he'd decided not to kill me, he would certainly have tried to discredit me. So, all in all, it seemed to me that the simplest course was to eliminate him while I had the chance.'

'While he was still weak from the beatin' that you'd given him in the skittle alley?'

'I'm not going to apologize for that. A good general always attacks when and where his enemy is weakest. He'd be foolish to do anything else.' Coutes climbed out of the hole. 'You should accept my offer to assist you in your career, you know,' he continued, taking a step closer to Woodend. 'If you don't, I might just have to turn nasty.'

'Meanin' that you might have to do to me what you did to poor Robert Kineally?'

Coutes laughed again. 'Of course not. Killing is the solution to his problems that a man resorts to in his youth. As he grows older, he finds other means to get his own way.'

'Like what?'

'I haven't properly thought through my options yet. But I could say, for example, that it wasn't *you* who discovered *me* digging up the body, it was *me* who discovered *you*.'

'That wouldn't work.'

'Why not? You were at the camp at the same time I was, and though most people would be willing to accept a Chief Inspector's word, they'd be even more likely to believe a Minister of the Crown.'

'There's two flaws in that plan,' Woodend said. 'The first is that I'd already left the camp when Robert Kineally disappeared.'

'And the second?'

'I've got a witness who'll swear that *I* followed *you* here.'

'That would be that sexy little sergeant of yours,' Coutes said. 'Monika, isn't it?'

'That would be Sergeant Paniatowski, yes,' Woodend confirmed.

'A good bluff,' Coutes said. 'But if she *is* a witness, as you claim, where is she?'

'She's around here somewhere.'

Coutes shook his head. 'No, she isn't, or she'd have made herself known long before now. My guess is that she's still in the car, because you thought she'd be safer there. That's always been a weakness of yours – wanting to protect other people.'

He took another step forward.

'I'd like you to put that shovel down now, Mr Coutes,' the Chief Inspector said.

'And if I don't?'

'Then I'll have to assume that you're up to your old tricks, an' act accordingly.'

Coutes threw the shovel to the ground with great aplomb.

'You really *are* living in the past, aren't you?' he asked.

'One of us is, anyway,' Woodend replied.

'You see,' Coutes continued, taking one more step towards him, 'you still haven't grasped the very simple fact that a man in my position – a Cabinet Minister – can find a hundred ways of getting out of his difficulties without resorting to violence.'

He must have had the short iron bar concealed up his jacket sleeve all along, but Woodend only became aware of it a second before it struck him forcibly in the chest.

The pain was indescribable. Woodend staggered backwards, clutching his ribs. Then he took a blow to the head, and he went down.

Coutes rolled him over, and straddled him.

Woodend felt the iron bar pressing down on his throat. He tried to raise his arms, but Coutes had them pinned down with his own knees. He tried to kick his legs, but there was no strength in them. He was starting to see black spots before his eyes, and realized that soon he would lose consciousness. And all the time the bar was pressing down, tighter and tighter.

'You were right, I should never have dug him up,' Coutes said in a voice that seemed to be coming from inside a tin can, somewhere far, far away. 'I think I'm going to have to put him back in the hole, and this time, he'll have company – you and your sexy little sergeant!'

So this was how his life would end, Woodend thought – in a small wood, next to a crime scene which was already more than twenty years old. He made one last effort to raise his arms – even though he knew that it was pointless.

He thought he heard footsteps, but knew he must be imagining them. Then he heard Coutes scream, and suddenly the bar was gone from his throat and the weight was off his chest.

He tried to climb to his feet, and only got as far as raising himself on one elbow before his body refused to move any more.

But at least he could see what was happening now – at least understand how he had come to cheat death at the last moment.

Two figures were squaring up to one another in a small clearing only a few feet away from him. The first was Douglas Coutes, the iron bar still held firmly in his hands. The second – her body set in the classic stance of a woman trained in unarmed combat – was Monika Paniatowski.

Coutes swung the bar. Paniatowski stepped back – and lost her footing. As she went down, Coutes swung at her again, and this time the bar connected with her shoulder.

Woodend made another desperate attempt to get up, and managed to raise himself on to his hands and knees this time. But he already knew that the pain would allow him to go no further – that whatever damage Coutes had done to him, it was more than a simple bruising.

Paniatowski had rolled away, so she was temporarily out of reach of Coutes. Now she was lying on her back, readying her legs – as the only weapons she had available to her – for when Coutes came at her again.

'We've got the bastard, Monika!' Woodend called out, in what he hoped sounded like the voice of a man who was only moments away from getting back to his feet.

Coutes turned to look him, and – despite the agony it cost him – Woodend forced himself into a kneeling position.

'He's mine, Monika!' the Chief Inspector said, through gritted teeth. 'You can help, if you like, but he's mine!'

Coutes looked back at Monika Paniatowski, quickly checked on Woodend again, and then dropped the iron bar and ran back through the woods, towards the road.

A thousand hot needles were attacking Woodend's chest, and his spine seemed ready to crack at any moment. Now that Coutes had gone, there was no point in staying in the kneeling position any more, and he lowered himself – as gently as he could – to the ground.

Paniatowski was back on her feet again, but from the curious way she was standing, it was obvious that Coutes had hurt her.

'Are you all right, sir?' she asked.

'I'll live,' Woodend told her.

'I'm going after Coutes,' the sergeant said.

'There's no point,' Woodend gasped. 'We've . . . we've got all the evidence we need – let some other silly bugger make the arrest.'

'I'm going after him,' Paniatowski repeated, and before her boss could argue further, she had disappeared.

Woodend tried to get up again, even though he knew there was no chance of succeeding.

'If anything happens to Monika,' he told himself, as fresh waves of pain tore through his frame, 'I'll never forgive myself.'

If anything happens to Monika, said the goblin in his head, you'll have *three* deaths on your conscience.

In the near distance, there was the noise of a powerful car engine roaring into life.

'Let her be too late!' Woodend prayed. 'Let the bastard make his escape before she gets there!'

The engine revved, the car pulled away. The still night air was filled with the screech of tyres.

He'd made it, Woodend thought thankfully. He'd made it, and Monika was safe.

Unless, before he'd driven away, Coutes had paused to deal with Paniatowski. Unless, even now, her life was seeping away from her at the edge of the woods.

The sound of the crash was sudden, violent and totally unexpected. First, there was the loud thud, then there was the sound of buckling metal and shattering of glass, and finally, there was the explosion.

The conflagration which followed, lit up the woods as bright as day. Trees, until now no more than dark shapes, stood out starkly in all their leafless glory. Shadows, only brought to life by the flames, danced dementedly.

And Woodend, finally giving in to the pain, slipped into unconsciousness.

Thirty-Three

The bed was nice and firm. The pyjamas – though not his own – were comfortable enough. And the view of the hospital grounds from the window was both pleasant and restful.

So this was how the other half lived, Woodend thought – a private room, and a smiling nurse just the push of a button away. He could probably get used to it, if he really put his mind to it.

The door opened.

'Visitor for you,' the smiling nurse said, before stepping aside to let him see that the visitor in question was a man in an expensive herring-bone suit.

'How are you, Mr Woodend?' Forsyth asked.

'I'm sick, Mr Forsyth,' Woodend replied. 'That's why I'm here in this hospital.'

Forsyth laughed, as if he thought Woodend had just been incredibly witty. 'May I come in?' he asked.

'Might as well,' Woodend told him. 'You look like a coat-rack standin' out there.'

Forsyth laughed again. He entered the room, turned the bedside chair around, and straddled it.

'Yes, you certainly do look as though you've been in the wars,' he said cheerfully. 'Still, even though you have a couple of broken ribs, there's no actual permanent damage.'

Ignoring the 'no smoking' sign, Woodend lit up a Capstan Full Strength. For a moment it was hard to decide whether the *pleasure* of inhaling was worth the *pain* that also accompanied the action – but it was an unequal battle, and his addiction won hands down.

'Breakin' ribs seems to have been Douglas Coutes's speciality,' he said. 'But how do you know that's all that's wrong with me, Mr Forsyth? Hospital records are supposed to be confidential.'

'And so they are. But nothing is secret from everyone – and I am one of those people from whom nothing is secret at all.'

'How terribly, terribly, epigrammatic,' Woodend said, in fair imitation of Noel Coward. 'Listen, Mr Forsyth,' he continued in his normal voice, 'I know we need to polish up this double act of ours before we take it round the Northern working men's club circuit, but I don't feel like rehearsin' right now. So why don't you say what you've come to say – an' then piss off.'

The man from the Ministry of Defence smiled, and this time he really *did* look amused.

'Forthright and direct,' he said. 'That's just what's written in your record. Or perhaps, I should say, that's the *gist* of what's written in your record. Your Chief Constable has chosen to express himself in terms which are a little less . . . what shall we call them? . . . a little less complimentary.'

Woodend sighed, then coughed, then took another drag on his cigarette. 'Get to the point, will you?' he asked.

'I'm here on a threefold mission. It's my job to provide you with the official version of the truth, and to issue with a warning about will happen if you decide to deviate from it.'

'I was never very good at arithmetic, but I make that twofold,' Woodend said.

'And thirdly, I am here to satisfy my own curiosity,' Forsyth conceded. 'But that comes later. The official version of events is as follows: The body discovered in the shallow grave was that of Robert Kineally, though, of course, the Senator will be given the true remains – the ones recovered from the woods – for burial. Robert was killed by a Southern racist by the name of Harold Wallace, who is now also deceased. The Right Honourable Douglas Coutes had nothing to do with any of this at all – his name did not feature even at the margins of the investigation. And lastly, it is with great regret that we announce the death of the said Douglas Coutes, which was the result of a freak driving accident – invaluable service to his country, promising career cut tragically short, etc, etc.'

'Neat,' Woodend said.

'I thought so,' Forsyth replied. 'Do I need to make the threats now, or will you take them as read?'

'I'll take them as read,' Woodend said. 'As far as I'm

concerned, justice has finally been done. But can you really seal it all up as easily as that?'

'Oh, yes,' Forsyth said confidently. 'The Cousins are terribly apologetic about the whole sorry business. According to them, the operation was all the work of a tiny rogue element in the CIA.'

'An' was it really?'

'Who knows? But whatever the case, a few low-level operatives in Langley will lose both their jobs and their reputations, and we'll pretend we've put it all behind us.'

'But you won't have?'

'Oh dear me, no. They've been caught with their trousers down, and everybody knows it. The American Airforce will take the bases *we* want them to have without complaint. And later on, some other concession will have to be made. It may not be of a strictly military nature – it could involve something as interesting as computer technology, or something as mundane as soy bean imports – but whatever it is, it will be markedly advantageous to us. Then – and only then – will the accounts be balanced.'

'You seem to be takin' all this in very good part,' Woodend said.

'What choice do we have?' Forsyth asked. 'The Americans are the senior partners in our alliance, whichever way you look at it, and if they treat us as a second-rate power, that's because we are one. But even so,' he continued, suddenly gloomy, 'I do sometimes wish that their intelligence services would stop trying to manipulate us as if we were some tinpot South American dictatorship.'

'I'll bet you do,' Woodend said.

'Well, that's the official business over and done with,' Forsyth said, perking up. 'Now let's get on to the part that really fascinated me. How *did* you know Coutes actually *had* killed Kineally?'

'That's easy,' Woodend told him. 'Throughout nearly all of the investigation, he was very calm – far too calm for a man with the weight of evidence stacked up against him. An' why?'

'You tell me.'

'Because he'd seen through the whole charade – he knew what levers were bein' pulled, an' why they needed pullin'. In other words, he was well aware that he was the victim of a CIA scam, an' so he knew that sooner or later he'd be offered a deal to get him off the hook. Now he might not have liked the situation he found himself in, but when you play dirty tricks yourself . . .' Woodend paused for a moment. 'I'm assumin' he did play dirty tricks, didn't he?'

Forsyth smiled. 'As one of his loyal civil servants, I feel obliged to say that my Master was above that kind of thing.'

'An' if you weren't one of his loyal civil servants?'

'Then I'd probably say he was one of the dirtiest players it has ever been my misfortune to come across.'

'I thought as much,' Woodend replied. 'Anyway, as I was sayin', when you play dirty tricks yourself, you probably learn to roll with the punches when other people play dirty tricks back on you. So while he didn't exactly *enjoy* what was goin' on, he probably saw it as no more than a necessary inconvenience – like missin' a turn when you land on the wrong square in a board game.'

'Very well put,' Forsyth said. 'Very well put indeed.'

'Besides, he might even have seen a way to turn it all around to his own advantage.'

'How?'

'He had ambitions to be Prime Minister himself, didn't he?'

'Undoubtedly.'

'An' if he'd helped the CIA now, he might have had the leverage to persuade them to help him later.'

'You think so?'

'I do. An' why *wouldn't* they have wanted to help him? He was their kind of man – one they'd know they could do business with. He might even have been able to get them to play a few dirty tricks on his rivals for the post.'

'Dear God, you could be right!' Forsyth said with feeling. 'But let me see if I've got what you've said so far absolutely straight. You're claiming he knew it was a CIA scam?'

'Yes.'

'How?'

'Because he knew it wasn't Kineally's body in the shallow grave. But he couldn't admit that, could he? He couldn't tell anybody that the *reason* he knew it was a fake was that he had first-hand knowledge of where the real body was actually buried.'

'I can see all that, but it's your own reasoning I'm finding difficult to follow.'

'Why?'

'Well, until you *did* find the real body, just a few hours ago, your theory was just that, wasn't it – highly theoretical?'

'Not really,' Woodend said. 'There were a couple of occasions when Coutes *did* panic, an' they were more than enough to tip me off.'

'Fascinating!' Forsyth said. 'Do tell me all about them.'

'The first time he panicked was at the very beginnin' of the case. In fact, it happened before my part of the investigation had even started. It was when he rang me up in Whitebridge, to tell me the body had been found. He sounded really scared. Now why was that?'

'I couldn't even begin to guess.'

'All he'd been told at that point was that Robert's body had been found. Not *where* it had been found, you must understand – just that it had. So he naturally assumed it had been found in the woods, because that's where he'd buried it.'

'But when he got more details, especially those concerning the shallow grave, he realized he had no reason at all to worry?'

'Exactly.'

'And when was the second time he panicked?'

'After I'd talked to Abe Birnbaum, the night before last, I went to see Coutes in his trailer. I accused him of abandonin' the jeep at the station, to make it look as if Robert Kineally had run away. He panicked *then* because he thought that if I knew about the jeep, I must also have known that previous to abandonin' it, he'd driven to the woods, unloaded Robert's body, and buried it. He might have confessed, then an' there, if I'd said no more. But I *did* say more, an' that spoiled it all.'

'How?'

'I said somethin' which indicated that I still thought that the body taken from the shallow grave was Robert's. That told him that I was as far away from the real truth as I'd ever been.'

'And what a relief that must have been to him,' Forsyth said.

'Of course, the cause of both of Coutes's panic attacks were a complete mystery to me at the time,' Woodend continued. 'That's because I didn't know that the body in the shallow grave was a fake. But once I *did* know that, I could see there

229

was only one possible explanation for Coutes's sporadic nervousness.'

'He had to really have killed Kineally,' Forsyth said.

'He had to really have killed Kineally,' Woodend agreed.

Forsyth stood up. 'Thank you, Chief Inspector Woodend, that was most illuminating,' he said. He walked over to the door, then stopped and turned around. 'There is one more matter I'd like to discuss, before I go.'

'An' what might that be?'

'I'd just like to run through the events which occurred in the last few minutes of the Minister's life, if you don't mind.'

'Which events are they? The event when he offered to bribe me to forget all about it? Or the event when he tried to throttle the life out of me?'

'The events I'm most concerned with occurred after both those unpleasant incidents.'

'Then I'm afraid I can't be very helpful to you. At the time, if you recall, I was on the verge of unconsciousness.'

'Quite,' Forsyth agreed. 'But before you blacked out, you were able to see the struggle that went on between the Minister and your Sergeant Paniatowski, weren't you?'

'Part of it,' Woodend said, suddenly cautious.

'You see, what surprises me about that particular incident is that she allowed him to get away.'

'She didn't *allow* him to get away at all,' Woodend said angrily. 'While they were fightin', she tripped an' fell.'

'Ah yes, but you see, that was all later,' Forsyth said.

'Later?'

'After she'd pulled him off you.'

'I don't know quite what you're getting' at.'

'Sergeant Paniatowski is an expert in some form of unarmed combat, isn't she?'

'Yes?'

'So what I don't see is why she didn't completely immobilize Douglas Coutes while he was still trying to kill you. She surely had the necessary skills to do that, hadn't she? And since he was concentrating all his attention on choking you, he must have been a sitting duck.'

'It was dark,' Woodend said.

'True,' Forsyth agreed. 'But I believe there was some kind of paraffin lamp burning. If that was adequate to dig up a body by, it would certainly have provided ample illumination for any manoeuvre Sergeant Paniatowski would be likely to contemplate.'

'This wasn't some competition held in the police gym. She was tryin' to save my life.'

'And I would have thought the best way to ensure that would have been to use her skills to maximum effect.'

'You weren't there,' Woodend said, with growing unease. 'You don't know what it was like.'

'And then, of course, there's the small matter of the Minister's car,' Forsyth said.

'What about it?'

'Strange that it should crash like that, don't you think?'

'No, I don't. Coutes was in a big hurry to get away, an' he made a miscalculation.'

'Perhaps he did,' Forsyth agreed, though he sounded far from convinced. 'Did I mention that I've had the boffins examine the scene of the crash. Not the local turnip tops, you understand, but the chaps who really know what they're doing.'

'No, you didn't mention it. An' who *are* these chaps who really know what they're doin'? MI5?'

'Something like that,' Forsyth said dismissively. 'At any rate, it looked on the face of it to be an almost impossible task I'd set them, given the vehicle had been completely incinerated. But then they had a marvellous stroke of luck. It appears that one of the back wheels was seared off at the point of impact, and managed to roll clear. And the interesting thing about that wheel was that the tyre had been slashed. Did you slash it, Chief Inspector?'

'No.'

'They also found a rather sharp knife – a flick-knife, I think they call it – which they believe was responsible for the damage. I wonder where that could have come from?'

From Monika's handbag, Woodend thought. It was more than likely that it was the knife Chief Inspector Baxter had given her.

'So this is the way I see it,' Forsyth continued. 'Firstly, Sergeant Paniatowski slashes the back tyre of the Minister's car, and then she deliberately allows him to escape from the woods, knowing he'll get into the car and drive away as quickly as he can. Now why should she have done that?'

I wish I could help you, Charlie, Monika had said in the van. *I wish there was something I could do to take away a little of the pain.*

'There could be a dozen ways to explain the tyre bein' slashed,' Woodend said. 'Coutes could have run over a broken bottle, for example.'

'If that had been the case, don't you think the crack forensic team would have found some trace of it?' Forsyth asked. 'No, Chief Inspector, you have to accept that any explanation other than the one I've just given you is completely implausible. And strictly speaking, you know, if Sergeant Paniatowski *is* responsible for sabotaging the car, she should be charged with manslaughter.'

'I lied,' Woodend said. 'I did shred the tyres. I suppose I might as well admit it now.'

Forsyth laughed. 'So the age of chivalry is not dead after all,' he said. 'But it *is* redundant.'

'What do you mean?'

'The CIA is not the only organization which is capable of doctoring reports, and I can assure you that neither you nor your sergeant will hear any more of this unfortunate incident.'

'That's very kind of you,' Woodend said.

'Not at all, my dear chap,' Forsyth replied. 'How *could* we charge Sergeant Paniatowski, without blowing our own carefully-constructed cover story. There would be all sorts of awkward questions asked by all sorts of awkward people. What was the Minister doing in the woods, for example? Why did he get into a fight with a senior police officer? It could be very messy.'

'True,' Woodend agreed.

'Besides – from a purely personal perspective, and stepping well outside the bounds of my civil service responsibilities – I'm more than happy to let sleeping dogs lie.'

'You are?'

'I am. The Minister was, as I think I may have told you previously, extremely effective *as* a minister. But as a man, he was what I believe you'd call "a thoroughly nasty piece of work". And let's be honest, if he hadn't had his unfortunate accident, there would have been no alternative but to bring him to trial, and that would have been quite embarrassing all round.'

'So you're not exactly broken-hearted that he's dead?'

'Just so. In fact, if I thought I could get away with it, I'd probably put Sergeant Paniatowski up for a medal.'